MELISSA ADDEY

None Such as She

None Such as She

First Paperback Print Edition: 2019 in United Kingdom
Published by Letterpress Publishing

Cover and Formatting by Streetlight Graphics
Map of the Almoravid empire illustrated by Maria Gandolfo
Map of Spain illustrated by Veronika Wunderer
Illustration of Tuareg jewellery by Ruxandra Serbanoiu

eBook: 978-1-910940-20-4
Paperback: 978-1-910940-21-1

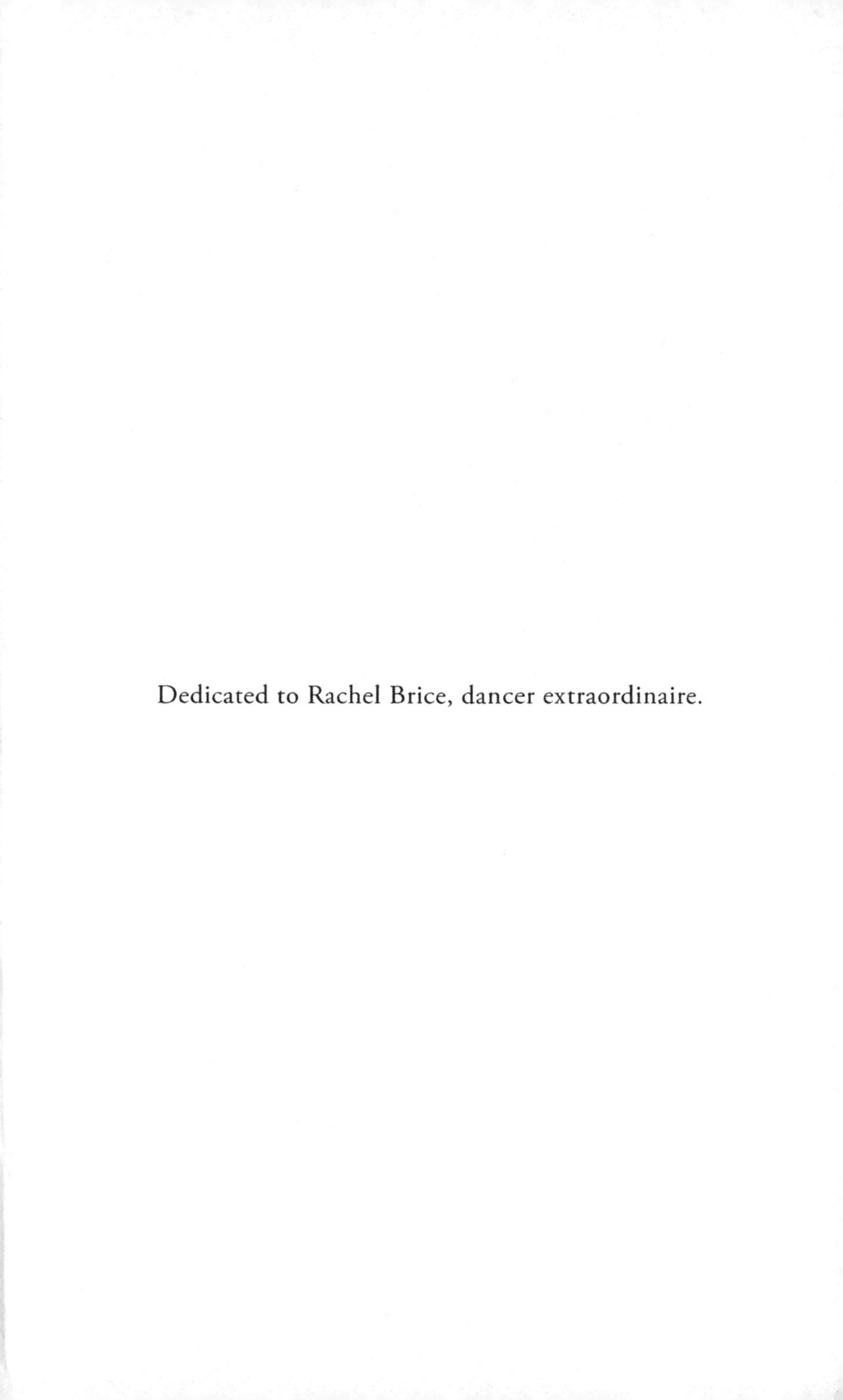

Dedicated to Rachel Brice, dancer extraordinaire.

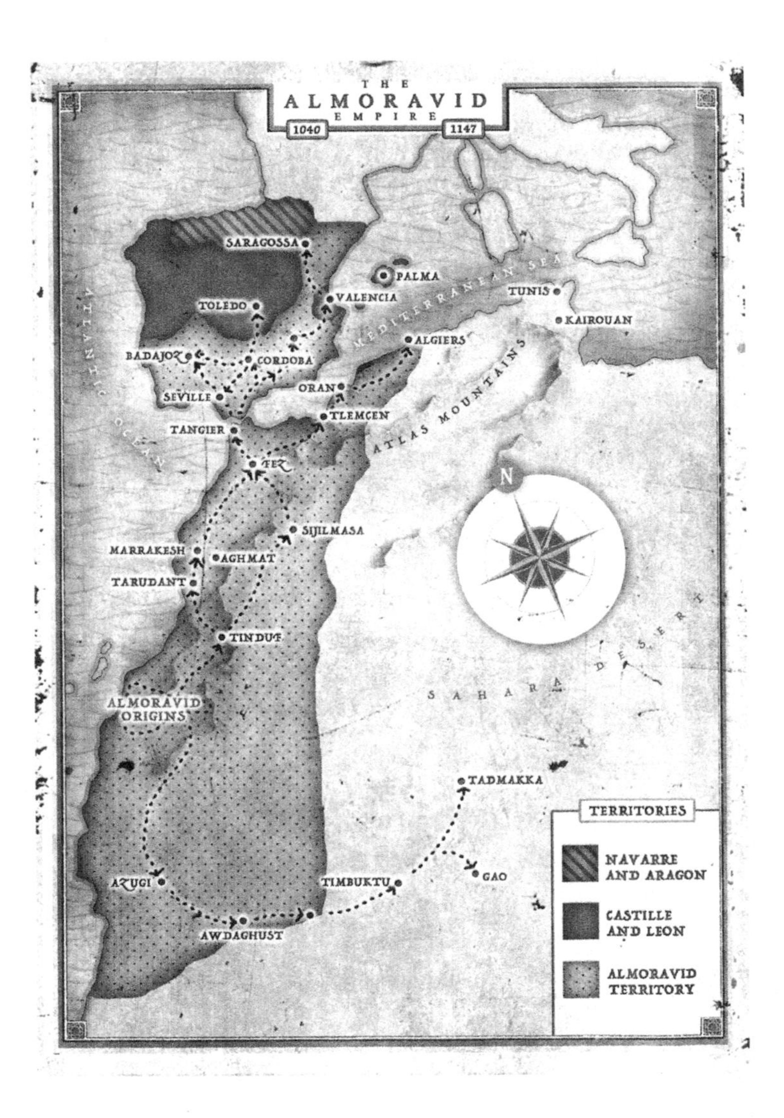
THE
ALMORAVID
EMPIRE
1040
1147
SARAGOSSA
PALMA
VALENCIA
TOLEDO
MEDITERRANEAN SEA
TUNIS
KAIROUAN
ALGIERS
ATLANTIC OCEAN
BADAJOZ
CORDOBA
SEVILLE
ORAN
TLEMCEN
TANGIER
ATLAS MOUNTAINS
FEZ
N
SIJILMASA
MARRAKESH
AGHMAT
TARUDANT
TINDUF
SAHARA DESERT
ALMORAVID
ORIGINS
TADMAKKA
TERRITORIES
NAVARRE
AND ARAGON
CASTILLE
AND LEON
ALMORAVID
TERRITORY
AZUGI
TIMBUKTU
GAO
AWDAGHUST

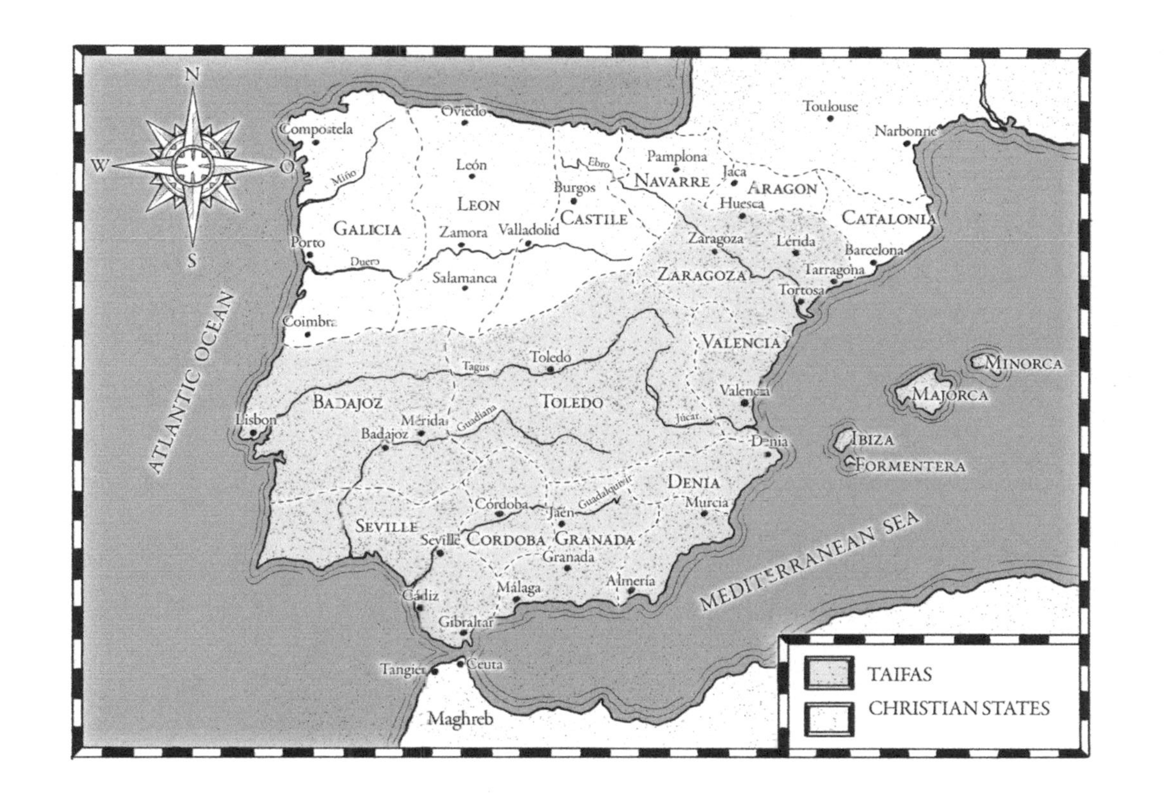
N
S
W
O
ATLANTIC OCEAN
MEDITERRANEAN SEA
Compostela
Oviedo
León
LEON
GALICIA
Miño
Porto
Duero
Zamora
Valladolid
Salamanca
Coimbra
Burgos
Ebro
CASTILE
Pamplona
NAVARRE
Jaca
ARAGON
Huesca
CATALONIA
Toulouse
Narbonne
Zaragoza
Lérida
Barcelona
Tarragona
Tortosa
ZARAGOZA
VALENCIA
Valencia
Júcar
Toledo
Tagus
TOLEDO
BADAJOZ
Lisbon
Mérida
Badajoz
Guadiana
Denia
DENIA
Murcia
Guadalquivir
Córdoba
Jaén
SEVILLE
Seville
CORDOBA
GRANADA
Granada
Almería
Málaga
Cádiz
Gibraltar
Tangier
Ceuta
Maghreb
MINORCA
MAJORCA
IBIZA
FORMENTERA
TAIFAS
CHRISTIAN STATES

After her childhood in Tunisia, Zaynab mostly lived her life amongst the people of North Africa loosely called Berbers (preferred contemporary name, Amazigh). The Berbers belong to many tribes and have various names for themselves, including Tuareg. They are known for their blue indigo-dyed robes and beautiful silver jewellery.

Amongst these peoples it is traditionally the men, not women, who veil their faces.

In her time there was none such as she: none more beautiful or intelligent or witty ... she was married to Yusuf, who built Marrakech for her.

12th-century text Kitab al-Istibsar

Murakush (Marrakech), c.1102

Walking pains me now. The distance to my rooms seems very great, each step jarring in my withered body.

Here and there I pass serving girls and slaves. They dip their heads in respect as I pass but I do not acknowledge them. I know as I move on that they make secret signs to themselves that they think I do not see. The slaves from the Dark Kingdom clutch at their amulets, hidden under their robes. The Christians make the sign of the cross and touch their crucifixes, amulets all the same. The others make their own gestures, murmur their own little spells of protection. They are afraid of me, as they have been these many years passed. They are so young they cannot even remember a time when I strode rather than shuffled, when my hair rippled down my back and my eyes were bright. But they have heard enough stories from the older servants, from whispers in the bright gardens and murmurs in the dark streets. They believe nonsense about me, believe that I command spirits and djinns.

The door to my rooms is protected by guards who spring forward to open it for me as I approach, heaving on the carved expanse of wood. Servants scatter as I enter and stand, heads bowed, awaiting my orders. When I tell them to leave they hurry to do so, for they have already heard the news, already know what has befallen me. The door swings shut behind them.

I trace the lines of my beloved maps with my fingertips. Every line fought for, every city's name grown great only because of my work and vision.

My legacy, turned to dust.

I open a carved chest that once belonged to Hela. My hands are stiff and pulling the stoppers from the tiny bottles I have chosen is hard.

The mixture smells foetid but I drink it all the same.

The city of Kairouan, Tunisia, c.1050

Daughter

THE SUN IS SINKING AND I am late back from the pools. My nursemaid Myriam is not her usual kindly self. She grabs me as soon as I come in and hustles me upstairs, gripping my arm in a painful way. I try to escape but she will not let me, hissing at me to be quiet and get into my bedroom, *immediately.*

"And wash that filthy mud off your legs!" she adds. "Where have you *been*?"

"The pools," I say as I am bundled, breathless, into my room. Myriam is already throwing open chests while two slave girls who have brought up large buckets of hot water are pouring them into a big basin.

Myriam barely hears me. "Faster!" she snaps at the slave girls and they flee the room with a pile of orders falling over their heads – more water, washing cloths, towels, robes, belts, hair pins. Myriam pulls my clothes off and flings them in a pile, then lifts me bodily into the basin. I stand up to my knees in water while Myriam scrubs me down and then shriek as she starts to brush my hair with none of her usual gentleness. She puts a hand over my mouth to stifle my cries. I squirm and try to bite her hand. This earns me a sharp smack on the legs. I stop shrieking and stand still, in dumbfounded pain. Myriam hardly ever smacks. I cannot even remember the last time she smacked me, but it must be whole years ago.

"What is happening, Myriam?" I ask, through tears of pain. She is still working on the knots in my long hair while the slave girls rush back and forth with everything she asked for. A yank on my head forces it to one side and I see that the robes being laid out for me are new, and the finest I have ever owned. They are very long, and more formal than I usually wear. They are entirely made of silk, a fabric more usually reserved in such quantities for my mother's clothes, and they are of many glorious colours. Myriam is arranging my hair very elegantly. I am going to look like a miniature version of my mother.

"Myriam?"

I try to get her attention but she does not seem willing to share any information with me. She is putting on her outer robes now, preparing to leave the house.

"Where are we going?"

"Engagement," she says without any elaboration.

Well of course I have been to engagements before, but never dressed like this. I would be well dressed, but not so elegantly and expensively. I run through all our family members trying to think who it might be that is getting married, for it must be someone important to us if we are going to all this trouble, but I have heard nothing about this and surely my gossiping aunts would have told me if something so exciting was happening in our own family?

There is no time to ponder this, for Myriam is rushing me back down the stairs. I am just opening my mouth to ask some more questions when I see my mother and father standing by the main door, about to depart. They are surrounded by servants.

My father Ibrahim looks like a prince. He is beautifully dressed and looks very handsome. I cannot help smiling at him, even though I am still confused. He catches sight of me and nods, stretches out his hands to me. I reach him and he holds me at arms' length to examine me.

"Very fine, Zaynab," he says. "The image of your mother."

I look towards my mother Djalila. She is always beautiful, but today she is stunning. Her robes are magnificent. If my father looks like a prince, she looks like a queen. I thought my new robes were grand, but she makes me look like a beggar girl. She is not smiling, however. Her face is pale and still. Beside her stands her handmaiden Hela, who rules our household in my mother's name.

"You are late," says Hela.

Myriam bows her head without speaking.

Hela ignores Myriam's contrite face and turns to the servants. "Ready?"

They all nod. It is only now that I look from one servant to the next and see what they are carrying.

A large jewellery box.

Dried fruits.

A live sheep.

An engagement cake.

I look again, unable to believe what I am seeing. Jewellery. Dried fruits. The struggling sheep. The cake. These are the gifts that the groom takes to his intended bride on the day of their engagement.

My father is taking a second wife.

My mother has a beautiful mirror in her room. Sometimes when she is occupied elsewhere I snatch a peek at myself in it. My mother does not like anyone going into her room. Only two people are allowed: her personal maidservant Hela, who comes and goes at will. And my father, who makes his way to her rooms only rarely and with a slow tread.

When my mother is not in her room and I am sure no one will find me, I creep close to her mirror and peer at myself. I have long thick hair, although it is always tangled, for I twist and turn under Myriam's hands until she gives up and lets me escape. I have very large dark eyes, which Myriam praises and says are like my mother's. I am not sure she is right. My mother's eyes can gaze at you without blinking for whole minutes, whereas my eyes are always moving, seeking out curiosities and following movements around me. My mother is very still. I have never seen her run or move fast. The same is true for my aunts, but they are fat and like nothing better than to lie on their comfortable cushions and eat sweets and cakes, giggling and quivering with the latest gossip. They are my father's sisters and come often to visit, caressing their brother and praising him. They are polite to my mother but she does not join in with their sticky-fingered whispers. She ensures they have everything they need and then leaves them, retreating to her rooms and the songbirds who flutter in their ornate cages there. The aunts while away long afternoons on their visits, occasionally catching me as I run through our house. When they catch me they crush me to their warm, multicoloured breasts of velvet and silk. Hot roses and jasmine flowers pervade the air around them. They laugh and poke and ask questions, rewarding answers with kisses and tastes of honeyed treats, then let me race away, back to my own games.

The mirror reflects my mother's bedroom, a place of fine colours and rich scents, beautifully arranged objects, which I am not allowed to touch. So I content myself with observing them in the mirror, reaching out through the glass so that I leave each item exactly where I found it, for my mother would surely spot any small changes.

In her mirror I am a small scrawny girl of ten years, with scabbed knees and long dark hair, wide-open eyes and a too-large mouth. I am not yet grown to a woman, but Myriam swears it will not be long now. I do not care. I have no older sisters with whom to compare and find myself wanting. No brothers either. I am my parents' only child.

My father is a carpet merchant, and the carpets from his workshops are much prized. Kairouan is famous for its carpets, and my father's are the best in the city. His workshops are elaborate places, with beautiful intricate paper designs replicated in a thousand thousand tiny knots, tied by the deft hands of women, following the designs created by my laughing aunts. Some of the makers work at home, but many choose to work in my father's workshops where they can chatter amongst themselves as they work. His workshops are refined compared to those of the other crafts – the heavy beating of the copper, the stench of the tanneries, the wet muddy droplets and dust of the potteries. He is a busy man, so I see little of him. Sometimes when Myriam takes me on her shopping trips

I visit his workshops where I can stroke the soft carpets as they grow on the looms, but I am not allowed to go to the dirtier workshops in the city.

Our house is large. We have a shaded courtyard filled with a gurgling fountain, flowers and trees. We have slaves, and some servants who carry out the more important household tasks, such as Myriam. It is Myriam who washes me but it is the slaves who heat and carry the heavy buckets of water to my room, they who clean the house, and do the chopping and stirring under the watchful eye of our cook, Hayfa. Our rooms have beautiful carved ceilings, our doors are painted and have marvellous thick handles and bolts in heavy beaten metal which I could not even draw until I was ten. We have great carved chests of perfumed woods in which to keep our belongings, and my father, although he is not a scholar himself, has many books. Sometimes he invites scholars from the great university to eat with us, and then they talk of many things until it is so late that I am falling asleep, and Myriam is summoned to carry me to bed. I am still small for my age and she is like a stocky little donkey, able to carry a great burden with no effort. She hoists me in her arms, whispering kind words so as not to waken me. She carries me to my soft bed and leaves me there till morning. Mostly she spends her time exclaiming in despair because I am always running about the city getting my costly robes dirty and sweaty from the heat and the dust. A girl from a good family like mine should not really be out on the streets.

But there is so much to see, for Kairouan is surely one of the greatest cities in the world! The surrounding lands are fertile and so there are grains, olives as well as great herds of sheep who provide wool, meat and milk. In the souks you can buy anything you want and on the big market days many hundreds of animals are slaughtered to feed the thousands of people who live here. Aside from its glorious carpets, Kairouan is known for its rose oil, which smells very sweet and rich. People say that if you marry a woman from Kairouan she will fill your house with roses and carpets, and it is true, for my mother smells wonderful and our house is full of beautiful soft carpets. Some carpet merchants use only the poorly designed or badly woven carpets for their own house, those that did not turn out as they were intended. My father says that is a poor economy, for when visitors and fine customers come to his house to be entertained they see extraordinary designs and marvel at their intricacy and quality. Then they eat and drink and gaze at my beautiful mother, who reclines in silence on finely-woven cushions in her gloriously coloured robes. The next day they buy many carpets from my father, finer and in greater quantities than they would have done had they not been so well entertained. I usually attend these dinners but the talk is often dull and the customers are old and smack their lips when they eat. Often I make my excuses after dinner and leave them to it. My mother watches me go. Occasionally I wonder if she would like to leave too, but if she is bored she never shows it.

Kairouan is also a very holy city. They say that Oqba found a golden cup in the sand here which he had lost many years before in the Zamzam well in Mecca, so perhaps there was a river flowing between Mecca and Kairouan. The water which comes up in the Bi'r Barouta well here is therefore holy, and if you drink enough of it you are exempted from the visit to Mecca which all good Muslims should undertake. The water is pulled up by a blindfolded camel that goes round and round all day. I watch it sometimes and wonder what it must think, on its endless wheel of walking, unable to see the daylight. Perhaps it is as well that it is blindfolded. If it realised that its journey would never end it might give up its life in despair.

Above all the rooftops towers the minaret of the great mosque. Inside the prayer hall are columns, very many of them. It is forbidden to count them or you will surely be blinded, but the street boys say there are four hundred and fourteen exactly. I have not counted them. Some of the street boys are blind in one eye or both, and it could be that they were the ones who counted the columns. I am not taking any chances. I love to see. Everywhere there are new things to see, especially in the souk. True, I often visit the souk with Myriam, but visiting it alone is different. I can run, I can get lost, I can visit parts of the souk where the shops get darker and smaller and the wares sold are more mysterious. I can stand and stare at the healers and their wares. There are teeth, snake skins, skulls of strange animals, bottles of every shape and size. The healers whisper that they can cure any illness, even ones I have never heard of but which the men and women who sit before them seem to be flustered by when they hear them mentioned. If I stare when I am with Myriam I am quickly dragged away as she tuts at me for my 'morbid fascinations'. Later I return alone to have my fill of staring, slipping out of the gate of my home when no-one is looking.

Although I come from a good family I find the other girls I am expected to spend my time with very dull. They only want to talk of their clothes, and their jewels, and whether their sisters will be married soon. The older ones whisper about boys they like and the younger ones beg to be told their secrets and follow them like unwanted pets, creeping a little closer every time, only to be pushed away when noticed.

I escape whenever I can and run through the city with the street children, who are quick, funny and clever. I take sweet cakes from our kitchen and share them with the greedy boys. Our cook marvels at how I can eat so many cakes and always be so bony, but she likes to feed me. She says our house does not have enough children for her to spoil, and what is the use of cooking for adults, who are too refined to say they enjoyed the food. She likes the way I beg her for treats and how greedily I bite into them. She heaps handfuls on me and I run into the streets and spread their honeyed stickiness across the whole city.

Sometimes we go beyond the city walls to the great pools, the reservoirs of the city. They feed the city so that no one goes without water. Even when there are droughts we can still visit the hammams and our fountains can still play, soothing our heat with their splashing.

The pools are deep. In the centre of the largest is a beautiful pavilion. In the summer evenings the fine men and women of Kairouan come down and sit inside it, enjoying the fresh breeze blown over the cooling water. During the day, though, it is our palace. We play at being great amirs, waving our hands regally at our servants. We take turns being servants or amirs. Those playing amirs think up ever more ridiculous tasks and those playing servants undertake them as badly as possible, moving stupidly slowly or doing the very opposite of what they have been told, so that we all shriek with laughter and even the 'amirs' snort and then hide their mouths so we do not see them losing their dignity. And when I return from my adventures, late as ever, Myriam despairs of me.

Especially today.

We are gradually joined by friends and family as we walk towards the mosque for the sunset prayers. I pretend to pray, but my head is spinning. My father is taking another wife! Who is she? I never heard anything being discussed. I berate myself for not spending more time with the gossiping aunts, who must have known all about these plans. No wonder my mother looks so still, so angry. But she must have given her permission or my father could not have taken another wife. I shudder at the very idea of suggesting such a course of action to my mother. My father must be a braver man than I realised. Who is she? Who is this woman who is brave enough to come into my mother's home and marry my father under her still, dark eyes? I am afraid for her, even though I do not know her name.

By the time prayers are finished and we have made our way outside the mosque there is a huge crowd. Word has spread of the engagement. More and more people join us as they emerge from other mosques or their houses as we stand there, waiting to go to the bride. The sheep, held tightly by two of our servants, has given up struggling and lies quietly on the ground, sadly contemplating its fate.

Now the crowd begins to move. Slowly we walk towards one of the quarters until we come to a door set into a high wall. The crowd is excited. My mother's face is rigid, without expression. My father is his usual reserved self, smiling wryly at some of the more ribald comments from the crowd and waving them away but I notice his left hand moving constantly, clenching and unclenching while his right hand reaches out to pat people's shoulders, to gently steer my mother through the crowded space.

My aunts are at the front of the crowd, and they start to pound on the door.

A laughing voice calls out. "Who is there?"

My aunts answer as one. "We have come to ask if you will give your daughter to be married to Ibrahim an-Nafzawi!"

The crowd cheers.

Of course there is much demurral before we are allowed in. It would not do for the bride's father to seem too eager. More calls, more responses, until finally the door is opened and we are welcomed inside. A great crowd streams in, myself and Myriam getting lost in it so that we fall back from our front-row positions and end up towards the back as we enter the courtyard.

It is a pretty place, not so grand as our own home, but still pleasing to the eye. It is cool and there is a small fountain that splashes merrily. There are fresh-scented trees which later will bear sweet fruits, although right now they are full of small boys who have climbed them to get a better view while the first surah of the Qur'an is recited over the engaged couple.

"In the name of Allah, Most Gracious, Most Merciful. Praise be to Allah The Cherisher and Sustainer of the Worlds; Most Gracious, Most Merciful; Master of the Day of Judgement. Thee do we worship and Thine aid we seek.

Show us the straight way, The way of those on whom Thou has bestowed Thy Grace, those whose portion is not wrath, and who go not astray."

I have been craning my neck throughout this instead of paying attention, straining to see my father's new bride, earning myself several digs in the ribs from Myriam. I fail to spot them and now the crowd begins to depart, so we are buffeted here and there by the many moving bodies. I am regularly stopped by those leaving as they wish happiness and prosperity to all members of both families. Many women pinch my cheeks and smile, asking if I am happy with my new aunt. I can only smile and nod, the men patting my head as they pass, muttering blessings. I am hot, tired and hungry, for we have not yet eaten our evening meal. I am grumpy, too. Surely I should have seen this new aunt by now? Why am I at the back of the crowd?

At last the crowd begins to thin a little and I catch my first glimpse of Imen, my father's future wife. She is all curves and blushing smiles, with pink cheeks and bright eyes. She has tiny feet and hands, and stands well under my father's shoulder. I am about the same height and I am only ten. My mother is much taller than her. It is clear Imen is fond of good food and sweet things, and that one day she will attain the quivering mass of my aunties. I am sure my aunties have chosen her for this very reason. Her hair is long and shines silken in the sunset. Although she is shy now, I can see that she does not hold back from affection. She accepts with enthusiasm the many hugs and kisses and blessings as they fall all around her, and she looks truly happy. She even smiles at my mother. My mother looks away.

Our household prepares for the new bride. Rooms are set aside for her and the servants who will come with her. The house is in chaos as new carpets and cushions, drapes and a large bed are carried up to the rooms, which have been cleaned and repainted, their plaster carving and painted ceilings newly touched up. My mother keeps to her rooms, refusing to attend meals. Hela must carry all her meals to her and often they return uneaten. Meanwhile I try to find out more about my future aunt, and why she has come into our lives. The servants' whispers are, as always, most enlightening. I crouch in stairwells near the kitchens where I can hear our cook expounding her theories. Hayfa always has tall tales to tell, and the other servants act as her willing audience.

"*She* didn't give him a son, did she? What did she expect?"

She is always my mother when Hayfa or any of the other servants speak about our family. The other servants nod, their hands full of their appointed tasks but their minds mulling over the new turn of events which is causing all this extra work. The slaves whisper translations to one another of Hayfa's words. Some speak our tongue better than others, and they pass on her speculations to those slaves who have not yet learnt the subtleties of our language. Hayfa approves of this, as it increases her audience, and so she allows suitable pauses for her words to be fully understood. When she sees comprehension dawning on the slaves' faces she continues.

"A man has the right to expect a son," she says wisely.

"And Allah knows the poor man has shown patience. One daughter she gave him, just the one child, and she is fully ten now, almost a woman. No sign of another child. That woman takes care of her bedding but I would say it is more than likely that she no longer has her courses."

That woman refers to Hela, my mother's handmaiden. Hela is the same age as my mother. She came with my mother when she was married to my father. I believe she served her family from when my mother was a girl. Hela is devoted to my mother. She takes her duties seriously and stands over her like a guard, always watching, always ready. If my mother is in a room there is a certainty that Hela is close by. You may not see her at first, but she will be there, ready to serve. Where my mother is tall and slender, beautiful and regal in her bearing, Hela is built like a man, with broad shoulders and a thick waist. Not fat, for she would never indulge so much in the pleasures of life to attain such a state, but strong as an ox. Her thick dark hair does not fall down her back as does my mother's, it is wrapped up in a plain dark cloth. When Hayfa talks about Hela she has more than once reminded her listeners that an ox is an excellent worker, loyal and strong, but that should it be badly treated it may well turn on those who torment it and kill them outright.

"And after all," she always finishes triumphantly, "who knows what an ox is thinking?"

This always leads to wise nods around the kitchen. The servants steer clear of Hela. She is not included in their whispers and giggles, she is obeyed without question as a senior servant, but she is not liked. Just as the servants are wary of my mother, so they are wary of Hela, for they know that she is my mother's eyes and ears and that Hela, to all intents and purposes, manages our household.

They approach Hela only when sickness or injury fall upon them. For she is a healer, it is well known. Her hands are sure and certain when a bone must be re-set and her face does not respond when her patients scream with pain as bone grates on bone as she finds its resting place. She knows the properties of many herbs and traders seek her out, coming to our house and asking for her by name to offer her far-flung remedies to add to her collection of tiny boxes and bottles, kept safe in her own room.

She is educated, and this make the other servants distrust her even more. "She *reads*, you know," they say, making faces at one another. "Like a *scholar*." Scholars are men of learning and wisdom, not serving-women.

My mother relies on her. She never has to ask for an item, only to stretch out her hand without even looking, for Hela will always be ready to drop it into her palm. When my mother retreats to her rooms Hela accompanies her, and only she is allowed to speak with her, to bring her food and clothing. The slaves leave water outside the door and it is taken inside by Hela, then left outside again when she has done with bathing my mother. She it is who goes on errands for my mother, walking swift and sure in the mazes of the souk, returning with little packages of this and that, secrets of which we know nothing. When my mother wishes to visit the hammam it is Hela who goes with her to the hot dark rooms to wash her, rub down her fine skin, massage her with delicate oils, comb through her long hair with rose-scented cleansers. I hear them talk to one another sometimes in my mother's rooms, their voices low and hard to overhear, for their words are indistinct. They do not raise their voices, only continue the slow steady murmuring that teases my sharp ears.

The rituals have been going on for days, even weeks by now. There have been meetings, parties, gifts, discussions and the painting of henna in intricate swirls. In just a few days Imen will leave her father's house and come to my father as his bride, her hair crowned in a golden headdress. She will be his new wife, my mother's sister, my aunt. The servants have their own views on this and Hayfa is holding forth again. The slaves' allotted tasks do not seem to be any closer to completion.

"The new one, Imen – she's here to provide a fine strapping boy. Maybe several. I had a look at her the other day when she was in the souk with her mother. A fine girl. Young. Wide hips. Plenty of fat on her." Hayfa outlines this figure with her hands in the air and nods her approval. "Imen will bear him many sons for sure." She lowers her voice slightly. "If *she* lets her."

"What do you mean?" one of the younger servants asks, her eyes wide. The others lean in. I come down two more steps, silently edging closer but still hidden.

Hayfa shakes her head slowly, as one who has seen all manner of things in this wicked world. "Do you think she will stand by and watch?" she asks. "You think she will open her arms and say, 'Oh, sister, welcome to my home. Bear my husband many sons with my blessing!'? Of course not. *I* would not be Imen for all the carpets in Kairouan."

"But what can she do?" This from one of the men.

Hayfa considers. "I don't know," she admits finally. This breaks her storytelling spell. "Back to work, now, all of you standing about here cluttering up my kitchen with your gossip and nonsense."

They begin to disperse. I get ready to make my getaway before any of them come up the stairs. But before I turn away I hear Hayfa as she mutters while scooping out oil from a jar close to me. I hold my breath and press my back against the wall. No-one else hears her but me, and later I will remember what she says and feel a cold river run through me.

"Allah knows I am a good and honest cook, but if I were Imen I would not eat what was laid before me in this house."

I turn and run up the stairs, past my mother's bedroom door and back to my own room.

Imen arrives at last, soft and blushing. She is kind to the servants, who love her at once. She gives few orders, always glancing towards my mother to get her tacit approval for even the most minor of requests. But the servants would find ways to obey her even if my mother withheld her consent, for who would not wish to please such a sweet little mistress, one whose voice of command is gentle and whose smile of thanks is radiant?

Our routine changes. My mother is now absent from most meals. The only meals she attends are the important ones, when there are guests. Then she descends, a princess amongst mere commoners, elegantly dressed, her beauty undimmed. Frequently on these occasions it seems that

Imen is indisposed, and does not join us, leaving my mother and father to greet guests as they have always done, as though nothing had changed. But at breakfast it is Imen who sits by my father's side, who passes soft warm bread smeared with honey and butter, who pours tea and whose hair is somewhat dishevelled, her smile tender as my father wishes her a good day before he leaves the house.

At first I stay away from Imen, as my mother does. I think that my mother will be pleased if she comes to hear that I do not care for Imen, that she will see that I am her ally against this newcomer. But my mother stays in her rooms and I find it hard to avoid Imen. When I come to eat breakfast she is there, smiling, offering me sweet orange juice, fresh breads with honey. While I eat she pours herself more tea and stretches back on the cushions to enjoy the dappled sunlight of our courtyard.

"I have something for you, Zaynab," she says one morning.

I look up and see her pointing to a covered basket.

"Open it," she says, her eyes bright.

Inside the basket is a tiny tabby-brown kitten.

"It will need feeding with milk," she says. "It is still so young."

She shows me how to dip a little scrap of cloth into milk and drip it into the kitten's mouth, gives me some soft cloth from the chests in her room to line the basket and make a warm little nest for it. She has the servants bring fresh milk every day in a special container just for the kitten and giggles with me when it grows old enough to explore and is afraid of its own shadow or overbalances on our wall. My mother will not let me feed her songbirds, but Imen strokes my kitten and when I kneel by her side to hear it purr she strokes my hair too, and after a time I forget that I should be my mother's ally, for my mother does not smile whatever I do and Imen laughs so easily, it is easy to laugh with her.

My father has begun to smile when Imen is nearby. He seems happier, walking more slowly, speaking more kindly to the servants. His wrinkles, which were beginning to appear as the years went by, seem to be fading. Once as dusk descended I ran to his rooms to call him for the evening meal and found him buried under a pile of soft giggling silks, which turned out to be Imen, who blushed mightily when she saw me. My father only laughed and kissed her forehead, then rose and came with me to dinner. We had guests that night and Imen sent word that she was unwell and begged to be excused. My father accepted the sympathies of the guests with a charming smile while my mother, by his side as always when we have guests, said nothing.

Sometimes I see Imen drinking from a wooden cup, a faded reddish colour marked with worn carvings. I asked her once what it contained and she lowered her lashes a little and said that she hoped it would help her bear many brothers for me. Then she giggled and chased me round the courtyard with a long feather she had found from the storks who roost on the rooftops of Kairouan, seeking to pin me down and tickle me.

But the liquid in the cup must have worked its magic, for Imen smiles ever more broadly and now my father is very tender with her. Where before my mother ordered our food to her liking and Imen never presumed to countermand her orders, now my father has decreed that all food must be ordered by Imen. Everything must be to her tastes. My mother says nothing but bows her head and is seen even less, spending her days tending to her songbirds, whom I can hear tweeting. All our household now revolves around Imen. She giggles over all the fuss but enjoys her new status, basking in the petting from my aunts and the foods she craves. Sometimes she turns a little pale and clutches at her stomach, sometimes I even hear her retching, and servants hurry to her with clean cloths and fresh cool water, but the aunts only laugh kindly and say everyone must suffer so to bring forth a healthy child and he must be a boy to cause his mother such grief already. Then they offer Imen perfumed drinks to take away the sour taste of bile and fan her as she reclines on the soft cushions by their side. They amuse her with stories and the city's gossip and recite endless permutations of names that might suit my unborn brother. Imen still sips from the carved cup, but now it contains tonics for her baby's health, to make him grow strong within her ever-increasing belly.

"What shall you name him?" I ask.

Imen stretches out her bare toes in the dappled morning light of our garden and yawns. "I think your father has a name for him," she says, smiling. "He said he had kept it for many years for his first-born son."

I look down. "He will be pleased to have a son," I say.

Imen reaches out and pulls me to her. Her pale pink

robes enfold me and her body's warmth spreads out from her to me. I tuck my feet under her cushions and lean my head against her.

"He will be grateful to have a kind grown-up daughter who can take good care of a baby brother," she says. "Think how much the baby will love you – a beautiful older sister to follow about and play games with. It is good for children to have brothers and sisters. When we are all old and wrinkled the two of you will be young and strong and will share your festive days together with your own families."

I cannot imagine pretty Imen being old and wrinkled but I smile anyway.

"Perhaps," offers Imen, "you might give a second name to your brother. What is your favourite name for a boy?"

To make her laugh I think up dreadful names, names that sound like they are only fit for a slave or a peasant boy. She laughs until she cries and then she gets the hiccups and I have to bring her water to sip to make them go away.

It is night and I am fully asleep when Myriam shakes me awake. At first she is in my dream, one of the street boys tugging at my sleeve as he shows me new hiding places in the souk's maze of streets. Then I am pulled from my dream and open my eyes in the darkness. I yelp, for Myriam's face, too close to mine and lit by a dim lamp, is like some terrifying djinn, one eye hidden altogether, the other bulging outwards. Then I am awake and puzzled. It is far too dark even for dawn prayers. The light dims as Myriam moves away from me and grabs a plain robe which she throws at me whilst struggling to unroll our prayer mats.

"Pray."

I hold the robe, sit up in bed. "What?"

"Pray!" Myriam hisses back.

She does not raise her voice as she usually would, nor ask me if I need my ears stretching like a donkey to hear her better. She has succeeded in unrolling the mats and is taking her place on one of them.

I climb awkwardly out of bed, pull the robe over my sleep-warmed naked body which is now beginning to tremble in the cool night air, then kneel beside her. "It's not dawn yet," I say crossly. "The call to prayer won't come for *hours*."

Myriam ignores me and begins to pray. I follow along with little grace and much mumbling. I stumble over words that ought to come smoothly, since I have been repeating them for many years and overbalance so that I knock my head too hard on the floor. The prayers seem to go on forever, far longer than usual. At last I see she intends to keep going all night and I stop, sitting back on my heels defiantly.

"I'm not praying anymore unless you tell me why we're praying in the middle of the night."

I think Myriam might ignore me, or yell at me. She does neither. She sits back on her heels and I see her face is streaked with tears. She sits still for a moment or two while the tears roll down her cheeks and then speaks, very low, as though afraid of being overheard. "Imen is ill."

I frown. "She looked well last night when we went to bed."

Myriam shakes her head. "She said she was indisposed."

I shrug. "She always says that when we have guests."

Myriam nods. "But she started to have pains. She thought it was the sickness again."

"I thought that was only at the beginning. She hasn't been sick for ages."

"Yes. She should have told one of us. We would have known something was wrong. She did not know the sickness should not come now. She had pains like knives in her belly." Myriam mumbles something else, which I don't catch.

"What?"

Myriam speaks a little louder. "Blood."

"*Blood*?" Even I know this is not a good sign.

Myriam nods again. "She started to bleed. Her maid got scared and called for help. The doctors are with her. Everyone is awake."

I turn my face towards the door and strain my ears. I have very good hearing, but if everyone is awake then the house seems unnaturally quiet – in the daytime you can barely hear a conversation for all the noise that goes on – clattering pots and pans, feet running up and down stairs, orders being shouted out. Now there is only silence. I look back at Myriam, frowning. "I can't hear anyone."

"They are all praying," she whispers, her face pale in the darkness.

I say nothing, but prostrate myself, the words suddenly coming to me, begging for His kindness, for His mercy, for any help He can offer to Imen as her crimson blood drains away in the darkness and my baby brother's life is lost.

As the cold pale light grows the streets awake. The dawn

prayers are called and there is a brief lull before the bustle of the new day begins in earnest. Only our house is quiet. In the coming days we will find ourselves mourning twice over; for my brother who did not even have a name and for Imen, whose gentle nature was not strong enough to withstand the agony that gripped her, nor the tide of blood, which swept her away as though she was dust in the road.

Many, many months pass before our house seems normal again. My mother sits with us at all our meals again, and my father's hair is a little more grey. The rooms that were Imen's are not used for anything, their doors are kept shut and the dust is allowed to settle around the spiders, who rebuild their webs and await any foolish flies who mistake Imen's windows for a true entrance to our house. The flowers Imen had planted around her windows fade and wither, for no-one comes to water them.

I miss Imen. I miss her love of good food and her sleep-ruffled hair. I miss her perfumed robes in pale rippled colours, so different from my mother's dark magnificence. Most of all I miss her giggle, her embraces given without warning or reason, her delight in my father and his happiness with her. He is quiet again now, and I have not seen him smile for a long time.

I sit in a cushioned alcove in our courtyard and rip leaves into small shreds, following their marked-out pathways. There is no-one now to share these mornings with and I am bored.

My father is leaving the house, going to one of his workshops. As he leaves he crosses the path of Hela, who is carrying breakfast to my mother. They see each other and pause, then speak in low voices.

I lean forward to hear them. I am curious, I rarely see them speak to one another. My mother issues all commands to Hela and Hela barely speaks when others are present. My father and she do not pass their time conversing with one another.

"I have spoken with her father." I hear him say.

Hela shakes her head. It is a quick sharp movement, a direct refusal of whatever my father is proposing. A servant should not defy their master, my father would be within his rights to reprimand or even strike her. He does neither, only looks down at his hands.

"There will be only one," says Hela. "You must resign yourself."

"It is not only that," he replies. "It is..." but he does not finish his sentence, he seems unable to find the words.

Hela holds up one hand, the other still balancing my mother's breakfast, now going cold. "There will be no more new wives in this house," she says, and turns, walking away from him into the house, towards my mother's rooms.

My father stands still for a moment, looking down at the tiles of our courtyard. Then he makes his way out of the gates of our home, heading towards his workshops.

Sometimes I still go alone into the souks, but the street boys seem to have grown up all of a sudden. Many now work hard every day, fetching and carrying heavy loads. Some are apprenticed to their fathers or to a trade. By evening they are too tired to come to the great reservoirs and play at servants and amirs, and so I sit alone in the middle of the vast expanse of water and gaze over the side of the pavilion at my rippled reflection.

My face is becoming more like my mother's as time goes by, and I know that people say that I will be a great beauty like her. I gaze at my face in the water and hope that I will still look like a street girl – with untamed hair and a wide smile. But however often I look my hair grows ever faster and more silky, my eyes become wider and darker, my limbs longer and more graceful. I am becoming a woman.

Bride

I AM GROWN TO FULLY FIFTEEN now, and suitors seek my hand almost daily, or so it seems. Their families hope that my mother's beauty, if not her fertility, will have been passed down to me. I know that they whisper that I have all her beauty but that in addition I seem to have rosy cheeks and a warmer smile, that my grandmother on my father's side had more than one fine son and two lovely daughters and that perhaps, therefore, I will not only bring beauty but also bear many children, thus making my desirability complete.

I find it laughable that someone would want to marry me, for I feel like a child playing at dressing-up when I am paraded before would-be husbands or their emissaries. Each night when a guest is due for dinner with us I am dressed beautifully, my hair gleams and yet I am bound to tip over a drink or trip on the long brightly-coloured robes which now drape over every part of my body. I grow clumsy when I am shy, and it makes me shy to be stared at as though I were a delicious course laid at table. Sometimes I have to bite my lips to keep from giggling, and Myriam, who knows what I am thinking, will nudge me or shoot me a warning glance. When she does that I cast my eyes down, which must look delightfully demure to the visiting suitors, but in reality I am only trying not to laugh out loud.

I no longer sit in the reservoir pavilion at dusk, for it would be unseemly for an unmarried fifteen-year-old girl of a good family to wander the streets alone. It was tolerated, barely, when I was a child, but now neither my mother nor father will hear of it, and Myriam no longer makes excuses for me. She is too afraid of what would happen to her if my reputation were in any way damaged. So I can go out only when Myriam will accompany me, and she does not often do so. Besides, I grow weary of walking the streets when so many people watch me walk by and whisper my name to one another, murmuring my heritage, my beauty, my suitability for marriage. They speculate on my suitors, on which man will be chosen for me.

So most days I sit at home, alone and lonely. Sometimes I think I had better hurry up and get married. At least I might have someone to talk to.

It is boring. I am not allowed to cook, only to order the meals if I so wish, but if I venture to the kitchens it makes the servants nervous, for I am no longer a child to be hugged and spoiled with little cakes and tender meats, I am the young mistress of the house, second only to my mother. There are servants to do every possible task. Myriam only gossips about people I have no interest in. I play music and sing sometimes, or dance a little, but it is not much fun alone. All the little girls with whom I was encouraged to play as a child are no longer my friends after I ignored their company and favoured the street children for all those years, and anyway most of them have already been married off. My mother lives her own life with Hela, keeping to her rooms, waited on hand and foot. She emerges when her presence is required but otherwise ignores me entirely. My father is an older, sadder man now. He spends little time in our house except for the evening meals when we have guests, which, as always, are elaborate and elegant. No one ever speaks Imen's name and my memories of her have faded. From her short time in this house I remember only her laughter and the kitten she gave me, who is fat and slow now but still fond of being stroked and whose purr is still loud.

I pass the time watching the sun circle through the sky, being washed and dressed, attending fine meals, thinking up ever more elaborate dishes for the kitchen staff to attempt, watching the birds as they fly above our courtyard. In this last I am joined by the cat, who peers hopefully at them without the slightest chance of ever catching one.

I used to enjoy the heat and cleansing calm of the hammam and went there often to pass the time, but it has lost its charm now that my body is eyed up every time I disrobe. Gnarled old matchmakers sit in the dark corners and their eyes turn on me as soon as I enter, inspecting every part of me, from my hair to my toes. They note how much hair I have on my body, the size of my breasts, the length of my legs, the shape of my toes, the curve of my behind. I am aware that they think I am too thin, but other than that they concur that I have a fine body, well-proportioned and delicate for all my height. They mutter that I ought to eat more fatty meat and rich cakes, but they cannot say that I am not beautiful, and they admit that my mother is also slender and that therefore it may be something I cannot help – this is said in pitying tones, with much shaking of the head and pursed lips. At first I used to stare in my own mirror and think about what I'd heard them say about me, wonder whether my breasts were the right size to please a future husband and whether I would bear sons easily, but having heard them discuss every other girl my age I know there is no pleasing them, there is always something they will find to tut over – one girl is too tall, another too short, I am too slender and another girl too fat. I have grown resigned to the knowledge that my naked body has been described to all their fellow matchmakers across the land, for their tongues do not lack speed even if their wrinkled old bodies creak and groan when they move from their warm dark corners. It is their descriptions that have brought the suitors to our table, night after night.

The suitors come in all shapes and sizes, and most importantly in all ages and degrees of wealth. There are the young eager ones, who blush more than I do and whose fathers accompany them, their lusting eyes wishing they were choosing a bride for themselves rather than for their sons. There are the wrinkled old ones, scrawny and with missing teeth or with red faces and fat bellies. These leer at me, eat too much and smack their lips. Some are old colleagues of my fathers, who talk shop all during the meal, either barely glancing my way or else looking at me as they would at a fine carpet, expertly counting knots at a glance. When they look at me I see them counting up my assets – long silken hair, fine limbs, elegant features of the face, well-to-do family. Then they turn back to my father and the talks continue, bartering over prices – mine or the carpets, I am never quite sure. I am only another commodity, I suppose. For all the tales of great loves that Myriam is so fond of hearing from the storytellers in the marketplaces, I can't quite imagine any of these suitors inspiring any such feeling in me. There are a few rather touching ones, who have fallen in love – or lust – at first sight, and who return night after night, seeking to sway my father's opinion. They cannot take their gaze from my face, which grows wearisome when I want to bite hungrily into a piece of chicken or when something has become stuck in my teeth. I suffer them in silence and leave as soon as I can. In this way the poor love-stricken men see less of me than those who do not much care whom they marry, so long as the woman is attractive and of a good family.

They are all well off, of course, or they would not even attempt my hand. Even so, there are those who are sons of chiefs and amirs or indeed chiefs and amirs in their own right. The amirs, of course, do not come themselves. They send emissaries, wily men who look me up and down and mentally catalogue me alongside the other beauties they have seen on their travels to find the next queen of a grand city, the next wife for a rich and important ruler. They wonder how much favour I will bring them at a distant court if they bring me back to their lord.

The chiefs sometimes come themselves, unwilling to trust someone else's judgement. These are men who have fought for their chiefdoms, warriors, who trust no-one but their own sharp eyes and strong arms in battle. They are a little ill at ease in my father's house, full of rich carpets and fine foods. They are used to plainer fare and simple clothes, to sitting amongst men, not being joined for an elaborate dinner by women dressed in fine robes and jewels like my mother and I. Of course with my mother's past history the chiefs are often a little wary about my fertility. A son is everything to them, and if I should fail to provide one then all the beauty in the world would not be sufficient to entice them.

I could have been married a good year ago, for there have been plenty of suitors to choose from and many fine offers have been made. But my father delays my future marriage. He raises objections to the suitors, regarding their lineage, their wealth, their distance from our own city. And so the talks go on and on and yet more visitors come to our table. Word spreads, of course, that many have sought my hand and been turned away, and all this does is increase my value, my desirability. As time goes by only chiefs and amirs make their advances, their sons no longer deeming themselves worthy. The merchants, meanwhile, have long since fallen by the wayside, however rich they are. What at first seemed rather exciting – the idea of being wooed and married – has come to seem tedious and unlikely ever to actually happen.

Tonight my father has decided that for a change he will have an evening that does not feature a fawning suitor for my hand. He declares he is weary of the same conversations night after night. Myriam is happy, for she can go and visit her friends and not spend the evening beautifying me. Tonight my father has a customer for carpets. His name is Yusuf bin Ali, the chief of the Wurika and Aylana tribes, whose boundaries are close to the great city of Aghmat, very far to the South West. There he lives in a *ksar*, one of the fortified cities of the desert-dwellers. It is for his own home that he comes to buy carpets, but my father is keen to strike up a good trade with him, for it is known that he travels much and is a friend of many important men, including the amir of Aghmat and so if he should like my father's carpets it may well be that my father can expect patronage from the amir also.

I beg leave from the table. I, too, am weary of the grand banquets. I would like to be left alone, especially as this Yusuf has no interest in me – he has come to see carpets, not seek a bride. My father grants me permission to be absent. The servants can bring food to my rooms when I am hungry and I will have an evening to do as I please, an evening when I will not be stared at. I dress in my favourite robe, originally a stiff bright yellow silk for formal occasions, which over time has worn to a pale glow, soft and comfortable. I leave it loose. To be without jewels and heavy constricting belts is a relief. My hair falls free, untied and uncovered. My feet are bare. I lie on my bed playing with my cat, who enjoys sitting on me if I lie obediently still while she closes her eyes in happiness, gently kneading my stomach. Unlike other cats she remembers to sheath her claws and so the experience is a pleasant one and my robe is not pierced. I tickle her ears and sing to her, which is difficult when lying on your back with a heavy cat on your belly, but I try anyway and she purrs in sleepy contentment.

I awake in darkness and realise I must have slept for many hours. I had not realised how tired I was, nor how pleasant it is to sleep with a light stomach, albeit one topped with a heavy cat, rather than an uncomfortably full one. But now I am hungry and the house is quiet. The dinner must have finished some time ago and our guest will have gone away satisfied with his bartering and our generous table. Now everyone is asleep. If I creep quietly downstairs I will disturb no-one. In the kitchen there will be leftovers – fresh bread, olives, figs and butter. There may even be meat. My stomach grumbles. I set the cat aside. She keep her eyes shut and growls, annoyed at my having the audacity to move when she is still deep in slumber. I open the heavy wooden door of my room and make my way down the stairs.

In the kitchen I find everything I could wish for and prepare a plate of good food, my stomach making happy gurgles as it senses the smells around me. I dip into a large jar for fresh cool water and then decide to eat in our courtyard rather than upstairs. The night air is still warm and our courtyard is always a pleasant place, full of pale scented flowers in the darkness. My eyes have grown used to the night and I make my way to a low bench set into an alcove in the wall. I place the plate beside me, then eat hungrily. It feels good to sit here all alone and eat with real hunger rather than a false dainty refinement. My fingers get oily and I lick them clean and then continue to eat.

"What an appetite you have." The voice is a man's, low and amused.

I would scream but my mouth is full of bread and meat. I gulp and my throat hurts as the half-chewed food is forced down. I peer into the darkness. A shadow moves slightly in the alcove opposite me in the courtyard.

"If you come near me I will scream," I say. My voice trembles. I do not sound very threatening.

I hear a chuckle. I relax a little since the speaker has not yet moved from their bench. I consider running upstairs, but this would mean running past the man and I do not have the courage. I shrink back into the alcove.

"I would not dream of coming near the daughter of the house without her express permission."

"How do you know I am the daughter of the house?"

"Your robes sound like silk. You just helped yourself to food in the kitchens. If you were a servant girl you would be whipped if you were caught. Besides, a servant girl would not threaten a guest."

My shoulders drop with relief. I make my own deduction. "You are Yusuf bin Ali, my father's visitor."

I hear a slow, soft clap. "Very good."

"I thought you were only here for dinner."

"It got late. Your father is a kind host. He invited me to stay the night."

"On a bench in our courtyard?"

He laughs again. I am beginning to like his laughter, it is slow, as though he has all night to laugh. I do not often hear such laughter in our house. Besides, he is my father's guest, so he is not going to attack me after all. I am safe. "I bought many carpets. I think your father thought I was worth a room at least."

"Why are you not in it, then?"

"Too hot. I wanted some fresh night air as the day cooled."

We sit in silence for a while, on our opposite sides of the courtyard. When he speaks again I realise I have been waiting for him to do so. I like the way he speaks, unhurried, how I can hear his smile even in the dark. "Why did you not attend dinner?"

"I wanted a night without a banquet."

"Do you have so many fine meals then?"

"Yes."

"Always customers for your father's carpets?"

"No."

"What then?"

I am unwilling to tell him. It sounds like boasting. I mumble my words.

"What did you say?"

"Suitors."

"Suitors? Who for?"

"Me, of course," I say, a little indignantly. I did not want to boast but neither do I like his tone of surprise.

"How old are you?"

"Sixteen."

"Surely not."

"Why not?" I am put out, he sounds as though he thought I was merely a child to be entertained.

The shadows move. I hear him walk towards me. I should leave, of course, should not let a strange man approach me in the darkness, even if he is my father's guest, but I am curious. Why does he not believe I am sixteen? He comes closer and I move to one end of my bench. He comes close enough to be facing me were I standing and then stops, a tall form stood over me. I can smell him, a warm scent, of smoke and camels, a masculine smell tempered with a fleeting sweet perfume, something like orange blossoms. His robes seem to be dark. His face is mostly covered with a thick veil wrapped round his head, in the manner of tribesmen from the South. I can hear my own heart beating and my breathing seems very loud. I try to quiet it by breathing very lightly.

"You're very quiet," he says.

I breathe out more heavily, relieved that he cannot hear me breathing after all.

"Why are you sighing?" he asks.

I stop breathing altogether.

He sits down alongside me on the bench, although he is at the far end. If I were to reach out my hand I would just be able to touch him.

I tuck my hands into the sleeves of my robes and start to breathe again, but very quietly.

"So, these suitors," he says. He sounds as if he would like to laugh, as though he is talking to a child about a make-believe friend.

I feel myself stiffen with pride. "What about them?"

"Who are they?"

I will ensure he is impressed. He cannot fail to be. My suitors are the talk of Kairouan. "Amirs, mostly."

I hear him barely suppress a snort of laughter. "Really."

"Yes, really. Lots of them. They come practically every night, from all over the Maghreb. Asking for my hand." I know that I sound like a boastful child.

"How nice for you."

"Not really," I admit reluctantly.

"No? Why ever not? Lots of rich important men begging for your hand in marriage? I would have thought that was what every girl wanted."

"No."

"Why not?"

I struggle to explain. "They look at me... I have to dress up... they don't talk like..."

"Don't talk like what?"

"Like – like you." My face burns, I did not mean to say that at all. My toes clench.

His voice is softer, curious. He leans forward a little, trying to make out my features in the darkness. "Like me? How do I talk, then?"

"Properly."

"Properly?"

I squirm. But I have to explain now or he will think I am a mad babbling fool. Once I explain he will understand and I will not look like a fool. "You just – talk to me. Like a person. Like people who know me well. The suitors don't. They sit there and eat for hours, they talk to my father about boring things and sometimes they say polite things to my mother. They look at me as if I was a sweet cake but they don't talk to me. Just words that don't mean anything."

"Like what?"

"Like how gracious and beautiful I am."

He leans back, chuckling. "I'm sure you are."

I struggle on with my explanation. "No – not even as if they meant it. Just things you *say*, all formal and like a story. You know, 'the lady Zaynab, whose form is most lovely unto the eye and whose beauty must make the very birds of the air fly closer that they might see her better…' that sort of thing. They don't *mean* it. They just say it because you have to when you're asking for a girl's hand in marriage."

"Do you?"

"Yes."

He laughs out loud. "I shall remember that when I am next looking for a wife."

I laugh, but he suddenly stands up and I press back against the wall. He turns and walks away without another word. I want to follow him, want to say something else, although I am not sure what. A good-bye at least, it seems very rude for him to walk away without bidding me farewell. I get up too fast and my forgotten brass plate of half-eaten food crashes to the tiled floor. I gasp at the loudness of it and hear him chuckle as he goes up the stairs.

I stand all alone in the dark courtyard and breathe.

Myriam is grumpy and surprised when I wake her in the morning. It is usually she who wakes me, dragging me from my warm bed to say my prayers. Then I often return to my bed, asking for food to be brought to me, much to Myriam's disgust at my lazy ways. This morning I have already prepared our mats and as soon as prayers are over I run to my chests and pull out one of my finest robes, a rich pink silk with so much embroidery that it weighs as much as a heavy water jar. I normally object to wearing such clothes, complaining that they are too heavy and cumbersome, too formal for anything but a wedding perhaps. Now I insist on being washed, perfumed, and dressed not only in the robe but in all the additional items that go with it. Fine slippers, a heavy ornamental belt, a great deal of jewellery. I even kneel in front of my mirror and darken my eyes with kohl, put red stains on my lips and cheeks. I stand, satisfied, as Myriam holds up the mirror. I look much older than sixteen, and very beautiful, even I can see that. I turn this way and that, admiring myself, my cheeks growing pinker.

Myriam is perplexed. "Where are you going dressed like that?"

"Breakfast."

Myriam snorts. "Nobody dresses like that for breakfast. You look like you are going to a wedding." She considers my outfit for another moment. "In fact you look like you are the *bride.* You only need the gold headdress."

I smile a huge smile at her and walk slowly, gracefully, downstairs. This will show him. My clothes, bearing and beauty will show him that I am quite old enough to be married, that of *course* I have suitors clamouring for my hand. Last night he teased me as though I were a child, and then left without even having the manners to say goodbye. I am not a child, and now he will see this for himself. He will be obliged to behave better to me, more appropriately. He will have to notice that I am beautiful when I am dressed like this. The darkness was not my friend last night. I do not even know what he looks like, only how he laughs and the sound of his low voice.

My father is sat at a table in our courtyard, together with Yusuf bin Ali. I am relieved that my mother is not with them, she would only look at me with her unblinking eyes in a way that always makes me awkward and clumsy.

I stand for a moment and observe them before I make my presence known. I want to see this man who was so funny and interesting last night but who then walked away without even bidding me farewell. In the darkness he was only a shadow, a low, laughing voice and a scent that I would recognise anywhere if I smelt it again. Now I can see him by daylight.

He is tall, even sitting down he is taller than my father and I can see that he has long legs under his robes. His hair and eyes are very dark and he has strong thick brows. Much of his face is hidden, but his robes fall back from his arms as he raises a cup of tea to his lips and I see his forearms, which are thick with muscles. By his side lies a large sword, sheathed in a magnificent scabbard. He is a warrior, there can be no doubt about that. He must have fought for his chiefdom.

My father hears me coming and hears the servants ask me what I would like to eat. He has not yet seen me as I approach behind his back. Yusuf, however, can see me, for he sits facing my father. His eyes take in my appearance. I wait for his eyes to widen, for him to smile, as all my suitors, even the old and ugly ones, have always done. I am disappointed. He only raises his eyebrows, rises to his feet and bows politely. I might as well be an honoured and wrinkled old grandmother, hobbling to the table to suck toothlessly at some soft bread.

"It is an honour to meet the daughter of the house," he says without a trace of recognition or interest.

My father catches sight of me and looks surprised, but then waves me to a seat by him. "My daughter, Zaynab," he introduces me. "Very elegant, I am sure," he adds as he knits his brows at my clothes. He turns back to Yusuf. "Girls, you know, they do so like to dress up at their age." He pats my shoulder, not unkindly.

I am crushed. I sit at the table for another hour, eating a few mouthfuls and listening to my father and Yusuf discussing carpets – the patterns, knots, their transportation back to Yusuf's home. Payment, it seems, has already been dealt with. Yusuf pays no attention to me at all and I gradually lose my elegant posture and end up sitting slumped against cushions, stroking my lazy cat who is seeking comfort. When the time comes for Yusuf to leave I do not bother to stand up. He bows perfunctorily in my direction and leaves with my father for the workshops.

So he is gone. A rude man after all, certainly he seemed pleasant at first but his manners were very unrefined. I shall not have to see him again, so that is a good thing. I walk slowly back to my room and snap at Myriam to take off these hot heavy clothes, which she does without any expression on her face, for which I am grateful. I spend the rest of the day seeking out something to do and end up getting in all the servants' way as they try to complete their daily chores. Eventually I retire to my room and sit staring out at the sky until I fall asleep with boredom.

Tonight we have guests, not suitors but friends of my father's. There will be many of them, so I will be able to leave earlier. It would be rude to leave when there are just a few of us, but when we are many I can often sneak away. I do not wish to draw attention to myself when I escape so I discard almost all the robes Myriam offers, choosing the very plainest of my elegant robes, a dark blue silk, refuse most of my jewellery and present myself downstairs.

He is there. Yusuf. Talking and laughing with my father and his friends as though he has known them all for years. At ease, confident, full of charm and good humour. I keep well away from him, for the very sight of him makes me feel quite ill – why do I have to endure his presence again? He has behaved very rudely to me, so I will have nothing to do with him. Luckily he does not once look in my direction and I keep very close to my mother who eyes me with some surprise, for we do not generally spend much time together. But she tolerates me near her and when we have eaten and everyone has settled back to talk, replete with good food, I start to edge my way to the door. I creep outside and then breathe with relief and make my way up to my room. Inside I kick off my shoes, then decide to slip outside and sit by our fountain where it will be cooler.

"Was the company not to your liking?"

Yusuf is standing right outside my door. I yelp and leap backwards, slamming the door in his face. I lean against it, wondering what on earth he is doing. I can hear him laughing, not the low chuckle from the other night but a full belly-laugh. I open the door again in a temper. "Get away from my door! How dare you come near me again after your behaviour?"

He stops laughing and considers me carefully, as though surprised. "What behaviour?"

I am spluttering with indignation. The door opens wider as I enumerate his failings. "You made fun of me when we first met and then walked off without saying goodbye. Then you acted as though you'd never seen me before at the breakfast table and treated me like some old woman instead of…" Words fail me. "Well, anyway… and then you went off again really quite rudely, and then tonight, you barely looked at me."

He puts one hand on the doorframe and leans towards me. His face is close to mine and I breathe in his scent without realising it. His voice is low. "Did you want me to look at you?"

"No!" I say automatically, then stop. "I just..."

He looks at me and then reaches out one hand and cups my face very gently. "Lovely Zaynab," he says. His voice is so low that afterwards I am not sure that he really says what he does, although I cannot stop repeating it in my mind. "So very lovely. Do the birds really fly closer to the earth the better to see you?"

I do not know what to say or do except close my eyes that I might hear his words better. I feel his breath caress my cheek. Then there is silence. When I open my eyes again he is gone.

He comes again though, night after night, talking and laughing with my father, who enjoys his company. His trading in the city will be over soon but while he remains in Kairouan he is my father's guest, for my father will not hear of him going elsewhere in the evenings. Often he stays the night as well and I have to face him at breakfast. He is unfailingly courteous and charming to me, but he never again comes to the door of my bedroom, no matter how many times I try to tempt him by sneaking away in full sight of him as I did that night.

I burn for him. I had not known this was possible. I have liked boys, thought them brave or funny, clever or handsome, but I did not know one person could feel so much and not die. How to contain such feeling? I breathe and think of him. I sleep and dream of him. I spend some days in tears because he did not glance my way the night before, other days in ecstasy because he looked my way and smiled, because he passed me soft bread at breakfast and our fingers brushed together. I am being consumed by this man and he has barely touched me. I cannot even think of his doing so, for I become dizzy and have to lie on my bed, covering my face with my robes for shame.

The dark heat of the hammams is intolerable to me now, for I have heat running through me. I crave coolness. I dip my hands in our fountain, wipe my face with damp cloths ten times a day. I try to write a poem for him and burn my attempts, for they are laughable. I write him letters which I could never send for I have not the courage.

Myriam tuts and shakes her head. I cannot fool her for she knows me too well. I try to eat and leave all untouched. I grow thinner and Myriam mutters about no girl having ever been chosen as a bride who was so skinny. I try harder to eat, chewing and swallowing with disgust, feeling the food slip down me with nowhere to settle in my churning stomach.

When he enters the room I become very still, but every part of me knows where he is, even when my eyes remain fixed on another face. While I speak calmly of inconsequential things my mouth grows dry and I feel the heat flow through me as he moves into my field of vision. When he looks my way and does not even see me I move slightly to try and draw his eyes, a foolish gazelle drawing the gaze of the lion, longing for a crushing bite to drain my too-hot blood, to leave me cool and free of such emotion. When he leaves I make my excuses and leave also, that I might run up every step in our house to the roof and, panting, seek out his shape in the courtyard below as he goes to the rooms set aside for him. When he is out of my sight I often go to my room and fall asleep in exhaustion, a mere few hours of his presence too much to bear.

He is going home.

I will die, I know it. Although he spoke my name so low, although he called me lovely he has said nothing like that since then. He smiles occasionally, he attends all my father's gatherings but he does not spend his time with me. He does not speak with me even though I creep closer to the men as they talk and hope to be included in their conversations. When my father notices me he pats me gently and says a few words to me, but the men do not wish to talk with me. They admire my beauty but have no inclination to discuss their business with a girl.

He is heading back to his home, his tribe near to Aghmat, far to the South West, many many days' journey away. I do not know how to bear it. I may never see him again and if I do I will be married, fat and old. I will have many children and he will glance my way but once and then turn away to speak with my even older husband who will smack his lips while he eats.

It is night-time and the guests are leaving. I am exhausted from crying half the day and sitting for hours through dull conversation. I see Yusuf leave the room and the tiredness takes away all my inhibitions. I follow him without muffling my steps, without disguising my presence from him. He does not turn his head, nor acknowledge my presence until we are outside his door. Then he turns to me and leans back against the heavy painted door. He smiles at me wearily. He looks older than he is, his eyes are soft with a pained tenderness. "Zaynab."

"Yusuf." We gaze at one another for many moments. He is about to speak but I hold up a hand to stop him. My heart does not race. My breath is even. I have to speak now or it will be too late. "Take me with you."

He raises his eyebrows but says nothing. I press on. "I love you. I want to be your wife."

His gaze is steady.

"Take me with you." I cannot help a pleading note entering my voice.

"You have your pick of any husband in the Maghreb. And you have a home here which you should not be so anxious to leave."

I frown at him. "This is not a happy home. The men I am offered as husbands disgust me."

"What makes you think I care for you?"

My face burns but I will not be dissuaded. "I love you. That is enough."

"Is it?"

"Yes."

"Even if I never love you?"

"I will love you. And that will be enough."

He looks at me and reaches out with great gentleness. His hand cups my cheek. "Oh, Zaynab," he says and if I were older, wiser, I would hear a great sorrow in his voice.

I close my eyes and listen for the words of love that are sure to follow. They come in a soft whisper.

"How wrong you are."

I open my eyes but he has slipped inside his room and I am left staring at the painted panels of flowers.

Myriam orders me to visit the hammam. I have not been for weeks, washing only in cold water at home. I do not wish to go. The dark fills my mind with sensual images, the heat is stifling, any touch on my skin, no matter from whom, is too intimate to bear. Myriam sets her lips firm and insists. I cannot argue, it is too much emotion on top of what I already feel. I go with her.

In the dim light she scrubs my body until I am sure I have no skin left, combs the knots from my dripping hair. She rubs me with perfumed oils as I complain about the heat and beg for us to return home. Only when she is all finished does she allow me to go to the coolest part of the room I can find and begins her own ablutions.

"I want to go home," I moan at her. "It's so *hot.*"

"You don't want to go home," says Myriam indistinctly from under a steady stream of hot water.

"I do," I insist.

"You need to stay here," says Myriam firmly as she rubs her skin with a rough cloth.

"Why?" I complain.

"Your father and Yusuf bin Ali need to speak and they do not need you wandering into the room."

I catch my breath. My heart flutters rather than beating as it should and I put one hand over it, for it feels very weak. "What are they talking about?"

Myriam finishes pouring water over herself and flicks

back her wet hair. Her voice is flat. "He wants you for his wife."

I scream with joy. Every part of me is full of life, of happiness.

"Hush!" Myriam hurries over to silence me, nearly slipping on the wet floor. "What will people think?"

I escape her pinning arms and dance around the room, wet and happy. "He is asking for my hand? This very minute? *Now*?"

Myriam nods and starts to comb her hair. She does not seem very pleased.

"Aren't you happy for me?" I demand, sitting next to her again.

She looks doubtful. "I know you like him, Zaynab, but your father is not so sure about the marriage. You will live so far away. And you know so little about him."

Nothing can make me downcast. "I will be with him. I will learn all there is to know. I will be so happy, Myriam!"

Myriam rolls her eyes but this does not dampen me. I am carried away with my fantasies. I will be with Yusuf, and despite his protestations he will love me… my body grows flushed at the thought.

My father is overly formal when he tells me. I can barely stand still before him when I am summoned. Myriam stands behind me, having reminded me all the way to his rooms to behave with dignity.

"You are to be married, Zaynab. You will marry Yusuf bin Ali, chief of the Wurika and Aylana tribes close to the great city of Aghmat. Your mother and I have agreed that you may be married immediately, for your husband-to-be needs to return to his people and it has been decided that you will accompany him when he leaves here."

I am so happy that I do not even ask the obvious question and it is Myriam who asks it on my behalf.

"When is the marriage to take place?"

"In three days' time."

Myriam and I gasp together. This is unheard of. What about the rituals, the wooing, the prayers, the feasts? No-one gets married so fast. Myriam opens her mouth but my father is already speaking again and Myriam reluctantly closes it again.

"It is very fast of course but your husband-to-be leaves in four days and he insists that you should go with him. Fortunately all can be arranged for the ceremony and as for feasts and so on – " he waves his hand dismissively "– that can all happen at his home. You have many fine clothes and jewels and I will arrange that many more be made for you in the few days that we have left to us. Other things can be sent on. You will not go to him as a beggar."

Myriam and I open our mouths again but my father is still speaking, a frown on his face.

"I need to know that you desire this union, Zaynab. I will not force you into a marriage."

"Oh yes," I stammer, over-eager to agree. "Yes, I desire – I mean – I wish to be married to Yusuf."

He nods and then opens his mouth as though he were about to say something else, but then he shakes his head. "Very well," he says. "So be it."

With this he leaves the room, and Myriam and I are left dumbfounded, our two mouths still soundlessly shaping questions to the empty doorway.

In the days that follow all is strange to me. Servants rush to and fro, Myriam barely speaks to me except to tell me what I must do next, and all around us is chaos. My mother disappears entirely and it is Hela who commands what must be done, as usual. Clothes and jewels must made. I stand before the mirror for only a moment in each outfit, barely turning this way and that before they are folded away in great chests, household goods and animals bartered for then readied for the long journey which we will undertake. One carpet after another is brought from my father's workshops and added to the pile of goods I will be taking with me to my new husband's home.

My husband! We have been married, but it has been so quick I do not even feel myself to be a wife and all the wild joy I felt at the news that I would marry this man who has consumed me has almost been thrown aside in all the hurry and the strangeness of the preparations. The words were spoken, the prayers said over our two bowed heads, mine heavy from the golden headpiece that every bride wears. There was even a feast, albeit a very minor one considering what it would have been like had the marriage not been so hasty.

I will not lie with him until we are in his home, so I am only a wife in name, not deed. I am almost grateful for this. No matter how much I wished for his touch I was afraid too, and all was done so fast I should have trembled had he come to me that night. But I am showered with good wishes and many young women of our city and their mothers smile at me most tenderly, for now I am married all those who once sought my hand may be inclined to look elsewhere.

The day of our departure has come. Prayers are said in almost-darkness and it is cold. I am wrapped in layers of clothes that I can gradually remove without losing any modesty as the sun grows hotter. Veils will cover my face from the heat of the day. There is a whole caravan of camels ready to take me and my possessions to my new home – along with those other animals that will come with us – sheep and goats, their lambs and kids bouncing along merrily for now although they will surely be weary by the time we reach our destination. As will we all. We will leave here now and join Yusuf's caravan near the outskirts of the city, before our long journey together begins.

And it is only now, after four days of madness, that I realise that I am leaving my father's home forever, and that I will live very, very far away. Only now that I look around me and realise that these familiar faces will be replaced by strangers and that I will be alone.

My mother is very pale. She kisses me and murmurs appropriate blessings, but she bites her lips repeatedly and steps back from me quickly.

Myriam is beside herself. It has been decided that I will not take servants, Yusuf will provide for me. My loving nursemaid weeps and weeps, her tears more than enough for a hundred mothers. We embrace tightly and my shoulders and cheeks are wet with tears, hers and mine.

She steps away only when my father approaches me, his face creased in a frown. "Are you truly happy, Zaynab? You have only to say the word and I will stop all of this."

I am crying but manage to smile. It comes out as more of a grimace but I need him to know that I am happy, despite appearances. "I am so happy to marry Yusuf, Father, but so sorry to leave you."

He nods and embraces me again, his voice warm against me. "Dearest Zaynab. Dearest daughter. I wish you a lifetime of happiness and no sorrows to blight your days. I know that you marry for love and I pray Allah brings you nothing but love in your life. And she will be gone one day, so have no fears."

I pull back to see his face, puzzled. "Who will be gone?"

He hushes me. "You are a beautiful girl. Young, warm-hearted. He has five healthy sons and now he will have you. In due course it will be as though they were your own sons and he will love you as you love him."

My many layers of clothes are too hot. I step away from him and remove my heavy outer robe, blindly letting it drop, saved from the dust only by a quick-witted servant. There is sweat springing up on my upper lip and under my eyes, running between my breasts and making my hands wet. I clench and open my hands hoping for the cold morning air to dry them. My throat, however, is already dry. When I speak my voice croaks. "Sons? He has a *wife*?"

My father opens his mouth to speak but already hands are lifting me onto a high wooden saddle, covered in soft cloths to make a comfortable seat. I keep my face turned towards my father, who stands in silence. I try to shape a question but my lips are too dry. The camels turn and we begin to move. Myriam's sobs grow louder and I look back to see my father and mother watching me as I leave.

Behind them, in the doorway of our house, Hela stands alone, a dark outline caught in the rays of the rising sun.

Concubine

MANY AND MANY HOURS OF travel go by, many and many days. The sun beats down by day, the cold nights make us shiver even in our thickest robes and the tents which are erected for us each night by the servants do little to protect us from either heat or cold. Yusuf travels far ahead of us with his men by his side. The servants are unknown to me, some speaking strange tongues, all belonging to a different land, a different household. I speak to no-one and no-one speaks to me.

I am grateful for the silence outside of me, for inside there are too many voices. I do not see the landscape change as we sway onwards, nor seek out new sights and sounds as we pass through foreign lands. My body is very still save for the movement of my camel and my face betrays no sign of my thoughts. This is how my mother always looked, still and straight, her face unmoving, her body elegant but always controlled. Did my mother also have these voices screaming in her head? I will never know now, for it is unlikely I will ever see her or any of my family again.

I want to ask her. I want to run up to her and scream into her face, to see if her eyes would blink, if she would step back. I would scream and scream until her dark eyes flickered and she looked away. I want to shake her and see her elegance and poise vanish into fear.

Why didn't anyone tell me before it was too late? Why didn't you tell me? Why? Why did no-one think I should know that he had another wife, one more senior than I, one who has five sons and will never be put aside for me to take her place? Why did you let me dream and love a man who had a wife of whom I knew nothing? Why?

My *why* is for everyone. In my mind as the hours pass I turn to each of them standing in our courtyard bidding me farewell. My mother, my father, Myriam, Hela, all of the servants. I see them step back from my screams. I see them cast down their gaze in shame before me. Of course many men have more than one wife, but not to know? To enter a house believing you are this man's only beloved and to find another woman standing there, her five sons gathered proudly around her? *Why?* As the miles go by I try to understand. Myriam and the servants, of course, may not have known, although they always seem to know everything. But my mother and father did know, and they did not tell me. Hela knows everything and she did not tell me. Yusuf did not tell me.

We pass the great city walls of Aghmat in the distance and continue towards the mountains, and it is only now I realise we have been travelling for more days than I thought, for we are nearing my new home. A narrow valley is our destination, greener than the hot deserts and scrubland around because of the river that runs through it, giving its name to both the valley and my husband's tribe. Here the mountains rise steep on either side of the river and any small patch of land that can be cultivated is set aside for food. The river is channelled here and there to wet the earth. The crops do not lack for water even if they must be hardy to grow so high. The sheep and goats are obliged to fend for themselves on the steeper rockier outcrops, with only bushes and rough grass for their food, although they are forever finding ways to try and sneak a little closer to the greener plants grown for their owners' benefit. If they are caught at their tricks they feel a stick across their haunches and bleat indignantly as they make their escape to higher ground.

Above the river, set high so as to avoid its fast and dangerous flooding in the winter, are the houses. Some are little groups of humble mud dwellings, their roofs thatched. Some, where the valley shape permits, form larger outlines. In the largest such space there are smaller houses surrounding a kasbah, a fortified castle, its moulded and decorated turrets towering above the simpler homes of the tribe. In the kasbah live those of importance, the chieftains, their families, their closest and most trusted men. Should danger come, as it so often does, from the nomads of the desert or refugees from tribal wars, those in the smaller houses would run here, their animals driven ahead of them, the heavy wooden doors then pushed closed by many hands, made to open only from inside. Here people and their animals can live for many days before hunger drives them out, and the turrets and rooftops allow for an advantage in warfare. This, then, is my husband's home, and now it is mine.

The kasbah towers above us as the camels make their

final weary way up the hillside. The houses around it glow soft peach as the sun sets and their outlines offer a stepped silhouette following the shape of the valley sides. I look up towards the kasbah and see smiling faces at every window and on every rooftop leading to it. Their chieftain Yusuf bin Ali is home again after much time away, and every person feels some measure of relief that he is returned to protect them. Once they have looked at him their eyes run over the servants, all known to them of course, and at the many bundles of new goods that Yusuf has brought back with him. Then their eyes turn to me, the unknown woman in the caravan, dressed in fine robes, young and beautiful. The whispers run quickly from the base of the valley to its very summit, to the high turrets of the kasbah itself. It is clear what I am. A new wife for their chief. There are giggles between children, smiles between women and lecherous glances from the men at me behind Yusuf's back as we progress. The whispers all around me die to silence as we reach the kasbah and its great doors are flung open.

They stand in the doorway, five boys, little height difference between them. The eldest is perhaps only seven or eight, his cheeks round and pink as ripe figs, his smile full of delight at seeing his father. The youngest is only a baby, he cannot even stand alone but clings grinning to his oldest brother's robes. All of them come beaming towards Yusuf, who leaps down from his camel and embraces them one by one.

I scan the crowd from my place high on my camel. I see servants, soldiers, slaves and in the midst Yusuf and his sons. But I see no woman of high rank. Where is this wife who has won everlasting honour for having borne five sons in such quick succession?

One of Yusuf's men stands at my side and commands the camel to kneel. It does so with weary relief and I am lifted bodily from its back. I stagger a little, for I have been riding since daybreak. I am dizzy with fear.

Yusuf turns to me as I approach. The crowd's noise dims a little. He smiles at me. He is happy to be home, to be with his sons again. "Welcome Zaynab," he says. "Welcome to your home. These are your children now, as they are mine. Boys, welcome your new mother."

They make their welcomes to me, the eldest with a nervous but formal speech, the youngest with a grin that shows me his first tiny teeth, newly acquired.

I try to smile but I am watchful. Where is the mother of these children? It is dangerous to be enchanted by cubs when a mother is nearby and may rip you apart for passing on your scent to her offspring. But still there is no woman. Gently I greet each child. Then I am led through the gates and into my new home.

It is cool in my new rooms. The servants chatter excitedly to one another. They seem pleased by my presence, eager to welcome me. Yusuf and his sons have been ushered away, no doubt to visit his first wife, wherever she may be. Meanwhile I am brought fresh water to drink and for bathing, my belongings are unpacked at speed and distributed about my quarters. There is much admiration for my clothing, which is stupidly rich for my new life. My father's house was one of luxury and idleness. This is a community where there are farmers and warriors, where women work hard. Their clothes are of good quality but simple, of wool and sometimes linen in plain bold colours or stripes, not rich embroidered silks like mine. There are servants and slaves, but not as many as I am used to. They are more familiar, addressing me and smiling, trying to show me everything at once.

"Get out of the way, you fools, you're exhausting her."

The servants scatter and I see the woman who has entered. She is old, bent, but wiry and quick in her movements. She grins at me with a mouth missing many teeth and hustles the rest of the servants out of the room. She settles herself on my bed and pats it invitingly. I stumble slightly on my way across the room but recover and sit beside her. She smiles and puts one arm about me as though she has known me all her life.

"Cry if you like."

And I do. I do not speak, only sob against this stranger's shoulder, wetting her clothes, sniffling until I can cry no longer. She passes me water without removing her arm from me. I gulp it down and sit up, a little ashamed.

"S-sorry," I begin. "I – "

"Nonsense," she interrupts briskly. "What have you to be sorry for? You're only sixteen and you have been married off to a man who lives a very long way away from your home. You have travelled in the heat and you are tired. Too much for a child to bear."

I do not object to her calling me a child, for it is how I feel – a babe among strangers, disorientated and fearful, fretful for a familiar face.

She looks about the room. "Have you everything you need?"

I nod meekly.

"What do you need to know about this household that Yusuf has not already told you?"

I want to laugh. He told me nothing. He told me nothing at all and I did not ask. Because I was a fool. I begged him to marry him and swore that my love for him was enough. He took me at my word and brought me here and now I doubt my love is equal to this challenge.

I shake my head. I cannot even think where to begin. "Who are you?"

She smiles. "I am Yusuf's mother. My name is Khalila."

I am horrified. I try to move, to perform a gesture of respect to my mother-in-law but she only laughs and holds me tighter. She is strong for an old woman.

"No need for such things. I am too old to need them to feel important." I sit back in her embrace and we look at one another. She looks at my tear-stained face and asks very gently, "What do you know of Badra?'

This, then, is the unspoken name now made known to me.

"Is she..."

She nods. "Yusuf's first wife. Mother to his sons."

I shrug, eyes on the floor. I am not sure I want to hear anything about her, I am too afraid.

Khalila sighs but her tone is brisk, as though she means to tell me all quickly, with as little pain as possible. "She was lovely. Beautiful, light of heart, warm of smile. Yusuf loved her at first sight, he would see no other's face. But she refused him. She told him she did not love him, that her heart could not embrace him. But he would hear no refusal. He must have her. He swore his love would suffice for them both."

I turn my face back to her shoulder and feel the wetness of my spent tears. I cannot listen to this story, but Khalila continues. "So they were wed. Yusuf did all he could to make her love him as he loved her, for he was certain that her love would flow to him one day, if he could but make her happy. For her part she tried. She was fond of him and tender to him, but her love could not flow for him." She sighs again, as though this part is harder to tell. "A child came. And all rejoiced, Yusuf most of all. But after the child was born Badra's light heart and warm smile faltered. She grew sad. A sadness that would not leave her. The sun did not shine on her, food grew tasteless in her mouth, flowers lost their perfume. The years have gone by. She has birthed five sons, all healthy, all strong. She is honoured and loved like no other wife, but still her sadness has not left her, indeed it has grown greater with each child she has born. At last a physician said that she must bear no more children, for they do not delight her as they should a mother but instead make her eyes darker and her spirit heavier. Perhaps if she does not bear children for a time she will grow lighter of heart."

I pull away from her. "This is why he needs a new wife? To lie with rather than Badra, that she may not bear children?"

Khalila tightens her lips and nods.

A cold thought comes to me. "Am I to bear children also?"

She shakes her head slowly. "Yusuf has sworn not to hurt Badra's heart, for he loves her still. He will come to you when you will not fall with child. In this way he can satisfy his desires without risk of causing her greater grief."

I stare at her.

Gently she strokes my hair, with pity in her eyes. "He spoke with tenderness of you. He said you had a great sweetness in your eyes, that you laid your heart at his feet and he could not turn it away."

I shake my head and she gets up and softly leaves the room.

I lie back on the bed and stare up at the bare ceiling.

I have been taken as a concubine, nothing more.

I have been in my new home for three days when a servant comes to me and says that Yusuf will come to my room tonight. I thank him with grace and then give frantic orders for the preparation of my rooms, of myself. As the hours pass and evening grows closer my heart flutters still faster. This, after all, is why I am here, in this long narrow valley, perched on this hillside in my fortified rooms. I am here because this man took my heart in the darkness of my father's house, with only a few words. I am here because I am only sixteen and I fell in love for the first time with a man from another country, a man almost twice my age, a man who makes my body both hot and cold with nothing more than a glance. This is the man who is now my husband but with whom I have never yet lain. This is the man whose home I have tiptoed around, afraid to see his children's curious faces at every turning. I have kept to my rooms these past days, peering from my windows at the steeply-stacked houses below, unsure of my place in this new world. I feel Badra's shadow everywhere. I do not know how to proceed.

I long for tonight. Tonight I will welcome my husband to my bed and I will become his wife in more than name. His desire will raise my status within these walls and I will learn how I can claim my place in this new life. In years to come Badra may leave this world and he may grow to love me. Perhaps he will misjudge his visits to me and I will bear a child of my own.

I am clean and perfumed, dressed in my softest silks. My rooms, also, are clean and scented with incense, soft with fine carpets and wall hangings. They are warm and welcoming, as I am nervously trying to be. When Yusuf strides into my presence as the sun sinks and our mountain walls glow in the fading light I order food and drink and have to pitch my voice lower than I normally speak so that the tremor in my words will not be heard. When we are alone I shakingly pour water for our hands. We eat. Yusuf leans back, comfortable in his home, on my fine cushions, while I sit rigidly upright, afraid to spoil my fine clothes with creases or food dropped in ungraceful uneasiness.

"So it is true what they say," remarks Yusuf between mouthfuls.

"What do they say?" I ask.

I think 'they' must mean the servants, or worse, his sons. What might they say about me? That I stay in my rooms too much? Perhaps they think me rude or arrogant? In truth I am only very shy in this new world, but perhaps they do not see that, only note my absence and read into it something I do not intend. I look at him anxiously and wait to hear more. He takes a drink of sweet juice and grins at me.

"Why, that if you marry a girl from Kairouan she will fill your house with carpets and roses," he says, waving his hand at the soft patterned rugs and indicating the incense burner.

The breath I was holding in escapes in a laugh and he laughs with me. He offers me fruits and I take them from his hand. I am swept all over with love and desire. This is why I am here. I love Yusuf, and despite his first wife he must love me. Yes, he had another wife once, but she might as well be dead, for she does little else but sit in her rooms and gaze far away, or weep. He may mourn her spirit and he may have warned me he might not care for me, but he asked for me to be his wife and brought me here. I will live with him forever, loving, and in time, loved in turn. He moves closer to me, begins to disrobe me while he leads me to our bed. I, anxious to please, trembling with hope and fear, hold myself ready for whatever he may wish to do with me.

He looks at me, first at my too-fixed smile and then down to my meekly compliant body. He smiles and strokes my hair with tenderness, and then he reaches away from me, to where his clothes fell by the bedside, and pulls out two lengths of golden silk. He does not speak, but ties one round his eyes. With great care he ties the second piece about my own eyes.

In the darkness that has now descended on each of us he reaches out to my young, unknown body and holds his beloved wife Badra in his arms for the first time in more than a year. His strong voice breaks a little as he whispers gentle endearments that were never meant for my ears.

I see nothing. I feel only the man I love caressing me and with a moan I take him into me. The golden silk around my eyes hides my lover's face but in my mind I see Yusuf's eyes on mine. His face is filled with love, his arms wrapped tightly about my naked body. The endearments I hear whispered are for me and me alone. He is everything to me as I am everything to him.

His dark eyes are fixed on me as I cry out.

He comes and goes. He is away for long periods without telling me in advance, so that I am often wrong-footed when I inquire from the servants as to his whereabouts and received a puzzled response that he has been away from us for many days and that he will not return for a month – did I not know? After a few such embarrassments I have learnt to hold my tongue. If he is here I embrace him, if he does not appear then I am silent and wait impatiently for his unknown return, keeping mostly to my rooms. I do not know how to be with his sons. I eat with them sometimes, stumble through their games and questions. I am awkward and do not know what my place is. It is easier to retreat to my rooms, where my servants wait on me without question, without the need for conversation. Slowly Yusuf's sons learn not to follow me, not to demand my presence. They forget about me.

Khalila does not forget about me. She tries to coax me out of my rooms. She takes me to see fresh fruits being grown, introduces me to the people of the tribe, who welcome me. They see in me a hope for Yusuf's future, a freshness and youth that has been missing in his life and which they hope will turn him away from Badra's misery. The servants care for her, but they know better than to expect thanks or a smile. They make sure she drinks enough water in the heat of the day, that she eats when the family eats. At night they make her bed and lay her gently in it. She does not resist, she eats and sleeps when told to but she takes no joy nor rest from either.

It is dusk on the day when I go to her. I follow a steep flight of stairs that wind to the roof. Inside a flower-carved door are her rooms. They are filled with flowers and fruits. The setting sun sheds its last rays on her face as she sits on her bed, facing the view to the valley below.

She is older than I, of course, but her skin is soft and her face sweet. Her hair is washed and combed and lies on her back in gentle ripples. Her clothes are good quality, woven in bright colours. She wears fine jewellery. I wince a little when I see the traditional gifts of love – the fine beads of engagement, the heavy bangles given for a wedding gift.

I stand awkward in the doorway. I feel as though I should not enter for she does not acknowledge me.

"I am Zaynab," I begin.

She does not answer, nor even blink at my voice, too loud in this quiet room.

"Sister," I try again, remembering that I must show respect to her, the elder and more senior wife.

There is no movement. I edge into the room and carefully sit beside her. I sit as she does, looking out towards the window, trying to see what she sees.

There is only a clear blue sky, paling now towards white

as the sun's power fades. She does not look down towards the far valley where people tend to their crops and beasts. She does not look closer to the walls where her children play in the last light of day. She sits motionless and stares as blue becomes white and will soon become blackness.

I leave, and then return some days later, thinking perhaps to touch her shoulder, to sit in front of her so she may see my eyes and I hers. I come to the rooms at the very summit of the kasbah and stand in her doorway.

Yusuf is here. He lies with his back to me, facing her on their great bed, her face turned towards him so that I can see her from where I stand. He whispers soft words to her, caresses her shoulders and face with infinite love and tenderness. She lies immobile, does not respond, nor do her eyes flicker to meet mine as I stand shaking in the doorway.

I run back to my own rooms and weep.

I do not return to Badra's rooms again.

Yusuf has been gone a month this time and I am burning up for his touch. At least when it is dark and his skin is next to mine I can feel that he is mine and forget for a moment that he will be gone again by morning without a backward glance, with only the lengths of golden silk left on the floor of my chamber to remind me that he comes to me only to feel Badra's body in his arms.

I sit in front of my mirror and look at myself with rising impatience. I am sixteen years of age and nothing more than a concubine. So be it. If that is my role then I will be the best there is. I will not try to compete with his wife by having sons, for what more use of sons has Yusuf?

I heard the whispers in the bathhouses, I know what herbs I must drink so that no life will take hold in my womb. I will take another road. I will learn such things as will bind Yusuf to me forever. I will leave him gasping for my presence. He will not go away again like this, leaving me here alone and idle, a living being only when he is nearby, a lifeless rock the rest of the time, merging perfectly with my rocky surroundings here on the hill-tops. He will not sit at table laughing with his sons while I wait alone in my room, hoping he will deign to reward my beauty with his presence in my bed. He will not lie by Badra's side and whisper to her while I wait in my rooms, unwanted for my too-fertile body. This is not the life I wish to live. I want to be desired, loved. I want to be a woman of importance in this household, not a mere adornment to its master.

I will make Yusuf love me. I call for my servant. She is taken aback by my request, but gold has its uses. She will never have seen so much gold in her own hand in all her life, and she never will again. This is her greatest chance to change her fortune, her station in life. She assures me that everything I wish will be done and that my request will go with her to her death.

The woman, when she arrives, is not as I expected. I thought I would be sent a woman so perfect in her beauty, so renowned in her skills, that men would run to her side and pay her whatever she asked. But when the door closes on the growing darkness outside and we are alone she removes her heavy robes and in the flickering lights of the lamps I see before me a brisk, stout woman. She is my own height, so taller than most, but her waist is thick and her features plain. Her long hair has many strands of grey in it. I am dissatisfied, and it shows on my face. I was going to welcome her, to ask for her help with humbleness. Now I step back from her rudely and sit on my bed, disappointed and embarrassed in equal measure. My servant girl deserves a beating for sending me this woman. What can she have to teach me? I may be unskilled but I am beautiful – and young. I am sixteen, this woman is my mother at least once over. I fold my arms and lift my chin to meet her eyes without comment. She will see that she has displeased me and she will leave.

She stands before me, her eyes on mine. Her heavy outer wraps lie at her feet, where she cast them off. Her robes are quite plain, dark and long, shapeless. I had thought such a woman would wear finer, more colourful apparel, something to draw the eye. But her eyes are warm and bright, as though she were truly happy to be here in this room, standing before a young girl who is sitting sulkily on her bed, not speaking. It is then that I notice she is moving, but only very slightly. I seek out the source of the movement, for she seemed very still only a moment before.

Her hips are barely moving. A tiny ripple from the folds of her robe is all I see, but it is so slight as to make me look harder, to catch her at it, to see how she can move and yet move so little. As I watch the movement becomes greater and her hips sway in ever increasing twin circles, the dark fabric around her accentuating and yet somehow hiding the rhythm. As I watch her hips her arms begin to rise past her thighs, up by her waist, catching my eyes and bringing them up towards her breasts, which are suddenly exposed as she undoes some secret fastening. My head jerks back at the sight of them, so quickly laid open to my eyes. They are larger than mine and not so pert, rounded and a softer brown than her arms. Her naked skin gleams with a patina of many years of soft creams and perfumes, warm water and caressing hands.

I draw my feet in towards me, sitting curled up now, shy and yet fascinated. I am not sure where to look. Of course she is nothing but a common whore, and so I am free to look where I choose, but still I find I am curled ever tighter, my face now resting on my knees. I am not quite ready to look at her eyes again, but I watch her dance, transfixed.

She is oblivious to me, it seems. She dances in silence but so intent is she that I can hear the rhythm she is following as though the room were filled with musicians. Her head rolls backs to shake out her long hair and she turns first one way and then another, sometimes with her back to me entirely. She moves now fast now slow, her arms languorous while her hips shake so fast it seems impossible. Then her hips slow down and sway in a curve that takes forever to move from one side to the other while her hands, quick and darting, draw attention to every part of herself, my eyes following them helplessly. In doing so she has drawn my eyes back to her face and her eyes, which I now dare to look at. When I do I see I was wrong. She was in no way oblivious to me. Indeed, I am the centre of her world.

Her eyes have never left mine. No matter where I was looking, her dark eyes have been fixed on me, no matter how she moved, even when she had her back to me her head has always turned back to look over her shoulder at me, a warm smile on her face, a smile that invites me to look where I will without fear or embarrassment. She has no false shame, no coyness. She loves every part of her body, she knows that she can dance like few women can even dream of dancing. She knows that for all her grey hair and her thick waist, her sturdy arms and broad hips, at this moment she is more beautiful than I will ever be.

I want to cry. What chance do I have? I will never prise Yusuf away from Badra. I have only my beauty, and that will fade away. I will always be the second wife, the pretty, useless adornment until that gift too leaves me and I will be truly useless. I may not even bear children even if I should drink other teas, which promise many sons. My mother bore only me, a girl. Other women pitied her behind her back. My father was saddened by his lack of sons. My head drops down to my knees, my eyes close and burn with tears.

I can still hear the woman dancing, her footsteps and skirts are still keeping to her rhythm. It does not falter but suddenly she is by my side. She has danced her way round my bed, and now her hands reach out and touch me. Startled, I look up and move slightly away from her, but she is smiling. She holds out her hands to me and invites me to dance with her. I shake my head. She will not accept my refusal, though, and turning her back on me she begins to shake her body whilst gradually arching her back until her whole body is curved backwards. Her eyes, upside down, meet mine and she invites me again. She grows comical in her entreaties, until I cannot help but laugh, although my nose is blocked and my eyes still sting with tears. I stumble off my bed and take her proffered hands. Reluctantly and ungracefully I begin to copy her movements. She does not speak, only helps me to improve, lifting her skirts to show me how my heels must lift when I sway so that my hips can move further and deeper in their endless curves back and forth. When she shakes her body forwards and back it ripples. When I shake mine it judders but she places her hands on me and makes the movement softer, slower. She indicates I should now remove my robes gradually, but I shake my head and refuse outright. She only smiles as one who has all the time in the world and we keep dancing, my feet learning new steps as my arms accentuate each movement of my hips and waist.

She stays with me for five days. I dance until I think my back will break, until my arms burn, my feet ache. My neck feels as though it will surely snap as I whirl it round to allow my hair to fly through the air like a great flock of birds. By the last day I dance naked, I dance like this silent woman dances. I hurt all over. I forget where I am, I forget everything except my dancing.

We never speak. Perhaps she cannot speak. Perhaps she does not speak my language. Perhaps she has no wish to speak. So we do not speak. We dance, we eat and drink, we sleep. Nothing more. I do not even know her name. We stay in my rooms, my servant girl brings food and then leaves again. I do not join the rest of the household, but they are used to my absences and do not remark on it.

On the last day we are practicing an intricate step, allowing me to move backwards and forwards, then side to side. My feet move gracefully in time to the beat only she and I can hear. My servant girl knocks and enters without waiting for my invitation. Another woman enters with her. The dancing woman and she nod at each other like old friends, then the dancing woman dons her heavy outer robes and leaves with my servant. She does not bid me farewell. She does not even look back at me. The servant girl closes the door and I stand bereft, my new friend and teacher gone. It is all done in a few moments. I turn from the door to the women who has just entered and see that she is already entirely at home. She has cast off her outer wraps and is now sitting on a cushion eating dried fruits from the platter on my low table. She has helped herself to the cooling tea from the pot.

I fumble for a robe to cover myself and after days of silence I find my voice. It croaks. "Who are you? What are you doing here?"

She takes no notice of me. She sips the tea and grimaces. "Call a servant," she says. "This tea is cold."

I stare at her.

Her voice is harsh, she speaks with a strange accent. She sounds like a common street woman. Her skin is wrinkled and coarse, dry with the years. Her back is crooked. Her fingers are twisted with age. She speaks as though I were her servant. I am too confused to respond. She raises her voice to a shout.

"GIRL!"

I flinch, but sure enough there are quick footsteps and my servant girl opens the door without knocking.

The woman nods approval at her speed. "This tea is cold. Hot tea, quickly. And food, plenty of food. I'm hungry."

The servant girl has the audacity to bow to her and,

ignoring me, run back through the door, closing it behind her.

I sit on the bed. I need to be seated higher up than this woman. I have to find some way of regaining my status, which she seems to have stripped away from me in moments and with no effort. I settle myself and try to formulate a question that will identify who she is and what she is doing here since she ignored my initial question. My mouth moves slightly as I try to compose a sentence. I am about to speak when she interrupts me.

"How many positions do you know?"

"What?" I ask stupidly.

"Positions. For congress."

"Congress?"

She uses a very vulgar term for sexual intercourse, one used only by the crudest of the street boys.

I flinch.

"Oh, so you do know something, then?" She cackles and helps herself to more dried fruit, stuffing it into her mouth, cheeks bulging. She speaks with her mouth full. "Where'd you learn filth like that then, a lady like yourself?"

I gather myself. "Are you a whore?" I ask, haughtily. I mean to insult her, but she is not insulted so easily.

"Of course," she says. "Best there is."

I snort with laughter. I cannot help myself. She is an ugly old crone with appalling table manners and vulgar speech.

She raises her eyebrows and grins back at me. "Don't believe me?"

I shake my head.

She nods, still cheerful. "I'm the best there is. They

may shut their eyes and dream of a sweet young beauty when they're with me, but they always come back. No-one knows as much as me."

I still look doubtful. We are interrupted by the servant girl, who has managed to prepare a ridiculous amount of food in a very short time. There are chunks of spiced meats, a thick soup, roasted vegetables, cakes dripping with honey, fresh and dried fruits and hot tea with yet more honey to add to it. She places it all on the table and the old crone flips a golden coin into her hand. I am shocked. How can she have so much money and dress so poorly? If she has money to throw about like that she could be living in a palace with her own servants. Perhaps she does.

The servant girl leaves and the old woman attacks the food as though she had not just eaten handfuls of dried fruits and drunk half a pot of tea. As she chews on a hunk of meat she looks up at me where I sit, still incredulous, staring at her. She rummages through her robes and throws something at me, which I try to catch but fumble and drop onto the bedcovers.

"Make yourself useful," she says. "I'm not planning on staying longer than I have to."

She belches loudly and selects another piece of meat. While she puts it in her mouth with one hand she pours tea with the other. I am impressed she can pour it accurately from such a height with barely a glance at it.

"Stop *staring*," she says. "Begin. I'm not here to teach you how to pour tea."

I scramble through the bedclothes and find the item she threw me. When I see it I nearly drop it again.

She sighs wearily. "You are *married*," she says. "Don't be such an innocent."

I gape first at her and then back at the item I am gingerly holding. I have never seen such a thing. It is a perfect replica of a man's organ, carved in ivory.

"Well?" she says. "*Begin*."

"Begin what?" I ask, hardly wanting to hear her answer.

She rolls her eyes at me. "Now don't waste my time. I've got a lot to teach you and you need to learn fast. My time is worth a great deal of gold to some men." She laughs unpleasantly and loudly slurps her tea. She eyes me over the cup and then sets it down in a business-like manner. "In your mouth."

My eyes widen.

"Oh?" she says. "Indeed?" She sighs and settles herself comfortably on the cushions, adjusting them with small grunts until she is comfortable. "From the *very* beginning, then."

The days with the old crone are less than those with the dancing woman, but they are harder. I am made to practice until my jaw aches, and once she is happy with how I can manipulate the ivory toy then it is taken away from me without a word of praise and I am forced into many positions, both off and on my bed, an imaginary Yusuf above me, below me, behind me, to my side. She watches me critically and when she thinks I am not trying hard enough she will grab a limb and force it into a deeper pose, thinking nothing of my yelps of protest. She keeps up a disparaging running commentary on both my skills and those of other women that she knows, not least the dancing woman.

"What is the use of dancing if you cannot do what comes after? Dance all you wish, but once a man has come to your rooms he will hardly wish you to keep on dancing all night."

I nod meekly while attempting what feels like an impossible pose to hold for more than a breath. She makes me stay in the position for more than thirty breaths and shakes her head in annoyance when I collapse, sweating.

"And fine silks and jewels? What man has ever noticed such things except for a silk merchant or a gold trader? And they look at the cloth and the metal, not the woman underneath it all. Keep *still*, you useless girl. *Now* move."

When her time comes to leave me I am relieved but I am also grateful, and perhaps just a little sorry. I have grown used to her endless talking, her strictness, even her revolting table manners and snoring have become a comfort to me. I was not lonely, at least, while she was here. Now I am alone again. But at last I have new skills with which to draw Yusuf to me.

I await his return. When he comes I set aside the golden silks. He smiles at me and there are tears in his eyes as he gently replaces them about his own eyes, about my face.

I do not hold back. Every skill I have learnt is unleashed upon him, all at once.

When he cries out it is Badra's name on his lips.

What now for me? Am I to learn yet more skills? Is there anything new that I can learn even if it would make a difference? I sit alone in my rooms and see the future stretch out before me in my mirror, as I play out my part as concubine until my beauty fades. Perhaps I will mutter to myself as I tend flowers or birds, as old wives sometimes do who have proved childless, or form a great devotion to the days of fasting and praying. Then another girl will be brought here, shy on her camel, eyeing me up with pity, bringing dancers and whores here to teach her what she believes will draw Yusuf to her.

I move close to the mirror and place my hands on it. My breath clouds its surface so that my face becomes blurred. Who knows what the future holds? Perhaps there is another way. My heart leaps when I think about Yusuf and what might be of greater importance to him than nights of embraces. He is a chief. A powerful chief, beholden only to the amir of Aghmat. Might such a man not have greater ambitions? After all, many men marry to create those alliances and opportunities for advancement which take them from lowly leaders to great amirs. Yusuf is already married. His heart is Badra's. But if he could have a wife who would fan the burning coals of his ambition until they became a fire, sweeping all before it… might he then to turn to such a wife, a woman who might stand by his side in his future?

I choose my time carefully. I risk embarrassment by asking the servants many questions to ensure Yusuf will be at home. I make an announcement. I have a wish to know my new country better. Khalila is pleased with me. She thinks that at last I am emerging from my shell, that I will take part in the day-to-day life here. I say that I wish to visit the waterfalls that run close by to our valley. They are supposed to be a place of great importance, of strength and power. I order my servants to prepare my camel and food. As well as my own maidservants I take three male servants with me, chosen because they are strong but also ignorant and credulous. I set out with them, while Yusuf sits in council with his men and Badra sits silent in her rooms.

It takes us until the heat of the day is full upon us to reach the waterfalls, and they are indeed memorable. In a land that needs water, that cares for it and channels it, holds it and longs for it, this abundance of water, falling in multiple glimmering arcs, spilling on the rocks and earth, is a magnificent sight.

My servants prepare food and I eat. They eat a little way off from me and then I tell them that they may please themselves for a while. I say that I wish to sit quietly, that I have a headache coming on and my eyes cannot bear the bright light of the day. They arrange shade for me with blankets from the camels and then they move away from me, some of the men swimming, the women coyly pretending to turn their eyes away, paddling their toes daintily and shrieking when the men splash too close.

I prepare myself. My heart is beating fast. I mutter the words I have planned under my breath. I loosen my hair fastenings a little, such that they would easily fall out, take water from the water bags and sprinkle it over my brow. I am ready. I picture Yusuf in my mind, see myself by his side, his only beloved. In one quick movement, before I can think again, I bite down hard on my lower lip. The pain makes me cry out, and I do not smother the sound. As my servants turn I fall back, thrashing on the ground. My hair falls quickly from its poorly-placed pins and its thick darkness grows pale and dusty on the dry ground beneath my head. I taste salty blood in my mouth and wetness on my chin as my lip bleeds. I begin to pant as my servants rush to my side. They drown out my fast breaths with their panicked shouting at one another. Here is the new bride of their master, fallen into a fit, droplets of sweat on her brow, her body shaking in a frenzy, blood now spreading across her face as her hands flail. They are frightened. What if I die? How will they explain their negligence? Swimming, chattering, flirting, while their mistress, who had *told* them she felt unwell, falls into this state? They will be whipped for this, even if I recover. If I die… They try everything, they hold me down, try to pat my face clean with damp cloths. I can hear the women praying, hoping for some divine help.

I begin to moan, and this makes them even more scared. When words begin to escape me they lean in close, relieved that at least I am speaking. One of the men quiets the others and puts his ear close to my mouth. He listens, then draws back. I see his face from between my half-closed lashes. He has become pale. The others want to know what he heard. I save him the trouble of repeating it and speak again, louder and more clearly this time. They stare at me. I cry out my words one more time, this time so loudly that they fall back, letting go of my limbs. I arch my back.

"Zaynab!" My voice calls out my own name, echoing on the hills. "Zaynab! Lady to a mighty lord! Oh, happy man who calls Zaynab his bride! He shall be mighty indeed! Ruler of his own tribe, ruler of the Maghreb, ruler of lands beyond his own birth! Mighty is the husband of the lady Zaynab…"

My voice, so strong, fades away, and I fall still. My limbs lie loose and crooked upon the hot dusty ground.

I am quiet during the journey home, pale and lifeless in the litter they have assembled for me. The men carry me, the women urge them on, trot alongside me, applying cool cloths and trickling water between my torn lips whenever we pause.

I lie in my rooms for many days. I moan and clasp my head. At first I insist on darkness and cry out random words from my vision. Then, slowly, I begin to recover. Reluctantly I repeat my revelation to those that ask for it to be told to them again and again. The servants whisper, people of consequence in the tribe seek me out. I am becoming a person of importance. I am gracious with them. Soon I will be of importance in the eyes of Yusuf, and this is all that matters to me.

At first Yusuf does not come to me. I hear that he was summoned to the amir of Aghmat soon after my vision was known of, and I can imagine that the amir may want to hear of it for himself. On the day when Yusuf returns I dress in my finest silks and await his command. Perhaps he will come to me and tell me of his plans for our future together.

At last I am sent for and I go with joy in my heart. I am a little sorry for Badra, for she will be swept aside now that Yusuf believes that I am his path to greatness. But she is already lost to this world. I cannot help the delight that makes my feet light as I walk with as much dignity as I can muster to his rooms, although I long to run to him as fast as I can, to arrive gasping for breath. I will be first in his heart now, as he is in mine. I will be his only love, his only wife.

When I enter his rooms Yusuf is surrounded by his advisors. I smile broadly at him, for this is how I dreamt it would be. I will no longer be a pretty concubine, hidden away amongst my carpets and cushions, incense and sweet juice drinks. I will be truly a wife, an equal at his side. Even his most trusted men will acknowledge my part in his future greatness. That is why they are gathered here.

But Yusuf's face is grave. I am surprised, but then I adjust my expression accordingly. Of course, he may have some difficult decisions to make now. He will have to set aside his wife, who has served him well. Her sons will also be set aside, for he will want to have sons with me: his heirs must come from me. But I am sure he will treat them with kindness, for he is a good man. Perhaps they will be minor leaders in the region. Now that he can see a glorious destiny prophesised for him he may well seek to establish an army of his own and look for opportunities to increase his own lands and powers. His men will be glad of this. And I will be by his side in all.

"Zaynab," he says, and his voice is so tender that my eyes fill with tears. I blink them back and look at him full in the face. Now is not the time for me to be a foolish girl. I must show him that I am a grown woman, that I could be his finest ally, his loyal and true wife, supporting him in all his endeavours.

"Zaynab, this vision that came to you."

I nod, eager.

"You must take it back. You must say it never happened, that you were mistaken."

I stare at him in amazement. "Indeed, my lord Yusuf," I say, my voice clear and strong. "It did indeed happen, I swear it by Allah. I saw true then and I speak true now." I know that I am lying to him, but he must believe me, he of all people must believe me. He must believe that by tying his destiny to me and me alone he will fulfil his true greatness. His men must believe it also. I tell myself that I am sure that Allah will forgive me, for He knows I am trying to be a good wife to Yusuf, which must count for something.

Yusuf looks at me for a long moment, and I see to my astonishment that he also has tears in his eyes. He speaks again, and his voice seems thick, as though the words hurt his throat as they emerge. "My lord, the amir of Aghmat, has heard of your vision."

Now I see what has happened. I misunderstood the amir's interest. He feels threatened. He may have challenged Yusuf to combat, or be demanding displays of loyalty, out of fear of Yusuf's possible future greatness. Yusuf is more than capable of fighting a battle. But he must believe in himself. He must believe in me, in my vision. I lift my head proudly. "My vision was true. My husband will be the greatest leader in the Maghreb and even further, to lands as yet unclaimed by our kings. This is the destiny of the man who calls himself my lord."

Yusuf nods and lowers his head. When he raises it again his eyes have cleared. His muscles are tight. He has come to a decision. I am proud of him. This is the beginning of our future together. "The amir of Aghmat also believes you have seen truly, Zaynab. He does not doubt your word. He believes that if he takes you as his queen then he will be the greatest leader in the Maghreb and beyond. And so he has commanded me to set you aside that he may take you as his wife. I cannot challenge his command. I am his vassal. You will no longer be my wife. And when the right time has passed you will go to Aghmat, as queen of that city. Until then you will live in my home but as my ruler. All care will be taken of you whilst you are in my protection, as befits your future status. I have promised that I will deliver you to the amir myself when the time comes."

He rises as I fall, standing above me as my costly silks cover the ground at his feet and my body shakes. My hands touch the cold floor and my eyes roll up to his face. He stands still and looks down into my eyes for a long, long moment. No-one in the room moves until Yusuf leaves the room. Then they all leave in haste, for my screams are unbearable, even to hardened warriors.

That night I seek out Yusuf in his own rooms, with servants busy at their tasks and a few of his men. When he sees me he stands and bows, as if I am already queen.

"Please dismiss your men and the servants," I say, my voice shaking. My eyes are bloodshot with crying.

"It would not be proper for me to be alone with you now," he says.

"Please," I say, more tears dripping fast down my face and onto the floor.

"I cannot," he says, his own voice grown thick. I can tell the servants are all ears and that his men are curious, even though they look elsewhere. But I have to speak. I stand very close to him.

"I lied," I whisper.

Yusuf stands. "You may leave us," he says.

The men and his servants hesitate, but the look on his face makes them obey without a further command. When we are alone I summon up all my courage.

"I lied," I say.

"Why?"

"I wanted to be important," I say. "I wanted to be more important than..." I do not say her name. I do not need to.

He closes his eyes for a minute, as though in pain. "I know," he says at last.

I gape at him. "What?"

"I tried to make you tell the truth," he says. "But you swore in front of everyone that it was true. Now it is too late. The Amir believed you. He is a man of great ambition, a man who believes that through you he will gain great power."

"Tell him I lied!" I say, clutching at his arm. "I do not care if they laugh at me!"

"It is too late now, Zaynab," he says. "He would not laugh at you. He would not believe you. He would think you were lying to stay with me. And if he did believe you then he would have us both put to death for seeking to deceive him, for making a fool of him."

"I would rather die than leave you," I sob.

He cups my face as he did that first time, his eyes full of tears. "Ah, Zaynab," he says tenderly. "I should never have brought you here. I have done nothing but make you unhappy. It was not my intention. I hoped your love would bring light into my life but instead I have brought darkness into yours."

And so there is nothing to be done. Yusuf stays away from me. My time goes by. There must be a period of time between one husband and the next of course, this is how it is done. It would be unseemly for the amir to take me to him at once as though I were some slave girl claimed as the spoils of battle. All must be done correctly if I am to be his respected queen, if my vision is to come true.

I pass the days sat on my bed, my eyes unfocused. I eat what is put in front of me, I drink when water is offered. I taste nothing. I hear nothing. I see nothing. When darkness comes I lie down and when it is light I sit up. I do not know if I sleep, perhaps I do. I cannot tell if I am awake or asleep. Either way I do not dream. There is only darkness inside me.

I know that sometimes Yusuf comes to the door of my room, that my servants hover behind him and whisper assurances that they tend to my needs, that I am washed and dressed each day, that I am fed and watered, that my bed is soft and warm. He nods, but he does not speak. I try not to look at him when he comes. There is nothing to say. Nothing can stop what is already decided. If the amir of Aghmat wants me as his queen, then it will be so. I have given my consent, as I am required to do, though it is given just as Yusuf's consent was given: our ruler has spoken and we cannot disobey. Already many of my possessions have been taken ahead of me to the palace. My rooms here grow bare as rooms there grow more elegant day by day. Already,

I know, courtiers are preparing themselves for a new queen, shifting this way and that to curry favour, to take positions in my household of benefit to themselves and their families. Already the poets and singers are making ready to sing my praises – even if I were ugly or old, stupid or crippled, their songs and poems would wipe away my faults. How easy for them, then, when I am known to be a beauty and oh so young, without physical blemish. As for stupidity? They will have to wipe away that at least, for who can be so stupid as I? What woman, married to a kind husband whom she loves, with a silent and all-but-invisible co-wife, would be so stupid as I have been?

The day comes for my departure. I stand in my room as servants take the last of my belongings to the escort that waits below. One servant hurries by and I stop her. I reach into the basket she carries, items to be taken back to Khalila for household use and draw out the two lengths of golden silk. Slowly I turn them over in my hands and then I leave the room, my pace almost a shuffle.

I walk up the long steep flights of stairs and when I reach Badra's room I do not waver in the doorway. I look at her and see myself, sunk in a dark misery. I walk towards her and without pause I lay one length of golden silk on her lap. Then I turn and leave her to her silence and stillness.

Downstairs, at the great gates where I first saw Yusuf's sons, I am lifted into a carved saddle. The boys stare at me, clustered around Khalila. She tries to catch my eye but I stare at her as though I do not recognise her. Ahead, Yusuf gives a command and my mount turns, as do those of my escort. We begin our journey to Aghmat, Yusuf delivering me himself to my new husband, my new lord. I sit slumped, shoulders hunched over, my hands twisting the second length of golden silk.

I am only just seventeen and my destiny has changed. I am to leave the man I love to become queen to Luqut al-Maghrawi, the amir who rules over the great city of Aghmat. Its riches will be spread at my feet, the people will call my name and my every wish will be obeyed.

I think my heart will break.

Queen

THE BIRD'S TALONS GRIP MY wrist so tightly I fear it will draw blood even through the thick leather of my glove. It looks this way and that, the wind ruffling its feathers, making it impatient. It shifts its feet and stares at me boldly, a challenge to my supposed authority over it. I whisper to calm it. There is as yet no prey in sight, it must contain its desire for freedom. I turn my horse a little and glance towards the falconer. His eyes scan the horizon and narrow at a glimpse of movement. His face is grown like that of his birds, I think, and stifle a smile. He nods and I lift my wrist in a quick swift movement, launching my falcon into the air. It sails away from us, strong wings beating, seeking out a trembled movement below.

"A good bird," says the falconer.

I nod. We wait, companionably silent together, watching the bird turn this way and that in the wind, feeling its way through the air currents holding it aloft.

He is one of the few servants who does not bow and scrape before me. He likes me because I enjoy this rare time outdoors; enjoy the soft feathers and hard eyes of his charges. He treats me with respect but does not fear to instruct me in how to manage my falcon.

One of my only pleasures here is falconry. There is a

great festival in the spring for which many birds of prey are caught and trained. During the days of the feast itself many gather to see their feats in the air, their power and agility, their ferocity and courage. When the festival is over there comes the moment for which I long, every year of the last twelve years as the queen of Aghmat. At the end of their time in captivity most of the birds are released, to fly free once again. They take wing above the palace and leave us, never to be seen again. Each year I watch this moment, and then I withdraw to my rooms. Everyone thinks I am tired, for I am much in public demand during the festival, but when I reach my rooms I dismiss my servants and weep. I permit myself only this one moment of weakness, every year.

When I have finished weeping I stretch out my hand and Hela is there, unbidden, to pass me water to wet my dry throat. Then she will bathe me and put cold compresses of cooling herbs on my eyes, so that the redness will not be seen. I will come to dinner as a queen should, in fine clothes and jewels, my head high and a gracious smile on my face. No-one else witnesses this precious moment of weakness, only Hela.

I had only been queen for a year when word came of the fate of my childhood city of Kairouan. When the Zirids declared their conversion to Sunni by giving allegiance to Baghdad, the Fatimid Caliph sent as punishment great hordes of Arab tribes to invade. They burnt, they killed, they reduced buildings to rubble. They so utterly destroyed

Kairouan that it was humbled in the dirt, a once proud city made nothing.

All of them perished. My father. My mother. Even loving Myriam. As for the street children with whom I used to play, now the men and women of that city, who knows who fell and who remained standing? Hela could not tell us.

She stood before us, her face grown old beyond her years, her body stooped, her clothes still streaked with ashes, smelling of smoke. The fall of Kairouan had taken her life away and left her a withered husk. She had come all this way to give me the news of my family. When my husband Luqut saw the way I shrank from her dark presence he at once appointed her my chief servant, as she had been to my mother. I did not argue. I had been married for only one year, yet I already knew the penalty I would pay should I defy him in any way. And so Hela came to be head of my household, my handmaiden as she was my mother's. And over the years I have grown used to her, her silent secret presence. I know my other servants are wary of her, just as the servants of my childhood home were. But they do not know what comfort it is to me to have one person who knows the truths of my life as queen, who does not exclaim or whisper but alters what she can and accepts what cannot be changed without sighing or wringing of hands. She makes me stronger than I could ever be alone.

That first night she came to me and dismissed the other servants. Already she had power over them, for they obeyed meekly. They brought all that she asked for, and then they left us alone.

She stood in the shadows and Luqut did not see her. She did not speak when she saw what he did to me. She had never been one for talking when it was unnecessary. When he left me a crumpled heap on the floor, then, only then, did she step out of the darkness and raise me up.

It still seemed strange to me that my family was dead. I did not weep, for I had suffered too much in the past year to weep, but my shoulders were stooped and my body was limp and unresisting in her hands. Had I not heard the news I would have been more uncomfortable in her presence. I remembered her strange forbidding presence from my childhood and how she had spoken of my father's second wife Imen. Her death had been sudden and unexpected and Hela's words at the time had frightened me, for they hinted at a dark hand behind gentle Imen's passing. I should have drawn away from her touch, but I stood still. I had never thought to see my family again, but still in my mind they had been alive, and now, suddenly, they were dead. It should not have made a difference, but it did.

I did not look down at myself, nor did I raise my head and look across the room at the carved mirror, which would have shown me what she now saw.

My body was covered in bruises. Not where they might show, of course. My neck and face, my hands and parts of my arms were made smooth and lustrous with fine creams and good food. My feet, also, were well shaped and delicate. But where my magnificent robes covered my body I was marked out in black and brown, yellow and purple. There were bruises that had almost healed and then had been marked again, so that there were layers of colours. And there were other marks.

Hela said nothing. She bathed me, standing close to each part of my body to stroke me with a warm wet cloth. As she did so she came even to my intimate parts, and she did not draw back at what she saw there.

When she had finished bathing me she went to a corner of the room. Here she had placed her two bags, both made of rough goat-hides. They were the bags of a poor serving woman, not a rich woman's favoured handmaid. She had never drawn unwanted attention to herself. From one she took several small pouches. Returning to me she extracted a few pots containing unguents, which she proceeded to smear on my body, different ones for different parts. Then she waved me to my bed, where I lay down. Hela stood over me. Gently, as though I were a child, she placed my covers over me, and then she looked down on me. Her voice was as deep as ever.

"How often does he come to you?"

I shrugged and closed my eyes. "When he wishes it. There is no pattern. Unless I have displeased him in some way. Then he will come until I have learnt my lesson."

"No child?"

I kept my eyes closed. "I know what to take to keep from having children."

"He does not wish for a child?"

"He has bastard children. He would think nothing of raising them up if he thought it would hurt me."

"Why does he want you then?"

I felt a tear creep from under my eyelid and make its way down my cheek. "For glory."

Hela was silent for a moment. "I heard about your vision. Every ambitious man in the Maghreb wanted you for a wife when they heard about it."

I did not reply but a tear made its way down my other cheek. I felt the wetness move down my neck.

"Do you often have visions?"

I did not reply, only lay there as the tears slipped down my face. Hela grew silent then and I heard her move softly away from me.

Life changed after Hela became my handmaiden. She ruled my household in my stead, lifting from me the burdens of managing servants, responding to supplicants, making arrangements for festivities and holy days. To me were left only the pleasant parts of being a queen – choosing fine clothes and furnishings, ordering the planting of gardens to delight me with colour and perfume, falconry, riding.

I was grateful for all of this of course, but it was one night that truly changed my life, only days after Hela came to me.

Luqut came to me and the servants fluttered round like shadowy moths as lamps were lit to make my bedchamber blaze with light. He needs to see to do his work.

I stood still and silent in the centre of my room. The servants did as they were bid. They did not stop to ponder the uses for the implements they laid out, nor count the bruises on my body as they stripped me bare. They had their orders, which had not changed since I had been brought here, and probably since before my time in this place. Those who disobeyed were likely to find out for themselves the meanings of these things.

I did not ponder them either. What would be the use? I thought of nothing else for months when I first came here, but after a year I was resigned. To protest would be to enhance his pleasure, to refuse would be to enhance my pain. I was better off imagining myself elsewhere, allowing my body to take the punishment that my mind could not withstand.

The first time, I screamed. I begged and cried for mercy. I tried to escape and found the doors barred. I had not known such cruelty existed, nor such men.

The second time I tried to avoid his sport by offering my own proficiency. Those skills I had learnt out of love and yearning for Yusuf I laid at the amir's feet to save myself. I hoped he might be enchanted and turn from his own path, but I was wrong. He laughed at my gentle offerings and continued along his own way, dragging me behind him, humbled in the midst of finery.

That first night Hela watched from the shadows. I do not know how he did not see her, but she has a way of melding with her surroundings. She saw it all. Not that this shamed me. I was beyond shame by then. Shame is for those who have been treated with tenderness.

Afterwards she did not commiserate with me, nor soothe me. She used her creams on me again and her touch was careful. That was all. But when the amir next announced his intention to visit my chambers, Hela dismissed the servants and made all preparations herself. She did everything without any mistakes, as though she had made such preparations all her life. Then she went to her own belongings and brought out her little pouches and a cup.

I stared. The lamps flickered and the cool breeze of the early night grew cold across my naked body. Reddish marks were etched into the worn wood. I found my voice although it came out as a croak.

"Where did you get that cup?"

Hela did not look up at me. She took pinches of substances, first from one pouch, then another, and combined them in the cup. Then she began to work them with a small silver pestle. The scraping noise made the hairs on my body raise.

"Is that Imen's cup?"

She shook her head. "It is mine. It has always been mine."

I shivered and wrapped my bare arms about my naked body as though their coldness might somehow warm me. "I have only ever seen it in Imen's hands."

She nodded.

"You gave it to her?"

"I gave her what was in it."

I felt my legs tremble. I tried to stop my voice from doing the same. I was feeling my way through a story whose ending I already knew. I was unsure whether I wanted to know where I would be taken, how much I truly wished to know. I tried again, hoping to hear that I was mistaken. "It put a child in her womb."

She nodded.

"And then..." I hesitated. She did not.

"Took it away again," she said. She stood and fetched water, a little of which she added to the cup.

I persisted, my teeth chattering. "The same mixture cannot have done both."

She looked up at me, frowned. "Of course not."

"So you gave her something that put life in her womb. And she was grateful to you. She thought you were helping her. Even though you were my mother's handmaiden."

She kept her eyes down. "Imen was a foolish girl. A trusting girl."

I turned away from her. A shadow moved opposite me and I gasped, then saw myself in the great mirror that dominates my chamber's wall, my body hunched with cold. I watched my face as she spoke behind me, her voice very low.

"She slipped away so fast there was no time for anyone to save her."

I whirled on her and cried out as I did so. "What is in that cup? What are you making? And for whom?"

She raised her face to me and her eyes did not flicker away from my fearful gaze. "I served your mother, body and soul, until she died. Now I will serve you until I die. You need not fear me. Only those who harm you need fear me."

I shook my head. "I forbid you to use that cup for anyone, Hela. I forbid it. He may harm me but I cannot kill someone. I cannot!"

She raised the cup. "Why would I kill him? Without him you would be in danger. How many other lords would seek to steal this city and the title of amir? How many men who heard of your vision would grasp this opportunity to take you as a bride?" She shook her head at me. "He made you queen of Aghmat. You have unimaginable privilege because of that position. You would be a fool to lose what you have for what you have to bear."

"You think what I bear is nothing? You who have seen?"

She raised the cup higher. "This will end your troubles."

"Without killing him?"

She nodded.

"How?"

She turned away, towards the door. "Trust me."

She left me then. Soon Luqut came for me. He had been at dinner. His eyes gleamed as he surveyed the room with all its apparatus and myself, standing alone in the midst of it, naked and defenceless. I bowed my head and braced myself for a long night of pain.

It lasted but a few moments.

No sooner had he begun than he was finished, his climax coming on him so suddenly, when he had barely touched my tender flesh with his instruments, that he was taken by surprise. He, who had always needed many hours to be satiated, was fulfilled so quickly that he gazed at me as though I might be expected to provide an answer to this mystery. But I only gazed back at him in silence and bewilderment, and he left me then.

He came often for a while, as though to wipe out that one time, but over and over again he was fulfilled with the merest touch, until he began to avoid me, seeking his pleasure elsewhere. I heard servants' whispers and once I heard a woman scream in another part of the palace, but I was tormented no longer. Hela's cup had done its work and I was free. True, I had to attend events with the him, maintain always the demeanour of a queen in public and still I had to endure his visits, but their intensity was so greatly diminished that I could feel once more that I was human rather than a beast.

That night was more than eleven years ago. I bore one year of marriage to Luqut alone, and these last years have been bearable only because of Hela. Without her I would surely have found a way to end my life, such as it is. My life is not happy now, but it is bearable. I survive. For what, I am not sure. In my secret heart I hope perhaps that Luqut will die. But this is an idle hope. He is older than I of course, but he has many years left to him. He is strong and healthy and he has me at his side. Zaynab, the promised consort of a great man, as foretold in a vision. What could bring him down?

This, then, is my life now. I am twenty-nine years old, and queen of Aghmat, have been so for over twelve years. I have no friends here, for my husband would not like that, nor can I take any servants save Hela into my confidence, for I know they may all be spies for my husband. I am childless, which might be shameful in another woman, but no-one cares about that. I was brought here for glory, not for childrearing, and certainly Aghmat basks in its glory.

It is a rich city. We are an important stop along the trade routes, and so we see the caravans come and go, swaying in and out of our gates from far away. Each trader might have a hundred or more camels, and their burdens comprise every wondrous thing that men might wish for, every good thing for which they are willing to pay. Rich cloths are spread out to catch the sun's rays. Wool and linen of course but also finer cloths, silks and those which have been decorated with shining discs of silver or twisted threads of gold. Delicate silken threads have been used for embroidering every manner of beauty upon the cloths – flowers and intricate patterns, even delicate script to spell out holy words.

There are sturdy iron utensils, plates or jugs of bright shining copper and twisted beaten precious metals studded with fine jewels, pearls and precious woods. More delicate than jewels is glass, heated and moulded in fantastical shapes, seeming lighter than air and yet safely holding water.

The smells of trade fill the air. The stench of camels and their long-travelled owners, the spices that enrich the foods cooked in the houses and at the market stalls, and the heady perfumes brought from far away to anoint the women of Aghmat. There is the dark smell of slaves too, unwashed, saddened and angry with their lot. I think I too would smell like this were my servants not forever washing and perfuming me to hide the smell of my sadness and anger.

There are sweets to tempt our tongues. Oranges, spices, sugar cane. Children beg for a little piece that they suck on all day long, chewing the soft spongy centre, strips of green fibre getting caught between their teeth. For the rich there is no need for such inconvenience. My own cooks will squeeze out all the sweetness and make rich dishes to tempt the amir and I.

The very best of all the goods are brought to me of course. I need not wander the hot markets, nor seek out one caravan or another, asking for favoured traders by name. When the best arrive, they come to the palace, where the quality of their goods are known and their faces are recognised. They do not enter my presence, they sit outside my chambers and wait for my favour to be made known to them by my servants. I can lie on a soft couch while goods from every part of the world are brought out and laid before me, I can dismiss or approve with a wave of my hand, a nod of my head. My husband is vain. He may dislike me and fear the rush that comes upon his manhood when he tries to touch me, but still my presence by his side, in his palace, promises great things for him and so I may have anything I want. We are to be denied nothing. He has the finest weapons, horses and women. I have the finest clothes, perfumes and furnishings. Our court eats the freshest and best foods, enjoys beautiful gardens and rooms bejewelled with coloured tiles in all directions, in patterns so complex they take experienced craftsmen months to create. Our court must be always magnificent so that the amir can be magnificent through its reflection.

Hela shops alone. When new traders arrive she will leave the brightly-lit palace rooms and go out into the dark streets. When she returns she will have replenished her stocks, carrying small bags of unknown items, which she will gradually use up over the coming months. The traders she uses do not come to the palace. They have perhaps four or five camels rather than over a hundred. They do not give their names, nor ask those of their best customers. There is no banter at their stall, nor much haggling. A simple nod, a few whispered words and gestures before coins and pouches swap hands. They know which cities to visit and their customers, like Hela, know where to find them when they arrive.

Later, servants will make their way to Hela's cool bright

rooms, adjacent to mine, and whisper their fears and pains, and leave clutching cures. I watch as they come and go and recognise the servants of rich merchant's wives and courtiers amongst those who ask for her help. She is as much consulted as a noble physician. Sometimes she looks up from her whispered consultations and sees me watching her. Then she will look away. I would stop her, fearful of what happened to Imen, but I know that those in her care thrive and are cured, so I hold my tongue. Sometimes she tries to teach me her skills, but I have not learnt much. I know how to brew the drink that I take to keep from bearing a child to the amir, but I knew that before I came here. I can name a few cures for simple ills – for burns, for wounds, for fevers and to soothe coughs, colds. I mix things with so little precision that Hela takes the mortar and pestle away from me, will not allow me to make much beyond a simple tea for women's pains or a headache. She herself is meticulous in her measuring and weighing, in her mixing and brewing.

There are often visitors to our court, some from far away, some closer to home. Today Yusuf is at court and I am shaking.

He rarely comes to Aghmat. He used to come often when I was still his wife, but since I became queen his visits have become less. I do not know why this is – if by command of my husband, or because of Badra, who still sits in her rooms and gazes at nothing as her sons grow into men. If it is by his own heart's wish then I do not know whether he does not wish to see me because I am a fool or because – and I am shaking even at the thought of this – because he longs for me and does not trust himself in my presence. Whatever his thoughts I know only that I lose my reason when he comes to court. I have maidservants who will pass me word of his coming in return for a little coin or trinkets. I pay more than they would ask for, for I must outbid my husband when it comes to paying for spies. When they come to me, pink-cheeked with whispers, I throw my chambers into disarray. I wear my finest clothes, my eyes are ringed with kohl. I come in state to the great chambers of the palace, in every way a great queen to those who behold me, in every way a foolish girl inside. Today he is at court and I am shaking still, even after twelve years away from his side. I have no-one else of whom to dream.

I sit carefully, the stiff silks folding around me as servants kneel before me to rearrange them more becomingly. They straighten and I try to appear at ease, as though I always look like this, as though every day I wear such formal clothing and sit in the state chambers of the palace rather than in my own rooms.

He enters and I catch my breath. As always he is dressed simply. He has little interest in finery and inwardly I curse myself. Why must I always appear before him so formally attired? Why does my nervousness at seeing him manifest itself in acting the part of a great queen rather than a young woman who was once his wife, whom he teased in the soft darkness?

But he, too, is formal with me. He sweeps a low bow, as he ought to his queen. "My lady Zaynab."

I incline my head, gracious, while the heat mounts in my cheeks. "Yusuf bin Ali. You are welcome to court."

He is seated and offered cool water to wash his hands,

then sweet drinks and cakes, hot tea. He takes them with courtesy. "Is your husband the amir well?"

I hate it when he calls him this, 'your husband'. I want to cry out *he is not my husband, how can he be when I was your wife and you are still living? He is not my husband, nor ever should have been! I am your wife, not his!*

I bow my head. "The amir is well. He is gone hunting and will return this evening. He will be glad to see you."

This much is true. He loves to have Yusuf visit us. When he does I am required to attend the meal. I must sit by my husband's side and smile while he and Yusuf talk. I must accept choice morsels from my husband's jewelled fingers into my mouth and smile. If he kisses my hand or compliments me I must smile. I must always smile.

He does not stay long, and when he leaves I do not know when I shall see him again. It may be only the rise and fall of one moon, it may be several. Once it was from one blossoming of the almonds to another. That time I thought I might go mad.

I thought that as the years passed I would no longer feel the same towards him. I was wrong. At first I longed for him because I still loved him as his wife. I was alone at court and I longed for his gentle touch now that I knew how cruel my new husband could and would be for the rest of my married life. When Hela came I was freed from that torment but was rarely touched at all, which brought a new desire – to be held, to be loved. Now, after all these years, I hope that perhaps he still thinks of me as I do him, and that if I can wait long enough the amir might die. If he were dead, Yusuf could take me back as his wife. This time I would know what I had in him and in his first wife – I would be grateful for a gentle loving life, even if it were shared with the shadow of another woman. But time passes and the amir is still hale and hearty, while I grow older.

Hela, meanwhile, goes about her own business. There is no part of the palace she does not visit, no place into which she cannot find her way. I have been here for over twelve years and yet I barely leave my rooms or the state chambers save to attend some festivity or other. Sometimes I summon the falconer and we take my bird to fly. I do not explore Aghmat, merely use its riches to pass the long hours of my life. But Hela knows every part of this city. She knows where the armoury is, the stables. She knows the movements of the guards, the name of every servant, the tiny winding streets where the poor live and their miserable dwellings. She has entered the homes of the merchants and the metalworkers, the rich nobles and their servants. She is called on to be everywhere.

Today she is returned from one of her outings. The other servants make themselves scarce when Hela attends me. She makes them feel ill at ease, for she watches their every move as a cat watches a lizard. Sometimes she reads from great tomes as well, and this also makes them uncomfortable, for surely a maidservant should not pass her days studying like a scholar or a physician?

"What have you found today, Hela?" I ask her.

She is busy washing out little pots in a basin of water, rubbing each dry with a cloth and packing them away again in a carved chest. She keeps all her secrets in that chest now, after I told her that the old goat-bags were not befitting to the handmaiden of a queen. The chest is very plain. I offered her one of precious woods, carved with every kind of flower, but she refused.

She does not answer. She rarely engages in conversation. I throw a date at her, which she ignores. I am bored. I have no-one to talk to but her.

"What secrets do you know today that you did not know before, Hela? Sometimes I think you are planning to escape this place. You know where the stables are, the saddles. The names and watches of all the guards. Are you planning to run away?"

She does not answer, only keeps washing her little pots, changing the water after each one, pouring from big copper jugs into the basin, washing, then tipping the basin's contents into a large tub before refilling with clean water. She is methodical, exact, focused.

I yawn and roll back on the cushions. "*Talk* to me, Hela. There must be some gossip you can tell me. Who is having a scandalous affair? Who is seeking a husband? Who a wife? How are the crops? Tell me anything."

Her voice, when it comes, is so calm and steady that I barely take in what she is saying. "There is an army coming."

I sit up. "What?"

She tips the last of the water into the tub, then takes all her clean pots and puts them to one side in her chest, ready to be filled when a new trader comes to the city. She locks the chest, careful to put the key away in the folds of her robes.

I lean forward, my bare feet touching the cool floor. "Hela!"

She looks round at me as though my interest is unexpected. "What?"

"You said an *army* was coming!"

She nods and gets up, crosses the room, sits down and takes up a book. It is a medical book, I have tried to read it but I do not understand enough of it. I can see I will have to drag every small bit of information out of her. "Where is this army coming from?"

"The desert."

"The desert? There's no-one there. Only a few nomads and the traders."

She shakes her head, still trying to keep her focus on the book. "The Almoravids."

I sit back, disappointed. I had hoped for something of interest to happen. Anything to liven up my endless life here. A battle would at least bring news, glory to our army, tall tales for the men to boast of their prowess at the evening meals.

"Hela, the Almoravids came ten years back. You remember. They took a few places on the trade routes and then as soon as they crossed the mountains their leader got killed. They had to retreat. So much for their holy war."

But Hela has closed the book and is stubbornly shaking her head. "They have a new leader. Two in fact, for they say his second-in command is also a great warrior and a leader of men."

"What's his name?"

"The leader is Abu Bakr bin Umar. His second in command is his cousin, named Yusuf bin Tashfin."

She knows that the very name Yusuf, common as it is, makes my heart beat a little faster and gives me a look. I make a face at her. "They are still intent on their holy war? Have they not learnt anything?'

"Perhaps they have."

I shrug. "When they cross the mountains they will be defeated again."

Hela does not answer, only goes back to her book, and then a servant comes to tell us that I am required to attend dinner this evening, and the whole tedious business of washing, dressing, being perfumed and bedecked with jewels begins again.

There is a time where we hear no more news of the army. At first I tease Hela and tell her that if she had been imagining handsome warriors marching into her arms she was mistaken, and perhaps she dreamed them. But she takes no notice of me, only goes about her business every day as though nothing had changed. I forget about the Almoravids.

Today I am summoned to the state rooms. Luqut wishes me to be by his side during council. This is a frequent occurrence. I am there as a figurehead, a promise. With me by his side the amir can plan for greatness, for my very presence is a sign of future glory to come. His council of men plan for the future. Alliances are discussed, maps are consulted. Perhaps if they were to be linked to this lord or that amir... perhaps if they were to take a small town to add to Aghmat's existing vassals...

These conversations bore me. After years of this I know the names of every lord and vassal tribe in the Maghreb and have met most of them when they visit us to discuss possible unions. I could draw the maps with my eyes closed. I know who is to be trusted and who is deceitful, I know who has large armies and those leaders who for all their bluster have little in the way of real defences. The endless petty skirmishes and associations followed by disassociations weary me, for nothing significant ever seems to change. Leaders rise and fall, territories change hands. So it goes on.

I arrive, am greeted, settle myself by Luqut's side. I try to make myself comfortable even in my stiff silks and prepare to be bored once again. A servant pours tea for me and I sip it, my mind elsewhere until I hear the word 'Almoravids'. At once, I am all ears. No doubt they have crossed the mountains and been defeated. I will tease Hela with this news. Looking around the room I see there is a tension I had not noticed. Luqut has commanded a messenger to repeat the news he brought just this morning so that all may hear it for themselves. The man bows low to us all, flustered at being faced with so many great men as well as the unusual sight of a woman attending council.

"My lords – my lady," he stammers awkwardly.

He is unsure of where he should look, or to whom he should direct his bows. Luqut waves at him impatiently to proceed with less formality. The men lean forward.

"The Almoravids, under the command of Abu Bakr bin Umar, have crossed the Atlas Mountains and taken some small towns."

There are nods. This is not unexpected. This is what happened last time, and they were defeated. They will be on their way soon enough. The crossing of the mountains is no mean feat. It will have left them tired, vulnerable. They have no stronghold city in which to rest and recuperate.

They must advance or flee, defeated. It makes them weak. They will be riding camels which are good for the desert but less fleet of foot now that they have reached more fertile plains.

"They have also taken Taroundannt."

There are gasps. Taroundannt is not much smaller than Aghmat. A pretty city, with mud-pink houses and white storks that nestle in its towers. It benefits from the shelter of the mountains and the rich fertile plain in which it sits, offering a large souk to those in the surrounding areas. Traders use it too, for it sits on the trade routes, as does Aghmat. If the Almoravids have taken it they are stronger than they were when they last crossed the mountains. Their leaders must be bolder, their men gathered in greater numbers. Now they have a stronghold. They can command food and water supplies, conscript men into their ranks. Their camels can be exchanged for horses if they wish. They are also commanding a city that sits on the trade route. They can confiscate gold and other merchandise with which to pay for their needs, raise a tax on merchants. Taroundannt changes the shape of this news. We are under threat. Aghmat is not so far away. It would be logical for them to attack our city next. Another rich city, another post on the trade route. A larger stronghold from which to create a capital should they wish. There will be a battle.

When the council is dismissed preparations begin. Fortifications must be made. Weapons must be assembled, as must be men. We will be ready when the army comes.

I tell Hela everything. While the other servants chatter and wring their hands Hela continues with her reading. She is unmoved by the news. I dismiss the other servants and move closer to her.

"Did you know about this?"

She says nothing but nods, keeping her eyes on the book.

"*How?* The messenger just arrived! He was brought straight to council!"

"I was with the amir."

"Why?"

She shrugs. She does not like being questioned.

"*Why*, Hela?"

"I was tending to a woman."

I turn my face away, thinking of the women in this palace who have paid for my freedom for more than eleven years with their own screams. But I cannot bring myself to look at Hela and order that she reverses her work, that Luqut should come to me again as he used to. I could not bear it.

I look at Hela and she looks back at me, sees my face. Sees that I will not give the order I should give if I were a good person, an honourable person. Nods.

I am ashamed. I have allowed Hela to take my pain and give it away elsewhere. I shake my head to rid it of my thoughts and return to the news.

"Are there truly many of them? They are stronger this time?"

She nods, eyes still on the page.

I move still closer and whisper. "Can they take Aghmat?"

She looks up at me, her dark eyes serious. Nods.

Three days go by and then word comes. The Almoravids have been seen. They are marching on Aghmat.

I climb to the topmost tower of the palace and look into the distance. I can see no army as yet, there are still too far off. By my side stands Hela. She does not scan the horizon. She looks at my face and then returns to my rooms. I follow her and sit down, watching to see what she will do next.

She looks at me and then speaks, abruptly, as though all her words have come at once. "They say their leader is a gentle man. Honourable. He has a wife, old of course, for he is old himself. But he has been a good husband to her these many years."

I nod, although I do not understand her meaning.

"If they are successful and take Aghmat it is likely you will be taken."

I look at her in horror. "As a prisoner of war?"

She shakes her head at my ignorance. "As a wife."

I frown. "They are not going to win, Hela. Luqut's forces are too great, his allies too many."

She ignores me and undoes the heavy locks of the wooden chest. She reaches in, takes out the carved red cup and holds it up.

Its worn surface glows in the rays of sunshine that enter the windows.

Widow

He stands before me in the chilly dawn light. Luqut al-Maghrawi, amir of Aghmat. My husband. Magnificent in his armour, he towers over me. I will myself to stand still and not tremble. After all, we are surrounded by servants and his men. He does not have the tools of his secret desires to hand. He cannot hurt me.

"Give me your blessing, Zaynab," he says. "I fight for Aghmat and for glory. If I win I will take the city of Taroundannt from the Almoravids even as I crush them and send them back into the desert to weep. And I will be one step closer to the greatness which you yourself foresaw for me, your husband."

I nod. I swallow and find my voice. "May Allah bless you, husband," I say meekly. "May the battle be brief and your victory glorious in His eyes."

He smiles. "I will be victorious," he says loudly. Then he lowers his voice so that only I can hear. "When I return you and I will be alone together so that you may feel my might and taste my victory."

I lower my head in submission and he turns away, satisfied. As he reaches the doors a shape emerges from the shadows. It is Hela, and she bears the red cup. I watch as she approaches him, the very picture of submission, the faithful servant to her lord and master.

She speaks and her voice is low and soft. "My lord, I have prepared a drink to fortify you in battle."

Perhaps I hope that Luqut will refuse without my having to intervene. He barely knows Hela except as my handmaiden. If he refuses all will be well. I will not be obliged to cry out and warn him against the red cup.

But he takes the cup from her with a warm smile. "Thank you," he says. He speaks with courtesy.

I see him nod to one of the senior servants and they nod back. I have seen this gesture too many times not to know its meaning. Hela is to be given coins for her trouble. I frown. Why does Luqut trust her and pay her for her potions? Somewhere, at some time, I have missed something that has happened here in this palace. Somehow my husband trusts my handmaiden even though I know she has given him a potion which has made him unable to satisfy his dark needs with me. I knew she had escaped detection for this treasonous offence but it seems she has done more than just escape his eye. Somehow she has pleased him. Has she taken away his potency with me only to strengthen it with other women, the women who scream in distant rooms? Something in me knows this is true.

He lifts the cup.

I have one moment to choose. One chance to redeem myself. If I warn him now I will save his life. He will be victorious, I am sure, for he is on his own ground here, with a brave army at his command. He will return glorious. I will be at his mercy again, for I cannot continue to permit those other nameless women to take the screams from my mouth and place them in their own. If I speak now I will save his life and later save the pain of many women even if I pay with my own pain, my own life.

If I am silent…

If I am silent he will die today. I am sure of this. I do not know what is in Hela's red cup this time, but I know from her eyes that once he drinks from it he will die.

If I am silent he will die, and the women's screams will stop. If he is dead I will be a widow, and perhaps Yusuf will come to claim me for his own again. If I cry out…

I do not speak.

He drinks, gives the cup to Hela.

Raises his fist.

His men shout out a war cry and together they leave the chamber.

The red cup sits, empty, on the table by the door.

All is darkness.

I awake in my own rooms, on my own bed. The lamps are lit. Outside the windows is darkness. Hela sits in a corner by her chest, rearranging her little jars. I try to sit up in bed and she looks at me.

"Better if you lie still for a while. You fainted. I gave you something to help you sleep."

My heart begins to beat too fast, grasping at my breath. "Is there word yet from the battlefield?"

She puts down her work, turns fully to face me. "How long do you think you have slept?"

"A day? It was dawn when he left. It is dark now."

She shakes her head. “You have slept for three days and nights. The battle is over.”

I leap out of the bed and run to the window. The city is very dark and quiet. There should be people in the streets in the evenings and even late into the nights, lamps in the houses. Aghmat is a large city, it does not rest, even at night. I can barely see the outlines of houses. I turn back to face Hela. She is standing right behind me. Our faces are so close I can feel her breath on my lips.

I cannot raise my voice above a whisper. “Where is Luqut?”

“The amir is dead.”

My skin grows cold. Luqut, whatever he did to me, was a strong brave warrior. He had a large army. He knew his own land. To be defeated by a ragged band of fanatical believers from the desert… I see again the cup in his hand, the faded carvings, as he drank. “What happened?”

She speaks as a messenger to a king, no emotion, only the facts as they happened. “The amir was in the midst of battle when he grew dizzy and disorientated. His strength left him and he fell. The generals fought on, but they were lost without him. The army of Aghmat was overthrown. The Almoravids were stronger than anyone expected. They have many more men than before. Better weapons, better trained, commanded by powerful leaders. They took Aghmat yesterday. There is a curfew tonight. Their guards are everywhere. Their leaders are within the palace. Tonight they hold council. Tomorrow they will begin to establish themselves here so that they may reach out and grasp other lands. Much of the city is ruined though, they may choose another city to serve as their seat of power.”

Everything is swept away. The city, Luqut, my status.

My status. "What am I, then?"

"A widow."

I am shaking. "A prisoner of war?" I know what happens to female prisoners of war, especially beautiful ones.

Hela smiles. She sees my thoughts before they are spoken. "It would be good if their leader were to be in need of a wife."

I shake my head.

Hela is serious. "It would be your best chance to stay safe. To be queen again. Marry their leader. Many have heard of Zaynab, the woman who will be wife to the man who conquers the Maghreb and more. Do you not think that is where their eyes turn now they have taken Aghmat so easily?"

My jaw moves without my command, my teeth strike one another and I cannot stop my whole body shaking. "T-there may be others who might ask for my hand…"

I can see Yusuf's face in my mind, hear his low laugh in the darkness of my family's courtyard all those years ago. Now, now he might claim me as his own again. Why does Hela not suggest him as a husband when she knows how I long for him?

A terrible thought strikes me. Hela sees the question forming before I speak my beloved's name. She shakes her head and grabs my waist tightly as I sink to the floor.

They are both gone. The husband who made me tremble and the husband for whom I still yearned. I am a widow twice over in one moment and worse, I am conscious of my precarious status. A widow is no-one. A prisoner of war who is a widow is less than no-one. She is in danger.

I am in danger.

But Hela seems unconcerned. It is coming close to dawn, a pale light begins to grow. Soon I will be able to see outside and then there will be little time left before I must face a new day and find out my new status.

"What will I do?"

"You are commanded to the council at first light, after prayers."

Hela is preparing my robes. She has chosen robes of state, magnificent, jewel-encrusted. A queen's robes.

I gesture to them. "You can't think I should wear those when I meet them. I am a supplicant to them. Not a queen. I am at their mercy."

Hela shakes her head. "You are the queen of Aghmat. You possess great riches. You are beautiful. It is foretold that your husband will conquer great lands. You have one chance to negotiate your position."

"How do I do that?"

She eyes me up as though she doubts my abilities. Her voice grows serious. "One chance, Zaynab. Their leader is a man named Abu Bakr bin Umar. He has only one wife, and she is not with him at present. Many of their wives were left behind when the army marched across the mountains. He is much older than you, but they say he is a kindly man – "

I interrupt her. "A kindly man who has just led a savage army of warriors to our gates and taken our city? A kindly man who has just killed my husband as well as the am – " I bite my tongue. I was about to say 'my husband as well as the amir' but I correct myself "– who has just killed my husband and one of our finest allies? You want me to marry this man?"

Hela shakes her head. "You need to think like a woman and not like a child, Zaynab."

I frown at this insult.

Hela ignores me. "You need to keep your wits about you. You must think about what is best for you, who your friends and enemies are, and then you must act to eliminate your enemies and bring your friends close to you."

I laugh. "Eliminate my enemies? You make me sound like a ruler of a great land, not a widow, not a prisoner of war!"

She shrugs. "It is how you should think. Everyone has enemies, opportunities for greatness, friends who can help them achieve their ambitions."

"Like you did for my mother when Imen came to my father's house?"

She does not recoil from the accusation. She bows her head and does not answer.

I have to know, have to ask one more question. "Like you did for me when the amir went into battle?"

She lifts up my glittering robes. "You need to get dressed. Abu Bakr needs to see a queen, not a supplicant. He must see in you a powerful ally, a symbol of his conquest. Not a widow, not a prisoner of war."

I allow her to begin dressing me. "I have nothing to offer him except my body and the empty promise of a false vision."

Hela sighs. "Forget about the amir. Forget about Yusuf. They are gone and you are alone. You have only me by your side. You need a powerful man to protect you. All women need this. You have one chance to secure him. You will go to him dressed as a queen. If he takes you as his wife he will have a beautiful woman in his bed, the promise of greatness in the future, a symbol of Aghmat fallen at his feet and the treasures of Aghmat at his disposal to pay for more men and more weapons. You are a prize and nothing more – a glittering prize which they can hold up to show their might. You need to be the legend that they can tell to their men and their enemies. But you will be safe if you do as I tell you."

And then she tells me what she has planned. What I must do.

I walk through the gardens and courtyards of the palace. Flowers bloom, fountains play in the sunshine that grows in strength and heat with every moment that passes as it approaches its zenith. All is peaceful. But if I turn my head as I walk I see glimpses through windows and gates to the city beyond.

It is ruined. There is rubble in the streets, broken pots and animals wandering without their masters. Many doors are splintered yet all are firmly closed. It seems the curfew goes on, or else the people are simply too afraid to walk the streets. I glimpse tall figures wrapped in thick blue robes carrying unsheathed swords. These are our new masters, the Almoravid soldiers. Their faces are mostly hidden although one or two catch the movement of my robes and glance towards me through gaps in the walls. They will know who I am, of course. Hela was right: my clothing, for now, is my protection. Any other woman would be shouted at, sent back to her house. The grandeur of my robes marks me out as the legendary Zaynab, until three days ago queen of Aghmat, now of as yet undetermined status.

I pass my servants, who serve new rulers now. Those I see are carrying food and drink, scurrying back and forth, cowed but knowing that, like myself, if they please these new masters they may yet keep their status. They see me pass but look away quickly, unsure what to do were I to command them – would obeying me be seen as a punishable offence under this new regime? Or if they refused to obey and then found my status unchanged – what then? Either way they risk punishment and so they avoid my gaze, hurrying onwards with their given tasks, hoping to avoid an error of judgement that might cost them dearly.

I come close to the great state chambers. There is only one guard, who bears a shield almost his own height and carries a sword. His robes are thick, dark and heavy, covering every part of his face but his eyes. He does not acknowledge me, only lets me past without hindrance.

I pause outside the door to the council room. I will have to face a room full of men now. Soldiers, the conquerors of this city, the murderers of the amir and of my long-lost husband. But I cannot accuse them, nor can I weep. I must hold my head high and charm them, make their leader believe that marrying me would enhance his status and ensure his claim to Aghmat is upheld. I lift my hand and steady my trembling, push the heavy door. It opens slowly and without sound.

The room is empty. The soft thick rugs on the floor and the bright glittering wall hangings have gone. There are no silk cushions on which to recline. The great jugs of shining copper and brass, which were used to hold many cups of sweet drinks and cool water for feasts and council meetings, have been taken away. It feels cold, as though the doors and windows have been open all night. The blue morning light enters the room, which is now decorated only with the white plaster carvings on the walls and the carvings on the doors. Below my feet the detailed tiles are still there, but they look strangely out of place now, overly gaudy in their newly-stripped surroundings.

I was expecting a room full of heavily armoured men, wrapped in their thick robes. Men ready to observe me, to pass judgement on me. There is no-one here.

"My lady Zaynab."

I nearly scream. I turn quickly and see a man framed in the doorway through which I have just come. He wears heavy robes, carries a shield and a sword. The guard I just passed.

"Who are you? And where is your leader?"

He rests his shield and sword against the doorway and pulls the door shut behind him as he enters the room. He discards his outer cloak and unwinds some, though not all, of the wool from his face so that I can see him better.

"I am Abu Bakr bin Umar, leader of the Almoravids. Praise be to Allah for His guidance, I am now also the new amir of Aghmat."

He is a short and stocky man, with a full beard as gray as his hair. He must be much older than I, perhaps as old as my father would have been by now were he still alive. He moves slowly, calmly, as though he has a great deal of time at his disposal. He does not stand in front of me, nor examine me as I feared he might. Instead he walks around the room, looking out into the courtyard with its sweet-scented gardens and splashing fountains.

"You have a very grand palace here, lady Zaynab."

"You have stripped it bare." It comes out too quickly, without my thinking. I bite on my lip, thinking that I must be silent. I must charm, not accuse.

He turns to me and smiles. He does not look angry. "It is not good to build up so much wealth, to live in splendour whilst others live in poverty. Allah says all men are equal – why then should some have so much and others have so little? A king should live as his people do."

I try to hold the words in but I cannot. How dare he come here and take my city, kill my people and then lecture me on how my life should or should not be lived? "Do you live as your men do?"

"I am happy in a simple tent, as they are. I pray with them, eat with them. We wear the same clothes." His mouth twists in a grin. "You thought I was a guard. You asked me where my leader was."

I blush and lift my shoulders in a gesture of resignation.

He grows serious. "And now? What is to become of you now?"

This is my moment. I should do as Hela told me.

I do nothing. I stand still. My life will change now, from one breath to the next. I tried once before to change the course of my life and it took me to a dark place. I allowed Hela to decide for me how to escape that place and that resulted only in the pain and death of others. I will let Allah decide now. I am unfit to make such choices. Let this man take my life into his own hands and make of it what he wills. His choices can be no worse than mine. His army has been given victory by Allah, who smiles on his endeavours. Perhaps if he chooses my life's path it will be smoother. I wait in silence.

He watches me for a moment and when he sees that I will not plead my case, that I will not choose to shape my destiny he comes closer to me.

"I have heard much about you," he says softly.

I risk a look at his face and see that he is smiling. He looks like a father speaking to a favoured child. He reaches out his hands and puts them on my shoulders and speaks directly to me.

"I have heard that you married a man who had a first wife. That you appeared unhappy in his household despite this husband having been your own choice, despite his first wife not treating you ill. It seemed that you could not find your place within that household." He pauses. "And then you had… a vision."

My eyes flicker and drop. I raise them again with difficulty and he nods as though I had confirmed something to him that he already knew.

"You had a vision that your husband would be the greatest in the Maghreb and beyond. And then something strange happened."

I chew at my lip.

"Instead of your husband keeping you by his side and reaching out for this promised greatness, as most men would have done, he divorced you, and gave you as queen to the amir of Aghmat."

His head tilts as he studies me. His voice is low and kind but his eyes miss nothing.

I squirm under his gaze.

"A man not known for his tenderness with women."

I feel tears well up but if I close my eyelids now they will surely fall on my cheeks. I open my eyes wider and meet his gaze, lifting my chin.

He steps away from me suddenly, paces down the room. His tone changes, becoming brisker. "Praise Allah for His mercy and favour, we have taken Taroundannt and Aghmat. Now we will reach out for more cities, more lands in His name. This is our intention. But we must have a place to call our own, a city that holds our strength as we march onwards. And we must have more men, more camels and horses, more weapons. And all must be fed. For this we need much gold."

He turns to face me and runs his hand through his grey hair. He looks older than he is, his mind on many things at once. He grins ruefully.

"So is this the time for me to be distracted by beautiful women, no matter what their promise of greatness? Why should I marry you, Zaynab? I know you need my protection but my men will whisper that I am allowing your beauty to blind me to the work there is ahead of us." He spreads his hands. "Give me a reason I can give my men, Zaynab. I am not an unkind man, I will be a gentle husband to you if that is what you need. But I cannot have my men wavering now. They have braved the desert and the mountains in the name of the most Almighty and I cannot let their faith turn to dust now that we are in the fertile plains."

It is the moment that Hela has prepared for me. It is this or no other. I turn and walk away from him, head held high. As I reach the door his voice catches me.

"Stop." His voice commands, it does not request.

I ignore him. I put both hands against the door and push, hard. It opens and the bright light of the morning blinds me.

Behind me I hear quick steps and a strong hand comes down on my shoulder. "I ordered you to stop. Stop."

He is angry now. He was kindly before but this man expects to be obeyed. I am no longer behaving as I ought. I turn to face him and before he can speak I take a strip of silk from my robes. It is golden, this silk, thickly woven. I take it and lift my hands behind his neck as though to embrace him. He steps back, surprised, but it is too late, I have blindfolded him. He makes to rip off the blindfold but I place my hands over his and lower my voice to a silken whisper, carried through the golden fabric to his ears.

"I will give you your answer, Abu Bakr, if you will trust me."

He hesitates. Trust the queen of a ruined captive city? Whose husband has been killed at his command? It is unwise, but his curiosity is roused. I know as soon as he hesitates that he will go with me, that he will step into the story I am telling him, take his place among the characters that I am bringing to life.

I take his hand. It is hard, calloused, and a little wrinkled. But strong and he clasps my hand with force. He must be a little afraid, I think. How long since he trusted someone like this, how long since he let himself be led somewhere unknown, at the whim of a woman?

We walk through the gardens, back the way I came a short while ago. Our robes brush against scented herbs and servants stare, but Abu Bakr does not know they see him, for he sees nothing. He walks gently, tentatively, but he does not stumble, for I guide him with care and he walks where I set his feet.

We do not speak. I had thought he would ask for answers, that he would demand our destination more than once, but he does not. We walk together, in the soft sunshine, hands clasped. We would look like lovers, were it not for the blindfold.

Hela is waiting, but as neither she nor I speak, and as her feet are shod with soft-soled sandals, Abu Bakr does not know another has joined us. If he thought about it he would think it was strange that we walk through doors that open with little effort on my part. But the world is strange to a newly-blinded man and he does not speak, does not acknowledge her presence.

We walk down stairs and through doors, then through winding passageways and down again. I am as lost as if I too were blindfolded, but Hela knows the way and I follow her as Abu Bakr follows me. When we come to a small door set in a rough mud wall Hela stops and indicates it. Then she turns and walks away. I want to call out to her, for I am afraid.

I do not call out. I push the small door and it opens a small crack. I have to push it harder to make it fully open and dust floats about us from the crumbling doorway.

We stoop to enter and when we are fully inside I close the door behind us. It is very dark now, and I keep one hand to the wall while the other clasps Abu Bakr tighter. He must know we are somewhere old and strange, for there is the smell of dust everywhere and it is very cold and silent. No perfume of sun-warmed flowers here, no trickling water. Only silence.

There is a soft glow but a few steps from us, and I lead him there. I push at the splintered wooden door, which opens silently, and I guide Abu Bakr through it ahead of me. Then I step through and close the door behind us. I swallow the gasp that rose to my lips as I entered. That would not be a part of the story I am telling.

I steady myself and then I speak. My voice is strong. It is the voice of the djinn in the tales told at night, commanding a mere mortal to behold a great wonder. Each word echoes.

"Remove your blindfold, Abu Bakr bin Umar."

His rough hands fumble with the fine silk and the blindfold drops to the floor. He makes to pick it up but stops. His eyes, so long denied the light, are glittering now as the room is reflected in them.

The walls are crumbling mud, the door is decaying wood. But the hundreds of lanterns which light the room are not there to light the walls or door. Their soft shining lights fall on the treasure held here.

There is gold and silver. There are rubies and pearls. There are gemstones of every hue, coins and ingots pouring out from chests, spilling onto the floor as though they were nothing but trinkets. They shine from every part of the room. The riches here are beyond any tale or conjuring of a djinn. They are boundless. Abu Bakr turns away from this sight and his eyes question me.

I speak again. "All that you see is yours. It is given from me to you, by the will of Allah. As he gave you Taroundannt and Aghmat, so he gives you as a wife Zaynab, whose husband will be blessed with greatness. Who will rule over the whole of the Maghreb. You need gold for your holy army. And Zaynab gives you this."

We gaze at one another and then he stoops. I think he will pick up a gem or a coin, for there are many scattered at our feet, but he does not. Instead he takes up the golden silk and hands it to me. I take it, and lift my arms around his neck once again. My robes fall back on my arms and my skin brushes his cheeks as I tie the silk around his eyes once again, and then he takes my hand.

As we leave I take one last look back at the room, at the many tiny mirrors, hidden here and there amongst the treasures, reflecting their glory a thousandfold to those who do not know how little wealth this room truly holds. Luqut was a spendthrift.

Afterwards it is easy. When we are far enough away from the room I remove the blindfold one more time. Our hands clasped, he returns me to my rooms in silence and there he leaves me with a courteous bow. Later I hear the whispers, here and there in the gardens and the streets.

"Abu Bakr is smitten with the lady Zaynab."

"She took him into an underground cavern full of treasures such as cannot be imagined."

"'All this is yours,' she told him."

"Now he is to take her as his wife and she will be queen once again, she who was a widow."

I am queen again and safe. Hela smiles and goes about the preparations for my wedding.

Even in this ruined city there must be a wedding. The people have been terrified, have lost loved ones, have seen their homes ruined but they must know that life goes on. That one thing, at least, has stayed the same in their newly-uncertain world. Zaynab is still queen of Aghmat. The people of the city cling to this one thought. If they ever doubted my vision, now they revere it. "It was foretold," they say. Now they believe it was His plan, that I was always meant for Abu Bakr's wife as the commander of this terrible army. My vision explains their suffering. It explains the new faith that has swept the city. Prayers are said with more conviction, there is more sobriety in dress, in behaviour. There is less dancing and flirting, more talk of war and conquest. The city that ran with water fountains and echoed with laughter now runs with the blood of animals to feed sacrifices and the army. It echoes with the beating of hammers on metal as new weapons are forged. The people of Aghmat can rail against the horrors they have seen or they can believe that this is His will, that a new era is coming and they will be placed at the centre of its power. They choose to believe.

I keep to my rooms. I look out of the palace only through the openings in walls; windows, small nooks and crannies, through the veils provided by elaborately worked gates. I cannot look the people of Aghmat in the eye. The servants know their place again and are reassured. I am queen, as always, and so palace life can resume, albeit with less grandeur.

How strange are these conquerors! Rough men, battle-scarred and pious all in one. They pray with a fevered devotion, all together, bodies swaying in rhythm. I have heard that Abu Bakr and his lieutenants pray with them, as common soldiers. Their clothes are lacking in any decoration. Made of thick coarse cloth, they cover their faces as do many of the men from local tribes, leaving them unknown, even to those of us who see them every day.

They take no delight in the riches and comforts that are now available to them. They make little use of the servants, who grow idle. They do not call for rich foods prepared by our skilled cooks. They do not lie on the soft cushions of the palace state rooms. Instead every room is stripped bare and even foot soldiers lie there to sleep at night, on the bare cold tiles, wrapped in coarse blankets. Perhaps to them this is luxury enough after their former life. They were trained for war in the desert, in the burning days and freezing nights, with little in the way of food but camel meat and dates, perhaps rough barley bread. Now, associating past hardship with their victory, they do not seek out the luxuries of city living.

Many of the men are encamped around the city. There are guards, too, who control who may enter and leave the city. They do not seek to halt trade, but naturally each merchant must pay them for the privilege of passing through what is now their own territory. In this way their reserves of gold are growing, their plans for the future alongside their new wealth. They can command more men, more camels and horses, more weapons. The army grows stronger and better fed by the day. The men are rested now, they have eaten well if not lavishly. They have time to train, to sharpen and repair their weapons. Their steeds, also, are better fed on our rich plains and running rivers. This army can go on to far greater things than poor ruined Aghmat. Already I have heard whispers that they may build a city of their own. *Murakush,* they murmur, *land of God.* They want a city in His name, a city from which they can govern and show their might to the world, for what is more mighty than to raise up a city where there was none before? Most conquerors would have been happy to build a bigger, better palace here in Aghmat and live in grandeur, but Abu Bakr and his commanders have bigger eyes for greater things.

They meet in the state chambers, but I am no longer required to be present. I am left to my own devices and to women's work in preparing for the wedding.

Abu Bakr remains solicitous of me. He sends servants to ask if I have all I need, and occasionally he comes himself to my rooms. He does not enter, does not stay long. When he visits me I offer sweetmeats and tea in my courtyard, by the fountain. He refuses the stickiness of the freshly-made sweets but accepts tea and sits with me for a little while. We do not talk much, sometimes he asks me about the crops that grow in this region or tells me about new arrivals – more men, more horses and camels and where they will be located within or without the city. I answer his questions and nod when he tells me about his plans, but I do not question him. I do not ask about the much-murmured new city, nor about how far into the Maghreb he wishes to proceed, how far he wants his message to be taken, his men to march. I am almost afraid to hear the answer. To me it seems I am about to marry a man who will in truth rule all of the Maghreb and it makes me afraid. That my false vision as a young girl, created in the heat of passion for a man who is now dead should come to life frightens me, as though I had unleashed a djinn from its hiding place and made a pact with it. Now it whirls away from me and I stand helpless, watching its progress and unsure of its intentions towards me.

I think Abu Bakr is a good man, kindly and calm in his manner. I will be safe with him, of this I am sure, but I know that ours will not be a marriage of passion. He speaks to me once of his wife Aisha, and I hear a softness in his voice which I take for love.

"I have not seen her for a long time," he says.

I do not know how to reply but let him continue.

"She is my first wife, of course, but she is of my own age and has borne me fine children. She will understand that the marriage between you and I is not a threat to her, nor to what has been between us in the past."

I nod and smile but my eyes fill up with unexpected tears and I busy myself in serving more uneaten cakes, in calling a servant to bring fresh tea. My eyes clear so that I can look at him again.

"I will have nothing but respect and love for my older sister," I say, for I know such a speech is expected of me.

He smiles sadly at me, seeing the slight redness of my eyes. "You will meet her one day and see that she is worthy of such feelings," he says, "and she will care for you with gentleness, as she has cared for our children."

My heart feels heavy. In truth I already knew this was how it was, how it will always be, but to hear it from his lips makes my eyes sting. A child. This is how he sees me. How I will be to him. He will care for me – and perform his marital duties of course – but nonetheless I will not be a true wife to him. There will be no passion, no shared dreams. There might be children, old as he is, but I doubt he will visit me often enough for that. I am a duty, not a pleasure to him. He longs for the familiarity of his first wife, a woman who has been by his side for many years and who can read his mind, who knows all of his history and understands his secrets. To begin again with me – to tell me each and every part of his life… the thought must only weary him. In truth, why bother? What need is there to truly make me his wife in more than name? We are unlikely to spend much time together. He has much to do. His wife will join him eventually. Besides, if he is to conquer more of the Maghreb I may well be left behind. Battles are no place for women.

I try to make light of these thoughts.

"I hope you have many tales to tell me, Hela," I say to her.

She is immersed in plans. The wedding is not far away now, and although my clothes are prepared Hela has her mind on more than my appearance. The servants have been cleaning for days. The gardeners have received a telling-off because the flowers, coming to the end of their natural lives, look less than satisfying to her critical eye. New ones must be planted. The pools must be emptied and their tiles scrubbed, then filled again so that they glisten in the sunshine. The servants mutter behind her back but as usual no-one goes against Hela. They are afraid of her dark eyes, her bent back, her closeness to power.

"What tales?" she asks impatiently, her back still turned to me as she surveys the gardens. She has already chastised me for showing little or no interest in this wedding. She says I should think of nothing else, for not until I am married will I be truly queen again.

"Oh, gossip and fairy tales, Hela. I do not think my husband will be here much." I make my voice even lighter, amused. "Why, it will be as it was before they came. Just you and I in my rooms and a husband I never see!" I almost laugh at the end, but do not have enough breath as I find I suddenly need to swallow at the picture that is forming in my mind as I speak.

Hela turns and looks at me. I avoid her gaze. She sighs. "What gossip do you want to know?"

I shrug, clear my eyes, breathe again and lean back on my cushions. "Oh, I don't know. Tell me about my husband's council."

"Why?"

"It's where he spends all his time." I try not to sound like a whining child but I can see that Hela does not think I have succeeded.

She does not seem interested in the topic I have selected. "They all look the same under those veils. Rough manners. Smell of camel. No idea of how to dress – all that thick dark wool when they could wear anything they wanted. More interested in prayers and armoury than food or women."

I laugh and pour myself a sweet pomegranate drink. "See, you can be amusing when you want to be. Tell me more. Who is his right-hand man?"

She looks at me as if I were stupid. "Don't you know anything about them?"

"Not really. I only see Abu Bakr. The rest are always in the distance. They don't come to my quarters."

"His right-hand man is named Yusuf bin Tashfin."

Now that she says the name I remember it. The name

Yusuf still makes me think of my first husband and my stomach clenches. I drink more pomegranate. I cannot mourn him forever. "Tell me about him, then."

Hela points out more unscrubbed tiles to a servant who sulkily returns to work.

"Makes Abu Bakr look like an unbeliever."

I choke on my drink and splutter with laughter. "No-one can be more holy than Abu Bakr!"

"*He* is. Prays all the time. Always looks disapproving about everything."

"Such as?"

"Pretty clothes. Women in pretty clothes. Festivities. Music. Dancing. Feasting. Any food that is not barley bread, camel meat, dates and water."

I laugh harder.

Hela waves her hand at the beautiful palace gardens. "Decorated palaces. Fountains. Jewellery. Anyone who doesn't pray, doesn't fast, doesn't do everything they ought to, when they ought to, how they ought to. He has no leniency, that's for certain."

"Is he a good fighter?"

"They say better than any man, better even than Abu Bakr. Trains harder and longer, rides for hours every day. Has no fear on the battlefield, doesn't seem to care whether he lives or dies – but it is always the other man who dies, never him. Fearsome."

"Is he married too?"

Hela nods. "Some tribal woman. Left her behind in some little village till he sends for her."

"Children?"

Hela shakes her head. "She lost a baby, they said. Kicked by a camel."

I picture her. An old tribeswoman like Abu Bakr's wife. A simple woman, surrounded by sands and camels. Left behind to await her husband Yusuf's summons or death, trusting only in Allah's will. Barren, probably, if he has no children by his age. No doubt these wives will arrive soon and I will be surrounded by toothless old women who look on me with pity, too young to share their huddled gossip, too old to have a chance of bearing many – if any – children. A not-woman, a child-queen, a figurehead and trophy of war. No more. I finish my drink and leave Hela to her scoldings, burrow into my bed and sleep.

The wedding is upon us. The day passes slowly but I am deaf to its sounds, seeing only images as time passes. The crowds. My jewels and heavy silken robes. Abu Bakr and all his men, as ever in their rough woollen robes without adornment. The prayers, rising and falling around me. The blessing. The feast afterwards. Simpler than it was for Luqut and I but still plates and plates of food, the rich meats and sticky sweetness of cakes, the fresh cooling drinks.

As the evening wears on I am brought back to my rooms where there are servants everywhere, lighting lanterns and candles until my bedchamber is ablaze with light. I stand amidst them all, unsure of what to do, how to be. I see myself in the great mirror and I seem small even though my robes take up twice the size of my real body. I try to stand straighter but this just seems to make me look wooden. I allow my shoulders to relax and watch my figure decrease in height.

At last Abu Bakr comes to me and our servants leave us. Even Hela makes her bows and disappears. We are alone.

I do all that I should. I welcome him with sweet drinks and delicate fruits, which he accepts even though I know they are not greatly to his taste.

"It is very bright in here," he says, smiling.

We make our way about the room, blowing on each tiny flame until the room grows dark, save for one lantern still lit by our bed.

I kneel before him to remove his shoes, rise again to help him disrobe. I struggle with the long wool wrap that he wears about his face and we smile at one another as at last his face is unveiled before me. I have not seen him fully unveiled before. His beard is thick and grey, his face broad and square-jawed. His eyes I know best, of course, a rich brown with many creases in the corners. His forehead, also, is much creased. Much of the skin on his face is paler than his hands and arms, since it is always covered from the sun's bright rays.

He in turn disrobes me. My rich silks fall to the ground and he looks over my body without shyness. He reaches out, but only strokes my shoulder, as though I were still fully dressed, before indicating the bed behind me. We make our separate ways to it and enter its luxurious covers. Once covered, we turn to face one another.

I am no fool. It has been a long time but I remember what will be expected of me now. I know, too, what I might offer in the way of delight to this man, but my courage fails me. His gaze is too tender, too much speaking of duty and care rather than desire or passion. I move closer to him and ensure our skin is touching, that my arms are neatly placed that he may embrace me with ease. I will be a good and dutiful wife, for what else can I offer? I had passion once and it was wasted by my foolishness. I have waited too long in fear and trembling for love to grow now for this man who thinks of me as a child to be cared for. But he is at least a kind man. I will be kind also. Our marriage may be one of convenience but perhaps it will also have tenderness. I have not had gentleness shown to me by a man for a long time. To be held gently will be something good in my life at last. Perhaps it will be a marriage more suited to two old people but that will suffice me. Perhaps he will not often come to my bed, but I will have some soft caresses and these will bring a longed-for warmth to my life.

Abu Bakr looks at me and cups my face in his hand. His gaze does not flicker from my face. "Now that we have a stronghold my wife Aisha will join us soon," he says.

I blink at his unexpected reference to her, but summon up the correct words. "I will be her respectful sister," I assure him.

He nods and strokes my face. I close my eyes. It has been a long time.

"Goodnight, Zaynab," he says gently, and turns his back to me. He blows out the candle and all is darkness.

I place one hand tentatively on his back. His skin is old, but the muscles underneath are still strong.

"Husband," I begin, tentatively.

"Goodnight, Zaynab," he repeats.

I withdraw my hand. "Goodnight, husband," I reply meekly.

I lie in the silent darkness.

I am a widow for a third time, in all but name.

Wife

I KNOW THAT THE SERVANTS WHISPER. To have been married three times, even in such unusual circumstances as mine – it is not done. They watch me when I pass and their whispers are added to all the whispers of my life. I know that the story of my life grows with the telling, that I am becoming a character from a legend rather than a real person.

A young girl, her hand sought by so many. Who chose to travel across the Maghreb, far, far away from her home and her family, to her first husband, a man still grieving for his dead-but-still-living wife. A woman who had a great vision at the waterfalls and was demanded as queen by the amir of Aghmat. Encased in rich robes, yet barren. Whose city was destroyed and yet who cast a spell over the commander of the conquering army, showing him riches such as are only dreamed of in this life. Made queen again from the rubble of a ruined city, lifted once again to greatness. Her vision coming true at last as the army prepares for domination.

When I hear the whispers I want to roll my eyes, but more often than not I shiver. I was only a foolish girl who married a man I had a burning passion for without finding out about his own crazed passion for a woman no longer of this world. I tried everything I could to bind him to me and in desperation made up a mighty vision, which only led to me being given in tribute to a monster. A monster killed by a man who I then tricked with mirrors into marrying me, to save me from a dishonourable fate, only to find out that my marriage bed, yet again, was cursed. Where is the glory, the fated destiny of my growing legend here? There is no glory, there is no wondrous life, only a stumbling from one place to the next, from one error to another. I cannot seem to find my feet, to stand strong, reach out my hands and take a joyful life. When I reach out to grasp the pure gold of happiness it turns to sand between my fingers, blown away by a hot summer wind.

Abu Bakr does not dishonour my name. He comes to my bedchamber, he sleeps in my bed. The servants leave us each night, content that at last my destiny has been fulfilled. Here I am, Zaynab, married to a great leader, one whose mighty army grows stronger by the day, whose reach may well grasp the Maghreb and beyond as was foreseen. A man who lies with me each night, as is right between husband and wife. They even hope for a child, the more credulous amongst them, thinking that such a child would show Allah's approval for this marriage, set a seal upon our joint destinies.

They can keep hoping for all I care. I shake when I think of my life. I spoke of a vision and here it is, growing before me day by day. I do not know how to stop it and I am afraid. I am like the heroes of the old stories, who open up the great jars contained long-imprisoned djinns and find themselves with a towering giant before them of unimaginable power. They reach out their puny hands to try to push back the stopper but it is too late and the djinn they created is free to wreak whatever havoc it wishes, leaving our heroes to watch, helpless before their unwitting creation. I do not know where this destiny is leading me.

It does not take long before Abu Bakr discovers my true worth to him. He is a clever man and nothing escapes his quick eyes. I glance at a map of the Maghreb laid out on a table at which he has been sitting and he sees my eyebrows rise. It is but a moment, but he is a man who must be alert to all moments, be they large or small.

"You are surprised by something, Zaynab?"

I look up. "It is nothing," I say hastily. It is not a woman's place to judge military strategies.

He smiles. "Tell me what you saw."

I shrug awkwardly and make a vague gesture towards the map. "The amir of that city…" I stop.

"Yes?" He has come to stand by my side.

I back away slightly. "He is known to be in the pocket of that amir." I point to a different part of the map.

He narrows his eyes. "And?"

I shrug again.

"*And?*"

"You would do better to attack that city first. The other will bow down to you as soon as the first city falls. The amir is a coward. He will not fight. He will gladly become your vassal if you will allow him to stay in his current position of power. He is a man of letters and has no taste for war. He will do whatever it takes to keep his scholarly life, so long as he does not need to fight." I am caught up in my thoughts now. The many, many hours of boredom spent in council as a figurehead for Luqut and his men are bearing fruit at last. I know every petty ruler and their strengths, interests, weaknesses. I know who is a fighter and who is a coward, whose favourite wife is sister to another chief, whose loyalties lie to one side or another. I point again and again. "This one, though, he is a fighter. You will need a strong army when you attack him. He needs to see all your might, all your power to realise that if he wishes to keep his honour he is better off making a treaty with you. If he thinks there is any chance of beating you in battle he will not stop fighting until he is dead and the ground strewn with the bodies of his men and yours. You will bear heavy losses if you do not overpower him quickly, for his men are as brave as he is. That one though – he is a fool. You can outwit him in battle, for his men are poorly trained. He is an idle man, too fond of eating and not fond enough of fighting. This one is old now, if you overpower him quickly by the time his son takes his throne you will be his masters and he will not question you." I look up. Abu Bakr is not watching my finger on the map. He is looking at my face. My eyes are bright, I am speaking quickly and with assurance.

"I did not know you were a military tactician, Zaynab," he says, grinning.

I try to back away from the table but he takes my hand and leads me forwards. He settles himself on the cushions by the table and gestures for me to do the same. We sit side by side, our heads close together, the map spread out in front of us, the names of rulers of every tribe and city laid out for us to consider.

"Tell me more," he says, and I do.

Now I attend council again, seated in honour by Abu Bakr's side. Perhaps I am not his true wife when we lie in our bed, but here I am his beloved. He praises my knowledge of the Maghreb to his men and although they are surprised they see quickly that he is right, my knowledge far surpasses theirs. They listen to me with interest as I share more and more information. As they file out that first day I see one of them gesture towards me and hear him mutter the name of Tin Hinan to another, who laughs. I smile. To be compared to a legendary warrior queen is no bad thing. My heart lifts.

The men leave the room while Abu Bakr and I stand looking down at the map we have been poring over. He is retracing various routes with his finger, considering first one plan, then another. I see a slight movement and look up to see one man still seated, at the end of the room from us. His dark robes and wrap cover most of his body and face. But his eyes are fixed on me.

Dark eyes, thick dark brows above them. The beginning of a sharp nose. Of the rest of his body I can see only his hands, which are hardened and calloused. He is playing with a dagger, this is the movement I saw.

We gaze at one another for a moment. I am curious, taking in what I can of him, face, hands, dagger, clothes. His gaze does not flicker. When I return to his eyes they are steady on mine.

Abu Bakr senses I am no longer following his muttered thoughts about the map and future conquests. He follows my gaze and smiles.

"Yusuf! I thought you had taken the men to training."

The name Yusuf has its customary effect on me, drawing up images of that first man whose voice teased me in the darkness. I clear away these thoughts. This, then is Yusuf bin Tashfin. In the crowd of dark-robed and veiled men it was hard to spot Abu Bakr's second-in-command. He did not take a place of honour, nor speak louder than the others, allowing each man to have his say.

Yusuf does not reply. He stays seated, draws the dagger from its scabbard and then slides it back in with a hissing sound of metal on metal.

Abu Bakr does not seem to take this as an insult. He looks down at the map and then back up at Yusuf. "Will our very own Tin Hinan bring us luck in our battles, do you suppose?" he says smiling and waving towards me.

Yusuf stands. It is done in one fluid movement, with none of the grunts or stiffness of the other men's movements after sitting in council while the sun moved across the sky. He stands in the doorway, black robes sweeping the floor and looks me in the eye. When he speak his voice is low and soft, but his words are hard. "As I recall Tin Hinan fought back against her Muslim conquerors and killed many of their men. Are you sure you wish for another such woman to be your tactician? Are you sure she is on your side?"

I open my mouth to protest but he has left the room. I see a glimpse of his robes as he rounds a corner of the courtyard outside and is gone. I turn to Abu Bakr but he is laughing.

"Yusuf is a man of war," he says. "A fighter. A true warrior in body and spirit. Now look again at this map, Zaynab, and tell me where we can most easily build a stronghold. Aghmat is not truly ours, here we are only conquerors. I want a great new garrison which in time will be our seat of government."

I look down at the map and see only lines. In my mind I see the dark eyes filled with suspicion of me. I shake my head and look again. "There," I say. "Close to Aghmat that you may use this city to provision your garrison until it is of a size to fend for itself. On the plain so you may see enemies approaching, where the water runs from the mountains so you will not thirst."

Abu Bakr nods. "It will be a great city," he says with satisfaction. He gazes at the map and in his eyes I can see plans being drawn up for a garrison, a fortified stronghold, a place from which to conquer the Maghreb.

"I shall call it Murakush," he murmurs. "God's land."

I smile and take his arm as we walk out to the gardens.

The council meets more often now and I am always present. There are many plans to be discussed. Aghmat, a once-glorious city in its own right, will become a mere tributary stream to the new city that is being planned. Abu Bakr wants his Murakush to be a new beginning. He is so eager for it to be ready that he will not build it and then move there. He wants to be there as it is built, and for this reason we will all move to an empty spot on the great plain and begin the work. Men, women, children, slaves, animals, everyone. He does not care that we will all have to live in tents rather than our homes. Aghmat will still have some people left, mostly craftsmen and those who produce much of our food and livestock, but even I can see that they will not stay here long. Why hold a market in a decaying city? Soon enough the traders will come to the new encampment, then the craftsmen. It will not be long before Aghmat will be a city of spirits only. This new garrison, city of the future, Murakush, will drain away Aghmat's very lifeblood to feed its needs.

Now that Abu Bakr has found a common ground with me our life together is easier. He still keeps to the memory of his far-away wife, but we are closer, like beloved cousins. We sit on our bed, surrounded by maps, discussing plans well into the night. When we come to council by day we are as one, our thoughts clear, our minds united on actions to be taken. Abu Bakr's orders are given with the confidence of one who has considered all options, our glances to one another make it clear that we are in agreement. I do not have to speak much, for all can see that I am as much behind the orders given as he is. The men seem to take this as well as can be expected. They might be uncomfortable with a woman such as I were it not for their childhood memories of legends told about the warrior queen Tin Hinan, and also for my own vision. They cling to these two myths and in them they find strength and faith, believing that my place in this council is a sign of greater battles to be won, greater glory for their cause. They look as much to me as to Abu Bakr for confirmation. Their respect for me grows. I see it in their courtesy to me, their care in ensuring I am heard in council and their nods or bows in the courtyards of the palace when they come across me.

But Yusuf is not happy. I am a thorn in his side, a snake in his house. He sits as far from me as he can in council and glowers at me throughout.

"You should sit closer to me, you would not be able to

see my face if it bothers you so. By sitting as far away as you can all you do is end up facing me for many hours, which I know is not to your liking."

We have arrived at the door to the council room together and are alone for a brief moment before we enter. I am laughing at him, for I know he does not like to be close to me and yet I am safe. I am the respected wife of his leader and even his loyal men have taken me into their hearts, ignoring his warnings about my possibly duplicitous nature.

He is ahead of me and puts one hand on the heavy door. When I speak he stops so suddenly that I almost step into him. He looks at me over his shoulder. "I sit where I can see you."

"So that you can keep an eye on me and my evil plotting behind your back?" I am laughing again.

His face darkens. "Yes," he says shortly, and pushes the door open.

We enter, take our usual places at opposite ends of the room and settle down to many more hours of gazing at one another as the talks go on, he balefully, I with laughter in my eyes which only serves to make him angrier.

My place by Abu Bakr's side is now kept only in council. His first wife Aisha arrives. He sent for her almost as soon as they arrived, and it has taken some time for her to make her way here. I await her with trepidation, afraid she will take more than I expect. I do not care if she takes Abu Bakr from my bed, for he has never touched me, but I am a little afraid for my place in his council.

The tall brown camel on which she sits has had an easy burden. Aisha is a withered leaf still golden in the sun. Small, wiry, her skin wrinkled, teeth missing here and there, her hands a little twisted and her shoulders hunched. But she has a warm smile and climbs down nimbly from her high seat, barely waiting for the unwilling camel to kneel. She comes straight towards me and enfolds me in a warm embrace, though she comes only up to my shoulder.

"A sister for me," she says, smiling.

I embrace her cautiously, feel her thin body and old bones, know as I do so that I may be younger, stronger, more beautiful but that I am not, never have been, a threat to her. She knows with one quick look that Abu Bakr has not lain with me as a true wife. She does not gloat about this, nor feel jealousy about my role in council, she accepts what she already knew and seeks to ease my humiliation – for each of us to acknowledge what the other brings.

"Our husband says you are his greatest strategist. He says with you to read the maps and Yusuf to lead the men there is nothing that cannot be done."

I cannot help laughing. No-one could be jealous of this little woman, only desire her as a friend and ally. She is too warm, too full of a quick bright strength that has come from many years as a beloved wife as well as her own self-reliance in being left without that husband for so long. "I do not think Yusuf would agree."

She grins back, her missing teeth making the grin bolder. "Abu Bakr said the two of you were not friends. He said anyone stepping between your gazes would be cut as by a dagger. But he also said you do not yet know one another's worth. Have you seen him fight yet?"

I shake my head.

She looks surprised. "Not even when they train?"

"I never watch them. I keep to my own apartments. Why would I want to watch them training?"

"It is a sight like no other. You should watch them one day."

I smile and call for hot tea and sweets. We sit together and talk of women's matters, our families and lineage, our rooms here at the palace. I offer her my rooms but she waves them aside. I take her to see other rooms nearby and she is content, calls for her servants to begin to unpack her belongings. I arrange for her to be bathed, give her fresh robes. She laughs at the fineness of my silks, asks for something simpler. It is Hela, unbidden, who steps forward with the bright striped woollens so much beloved of the desert dwellers. Aisha is pleased and when she returns from her ablutions she is restored. She asks to see the gardens, we climb up the walls that she may see the city from a height.

"It was beautiful," I say sadly, showing her the much-diminished glories of Aghmat. The signs of conquering are still much visible.

"It is still beautiful," she says gently. "But there will be new glories."

"Will there?"

She nods. "Abu Bakr does not fight for his own glory. He fights for Allah, and he fights for true faith. One day the wars will end."

We are interrupted, for Abu Bakr has been advised of her arrival. He comes across the gardens and takes her in his arms. I can only stand by and lower my eyes. After a few moments Abu Bakr turns to me.

"Zaynab, we will leave you now. Tomorrow I will see you in council." He smiles, his fatherly smile, and places one hand on my head, like a blessing.

I nod and smile at Aisha. I cannot even begrudge her this moment. When I saw how he looked at her and she at him I understood why he would not lie with me, no matter that she would have accepted it if he had. They are as one.

He begins to walk away. Aisha turns back to me and speaks softly. "Watch Yusuf," she says.

I raise my eyebrows.

She smiles at my incomprehension. "Watch him," she repeats. "Go to the walls when the men are training. Watch him fight."

She hurries to catch up with Abu Bakr as he reaches her rooms.

The doors close behind them and I am left alone in my courtyard.

I stand on the empty plain.

"It will be here."

I nod. "It is a good place," I say. I turn to look at Abu Bakr and we smile at one another.

"We will begin the move at once."

"Now?"

He nods, obliges my camel to kneel, helps me regain my seat and takes his own. On his command they both rise to their feet and we begin our journey back towards Aghmat, our escort of soldiers behind us. We have ridden since the dawn prayers and now we are in the heat of the day and it will be dark before we reach the city walls again. We have stood here for but a few moments and yet we know this is the right place. We have seen how the mountains will bring clear water to the planned city, how the earth underfoot is good and will support the animals who will need to graze to keep us fed. We will plant many trees – olives and almonds and dates will flourish here. By the time the city is fully built the trees will be bearing their fruits for the many mouths within its walls.

Now that Aisha is here I am more than ever Abu Bakr's child rather than his wife. I am a beloved daughter, favoured and treated almost as a son. I am a part of his plans, his strategies. He does not see me as a woman nor a wife. He does not see what robes I wear, nor how the sun touches my hair. He does not seek to touch my hand with his own when we walk together, only takes my finger and moves it to point at a different part of a map, the better to show me his thoughts on paper. He sees a clever mind, hears a quick tongue and treats me as he might one of his men.

I suppose I should be grateful I am excused training.

The day has come. We are going to Murakush. To an empty spot on a plain which we will fill with our tents and animals, our noise and plans for the future.

We look like dispossessed war captives rather than a conquering army about to build its stronghold. Battle-trained horses are loaded up like pack mules, hardened soldiers pack up belongings as though they were slaves. The slaves are worked almost to exhaustion. There is no time for good meals or fine clothes – we wear rough robes and slowly the palace empties of anyone and everyone of importance. A few soldiers are left behind to keep Aghmat safe but the army is on the move. Thousands of men, bright armour glinting here and there among their dark robes.

Many of the humble people come with us also. We have need of all – of women and children, of men and slaves. Even a garrison – for that is all Murakush is for now – needs bread, meat, vegetables, water, grains. Many hands are needed to feed many mouths. Craftsmen are needed to repair the armour of the soldiers and the saddles of horses and camels. Whole houses fall silent in a day and the streets are empty. Slowly, over many days, the procession away from Aghmat grows longer, while that empty spot on the plain begins to fill. Later there will be walls, buildings, a great city. For now, there are tents of all shapes and sizes. There is a great empty centre, which we leave for prayers since there is no mosque, for feasts and markets. Around it are placed the largest tents, those belonging to the people who command. Abu Bakr's tent is largest, for here is where we will hold council from now on. Our large cool palace rooms placed in gardens, tiled in a thousand bright colours, are very far away.

The work begins quickly. There are latrines to be dug. The shepherds must seek safe new pastures for their animals. Water must be brought. Already they are building the means to bring water to us without it being fetched jug by jug. There must be an acqueduct, and animals are brought to turn the wheels so that water will flow to us. It will be rough and ready for now, but later we can refine it, there will be a greater flow of water for the gardens that will be set aside to grow crops. For now, much of our food is preserved and brought from elsewhere. Abu Bakr's orders have been obeyed and the trade routes which pass through those cities they already hold are yielding a goodly source of taxes on the merchants who trade there and many goods are brought for our needs. Often we eat only coarse bread or couscous with dried dates and water. There is little time to prepare other foods. Sometimes there is fresh meat and it tastes better than all the great feasts I was used to in the palace at Aghmat.

"Not pining for your palace, lady Zaynab?" asks one of the men when he sees me emerge from my tent one day.

I am about to say that I miss it but other words come from my mouth. "It is a new life," I say. "But not a bad one."

The man seems surprised, no doubt expecting me to be fretting for my fine rooms, my cooling gardens, for a life of luxury such as I have been used to. He is right, of course. The tents are hot, there is little room inside them even though I have one of the larger ones. There is dust everywhere and chaos as more people arrive every day. Although I still have many servants and slaves to call my own they, too, are pressed into service to help set up the camp. There is new work to be done every day. Ovens have to be built that we may bake bread. Water still has to be fetched even if not from so far away. Cooking is not done in the big kitchens the slaves and servants were used to, but on campfires. Abu Bakr's men may be accustomed to desert life but the people of Aghmat have lived in cities for all their lives and their parents' lives before them, even their grandparents. This is a new, hard, life for them. They have come because they are needed and because as Aghmat empties it becomes clear that if they wish to rebuild their old lives they will need to be built here, in Murakush. Aghmat is a place of spirits now, each house gradually losing its living breathing inhabitants, being left for the winds to fill. There is still a souk, but it is becoming a desultory place, a quick stop-off for merchants before they come on to Murakush where their wares are wanted.

But I am happier here than I have been for many years. I do not live in fear. I am treated with respect by all and with kindness by my husband. I am wanted for my wits and my strategies, accepted by the men who matter most in this place. Even now there are tribes who are travelling here to meet with Abu Bakr, to see for themselves what manner of a man he is, how great an army he really has. When they arrive they are awestruck. Never have they seen so many men, so many camels and horses in one place. So many weapons. They are afraid at first but before they can become aggressive, as many men do when they are afraid, Abu Bakr's strong hand will be on their shoulder, a warm smile on his face. They are offered food and drink, taken to sit in council sessions, offered privileges if they will swear allegiance. They look about them and see that great things may be theirs if they agree, that their people will be slaughtered if they do not, and they agree. They leave Murakush with gifts and blessings, with safety in their hearts. They return home and as they do so they spread the word – Abu Bakr's army is not to be trifled with. It is better to be their friend than their foe. Then more leaders come to us, and so it goes on. We are fighting a war without bloodshed so far, in large part because of my knowledge. As the smaller leaders capitulate so the larger, stubborn ones are left without allies to call on.

There will still be fighting. I can see it coming when I look at the maps spread out before us. The leaders of the larger cities will not so easily roll over like trembling dogs. They will fight. But when they do they will find out what it is to fight the Almoravids, and they will suffer for their bravery.

Today Abu Bakr announces that he needs to focus on preparing his army for the next stages of conquest and so the rule of the camp's daily life is to be given to me. He has decreed that all who arrive in the camp must come to me first. I will direct where they are to set up their tents, where their animals are to graze, what work they are to be given. I have more slaves and servants given to me so that I may direct the camp's life with ease. When there are problems – when water is short or there must be a decision about grazing rights – I will be told and I must decide what is best for the camp. I am to be the ruler of my own garrison city. I am grateful for his trust and that of the men who agreed I should take on this role. Yusuf, of course, merely looks into my eyes and then away again. He does not agree, he does not disagree.

I smile at him as I leave the council. "We are both Abu Bakr's lieutenants now, Yusuf," I say, taunting him. I like to see him scowl at me. He is bad tempered and obstinate, still unwilling to acknowledge that I have been of great use to Abu Bakr's plans.

"You are a woman," he says, scowling as I had known he would.

"And you are a jealous man," I say, and move towards

him to leave. He does not move, so I push my shoulder against his. He will not give way and I have to force my way out, our bodies hard against one another. I laugh as I go and feel his anger mounting behind me.

Days go by where I give out endless orders. The camp is at last beginning to come to some semblance of order although I can see that mine will never be a simple task. New people arrive daily – soldiers, slaves, animals, merchants. Families. All must be housed, all must be fed in a garrison that does not have all the facilities of a city. Those men who are not training are needed to dig trenches and build walls, for this city of tents must nevertheless be fortified. Houses will come later, safety is more important. Tents must be erected to some sort of pattern that people may walk easily and quickly between them and I find myself drawing up little maps to show paths between them. There are lavish tents made of fine leathers covered with rich embroideries and tents so tiny and grey with age they barely exist. My own tent is fairly small but Abu Bakr has told me I should have a new one made. I order a very large tent.

"What colour?" asks the man who is organising this for me.

I wave my hand impatiently. "Black, for all I care," I say. "I do not care about the colour, I care about the size. It must be large, taller than a man inside, do you understand? I am sick of being bent over double, all this crouching and stooping. It is uncomfortable. It will be a long time before I have a building in which my own airy rooms can be built.

I refuse to be bent over like an old crone from now until then."

He nods and begins to walk away.

"And make it quickly!" I call after him. "My back is already aching!"

He laughs and promises that if it be Allah's will I may stand tall again very soon, very soon.

He is a man of his word. The tent is ready within ten days and it is gigantic. There are others more ornate but mine is the largest in the camp, as big as the council tent. It is a rich black all over, made with black cloth and skins and when I step inside I can not only stand at my full height but also lift my arms above my head. I am delighted. Abu Bakr laughs at me for my lavishness but I am happy. Hela is happy too. She makes up a bed for me and has my belongings brought to me. Meanwhile she takes over my old tent, which stands by the side of the new one and makes it her own, full of her chests of secrets.

The next day I wave aside all the usual demands on my time – the questions, demands, worries of hundreds of people who come daily. I appoint Hela in my place and watch in amusement as the crowd that always comes to ask me for decisions is changed into a crowd of those who seek her healing.

She looks over her shoulder at me as I walk away. "Where are you going?"

"To watch the men training,"

She turns back to the crowd, her hands already reaching for cures among her chests.

I speak with the foreman and he takes it upon himself to escort me to the first part of the walls to have been built, the part that looks out onto the training grounds. The men continue with the trenches and fortifying walls elsewhere, but at this part they are already built. There is much to-ing and fro-ing to find me something I can climb. One way or another, with many hands guiding me and the foreman holding his breath in terror at the thought of me falling and hurting myself, I am lifted up to the top of the wall, where I can sit, for the walls are broad enough for two large men to sit on, let alone my slender frame. I dismiss the foreman then and he backs away with many worries on his brow. I tell him I will call for him when I need to come back down. He nods but continues to worry and cast glances my way as he directs his men's work. Now that I am comfortably installed on the wall I can look out across the training ground.

Now I see what I did not see when they came to Aghmat, when I was taken by darkness. Here I sit on the fortified walls of a city, looking out to a conquering army. I have grown used by now to think of Abu Bakr, of Yusuf, of the army, as *my* army, *my* people, *my* plans for conquering. Now I look out and I see what others will soon see – a conquering army, the enemy, a fearful onslaught of weapons and men.

At first I struggle to form shapes within the sight before my eyes. Too many men to count – thousands had come to Aghmat but now there are tens of thousands. Camels and horses weave between the men, so that sometimes I almost see one being with a camel's body and a man's head, or the legs of a man with the head of a horse. Before they had used mostly camels, more suited to the desert and the mountains. Now horses arrive every day, for on the hard earth their hooves are swifter. All must be trained, just as the men must be. Many of the animals are fierce, fighting animals, not the docile slow beasts used for carrying women and goods. There is biting and kicking, neighs and grunts which the men must both temper and avoid.

Their weapons are everywhere. Within the camp I am used to seeing daggers on every belt, but here there are longer daggers, javelins, swords. There are shields that no common man could even lift, let alone fight behind. The hardened layers of skins shine in the light.

The men themselves I am better used to seeing around the camp. Seeing them all at once I am struck by their variety. They are of every size – the thin wiry short men, the tall loping men, the ones built like the very walls on which I am sitting. The ones who seem made of fat but whose size belies their strength. They are of many colours also. There are those so black that I can barely make out their features at this distance, those whose skin is honey-gold – they might have been even paler in their own lands but here the sun has made them its own. There are men who are so scarred by battles they might once have been of any hue. All glisten with sweat and all bear scars.

Now I begin to see individual shapes – where one man fights another, the better to learn their skills for the battlefield. My eyes move from one fighting pair to another. Sometimes they fight in larger groups. They fight with a strange mix of care and ferocity. They must truly fight if they are to be better fighters but they cannot harm one another for to do so gives greater strength to their enemies.

A shout goes up and is repeated. The men move at once and the shapes shift before me from little groups into tight, closed ranks. The foot soldiers are at the front, the mounted men behind – horses first, then camels, rising from the height of a man to twice that height. Seen like this the army is huge and terrifying. Too many men to conceive of defeating, so closely packed together that they look like one giant creature risen from dark dreams and made real.

They stand, immobile.

Then the drums begin. The beat is slow, the sound so deep it reverberates in my belly. I have heard it before, of course, but always when I was within the camp, with the chatter and noise of people and life around me, muffling its sound and making it nothing more than a distant thunderous rumble, which could be safely ignored. Sitting high on this wall the sound comes straight to me, strikes against me over and over again. The men begin to move, but no gaps appear between them. They are moving as one beast, forward, sideways, backwards. I know because I have heard that in battle they will not retreat, only advance, step after step, as slowly as is needed. In training, though, they must learn their part in this whole and to do so they must move in any direction without losing their connection, without allowing any gaps between them that could be exploited by the enemy.

In the sun's light their weapons shine and the drums add to the heat. The sound continues to beat within me. I feel myself growing dizzy and sick with it. I want to climb down from the wall but I am transfixed by the sight and though I feel ill I cannot look away, cannot raise my voice and call to the foreman who would be more than glad to see me return to the safety of my tent.

Then I see Yusuf. I had already spotted Abu Bakr

earlier and smiled to myself to see him, sweating and grim faced, dealing strong blows to his sparring partner's sword. Persistent, serious, doggedly carrying out the moves needed to keep his arm strong and his lungs powerful. I saw him step back to watch the men as they made their formations, eyes squinting in the harsh light, seeking to spot any weaknesses, calling out to his lieutenants when he spotted mistakes or changes to be made.

Yusuf sits within the cavalry, close to the ramparts where I sit. His horse is huge and black, a fine animal that snorts and paws the ground. It would kick those surrounding it and gallop away were it not held tightly back by strong hands that know how to manage such a beast.

I have never seen him like this. His eyes are filled with a strange light. He is like a man seeing a vision before him, looking neither to left nor right but only ahead, no matter where the mass of men shifts to. Once I spot him I cannot look elsewhere, for the other men's faces are tired, or stern, or bloodthirsty, but Yusuf's is none of these. Now I know what Aisha meant when she said I should watch Yusuf, that he goes to war as though he can see Allah's hand urging him on.

Suddenly the drums stop. The formation shifts, then dissolves into its component parts. I blink and look about me in a daze. The foreman comes hurrying over. I allow him to help me down and return to the camp where I wave aside all food or drink and stumble onto my bed to sleep. My head pounds with the rhythm of the drums and only sleep can quiet it.

I cannot help myself. Every day, now, I go to the wall and call for the foreman to lift me up. Every day I watch while the men fight and train their horses. I wait for the moment when the beat of the drums begins, when I feel sick and dizzy yet cannot tear my eyes away. It is like a drug to me. I look always to Yusuf's face, for that light in his eyes which draws me. In council, later, I stare at him, searching for that light, wanting to see it close to, but it is not there as he talks, listens, agrees, disagrees. He catches me staring and as ever, glowers back at me.

The council is in an uproar. There are tribes to the South who have dared to raise their voices against us, who challenge our rule. We had thought the South well in hand, a safe place for us. But this new challenge threatens our hold on the trade routes and this spells danger. An army of this size must have access to the trade routes – to the taxes on merchants and traders, to the gold and slaves from the Dark Kingdom. These are what sustains us, what pays for weapons and food. There can be no rebellion. It must be crushed. Abu Bakr has decided he will take men and deal with this himself. No-one understands this. There are many who could be trusted to lead such a contingent. Yusuf, for one. Or the third-in command, also a fine warrior and a man of honour. But Abu Bakr will not listen. He has decided he will go himself and as Commander his word is law.

He holds up his hand and everyone falls silent. "I may be gone for much time," he says.

The men shift and look uncomfortable. This means he is about to appoint a leader in his absence. They are afraid he will pick a man who will make them build Murakush rather than go out and conquer new lands. These men are warriors, they lead warriors. They are tired of a peaceful life, it is dull to them. They are longing for action, for battles.

"Yusuf bin Tashfin will lead the army in my absence."

Uproar. There is much back-slapping and hugging. Yusuf is buffeted about by his men's proud congratulations. He finds time to bow his head to Abu Bakr. The council session finishes and the men whoop as they leave. They are pleased. Abu Bakr will flatten the rebellion and meantime they are left with Yusuf to lead them. He is a warrior, so there will be battles again. They all but run to the training grounds. Yusuf, Abu Bakr and I are left alone.

I turn to Abu Bakr. "What about me?" I ask, laughing. "Am I to be left with no husband?" I mean it as a joke – I will wait here just like any other wife for him to return, naturally – although I do not imagine Yusuf will want me in council. My life may change a little but I have enough to do with the camp and Abu Bakr will be back soon enough. A few rebel tribes are no match for his men. Meanwhile I have Aisha for a friend. I like her bright eyes and her matter-of-fact acceptance of the strange twists and turns of fate. I will try to learn from her.

Abu Bakr though, is not laughing. "I have thought about what is best for you, Zaynab," he says kindly.

I do not like his tone of voice. He sounds as though he has made a decision without my knowledge, a decision that will not be reversed. I fix my eyes on him and wait to hear what he has planned for me, which way my life is turning.

"The rebellion in the South is no minor matter," he begins. "I may be away for a very long time. This is why it was necessary to formally appoint Yusuf as the army's leader."

I nod. I know this. We have discussed every part of this rebellion. I might as well saddle up a horse and go there myself to quash it, for I know all that has been planned.

"I have decided that Aisha will accompany me."

I frown and open my mouth to object but he goes on before I can speak.

"We do not wish to be apart again for so long. She is used to a rough life, living in tents, as am I and all my men."

My mouth moves again to say that I, too, have learnt to live in tents of late – has he not noticed this? Once again I do not speak quickly enough.

"I believe that with your understanding of the strategies we are preparing for our future conquests you should remain here. You will be of great help to Yusuf in his new position – "

I cannot help it, I laugh out loud. I see Yusuf frown at me but really, does Abu Bakr think for one moment that Yusuf will accept my thoughts? He has made it very clear what he thinks of me. The light I search for in his eyes is reserved for the battleground alone: certainly it is not for me. He will do nothing but scowl until Abu Bakr returns.

Abu Bakr smiles ruefully but he is set in his decision now and no one can turn him. May Allah give me strength, I am surrounded by stubborn men.

"Neither of you know the worth of the other," he says. "But you will learn."

He stands up with a grunt and leaves the tent. Yusuf and I sit opposite one another for a few more moments. I wait for him to declare himself – to either concede that we will have to make the best of this unwished-for situation or to make a stand and tell me he will turn his back on me as soon as Abu Bakr leaves and that I will have no other reason to exist than to wait for my absent husband to return. He says nothing. I sigh and move onto my knees, so I may rise and leave the tent, when Abu Bakr reappears. Half-crouched in the doorway of the tent he addresses us both.

"I have been thinking. My absence may be long – perhaps more than a year. Zaynab should not be left here without the protection of a husband and therefore – "

I grin triumphantly at Yusuf. I will not be left here for him to crow over after all. I will go with Abu Bakr and Yusuf can think up his own strategies without me. If he can.

"– therefore I have decided that I will set Zaynab aside. After three months she may remarry and it is my wish, Yusuf, that you take her as your wife. In this way she will be protected and you will have a capable woman at your side. I will arrange for the divorce to take place as soon as possible."

He ducks out of the tent and leaves us again.

My grin freezes on my face. Yusuf's face is still, entirely without emotion. Slowly we each rise and leave the tent, one in one direction, one in another, in silence.

I try to object but Abu Bakr will have none of it. He is kind but he does not listen. No, I cannot go with him. No, I cannot wait for him for who knows how long. No, I cannot remain here unmarried. No, there is no-one more suitable for me to marry than Yusuf. The divorce takes only moments. I stand in my tent afterwards, speechless.

Hela is sitting by my bed, sewing. "He's younger, at least."

I turn to her, still agape from what has happened. "I don't want him! I don't care if he is younger than Abu Bakr!"

"You might have a real marriage," she offers matter-of-factly.

"Allah save me! You mean not only will he glower at me all day but he has to come to my bed as well?"

"You might have a child. Would you like one?"

"I am too old for that."

Hela sniffs. "Never too old," she says.

"Enough of your potions!" I lie on my bed and kick my heels in frustration. "Abu Bakr might not have lain with me but he was kind! He cared for me! He respected me! I sat in the council, I was honoured."

"You can still do that."

"With a man who hates me?'

Hela does not answer, only goes about her business leaving me to punch my cushions in a fury.

I sit on the wall and watch this man. In only a few months he will be my husband. If I thought that same light might shine in his eyes when he looked at me I might look forward to that event with more enthusiasm. As it is I shake my head and climb back down, return to my tent and bid a mournful farewell to Abu Bakr and Aisha as they leave.

Aisha is all smiles. "Be of good cheer, Zaynab," she

whispers to me. "My husband has left you in his most trusted pair of hands. He would not see you unhappy."

"I am unhappy," I retort. "And I will miss you. So I am doubly unhappy."

We embrace.

Abu Bakr comes to me. "I know you think I have wronged you, Zaynab," he says. "But you must trust my judgement."

I accept his embrace and do not argue. It is too late to argue now.

The camp feels strange, with tents missing here and there and a new leader in place. There is an unsettled feeling and I am more unsettled than anyone.

I cannot sleep tonight. I lie miserably awake, reliving every word or look Yusuf and I have exchanged. None have been kind or even courteous. He will be my fourth husband. I choke back a sobbing laugh. What is this torment of my life? How many more husbands am I to have? How many more marriages that are not true marriages? At least with Abu Bakr I felt safe and respected. The image of Luqut rises before me. What will it be like to have a cruel husband again when I had thought myself protected?

I rise. Outside all is dark and peaceful. From the tents come soft sounds of snoring, of lovemaking, of babies whimpering for milk.

I walk. Through the maze of tents, to the parts of the walls as yet unfinished, where there is still no need for gates. To one side of me, a high wall, to the other, nothing. By my feet remnants of clay, buckets of water, tools. I step past them all, walking until I am outside the camp, out on the plain where the animals graze. I can see them, those that cluster nearby, some eating, some lying peacefully chewing the cud. Those closest scatter as I walk by, those further away take no notice.

"Where do you think you are going?"

I almost scream as a man's rough hand grabs my arm. In the darkness I cannot see who it is but when he speaks again I know his voice.

"What are you doing out here?'

"Yusuf!"

"Well?" He has let go of my arm now and we stand facing one another, though neither of us can make out much more than a shape in the darkness.

"I needed to walk," I say. It sounds foolish.

"It is not safe," he says instantly.

I bristle. "Who are you to tell me what to do?"

I can hear the frown without even seeing it. "I am soon to be your husband."

"Perhaps. But you are not my husband now."

"No 'perhaps'. I might as well be your husband now."

Everything he says makes me want to challenge him. I draw myself up to my full height. When I do this we are the same height, for I am a tall woman.

"You will not be my husband until you lie with me," I say sharply, and turn to walk away.

He moves faster than I would have thought possible. He takes my arm and pulls me round to face him. He is stronger than I thought and I am a little scared at how easily he moves me with only one hand. With his other hand he pulls at the wrap around his face and then his lips are pressed to mine.

I struggle in terror, for this treatment reminds me of Luqut but then I feel his arms about me and although he is strong he is also gentle. He is not hurting me and his mouth is soft on mine. I have not been kissed upon the mouth for many years now. I stand still for a moment and then I tentatively place one hand on his arm before slowly returning his embrace. I am not as passionate as he at first, but I feel desire growing in me and I grow more bold. My embrace tightens.

He pulls away. We stand in the darkness, our breathing a little fast in the silence and then he walks away from me, back inside the camp. I cannot think quickly enough to follow, so I stand motionless in the cold air and breathe until my heart slows. Then I make my way back to my tent. I see his tent close by but I dare not even think of entering. My mind is confused with all that has happened tonight and sleep is long in coming.

In the bright daylight the darkness inside the council tent makes me blink. I pause, for on stooping to enter I find that Yusuf is seated in Abu Bakr's place. My eyes flicker. Where should I sit? Abu Bakr welcomed me always to sit by his side, a place of honour and privilege. Side by side we could see the same things, confirm our thoughts with a quick glance to one another.

Now I am facing Yusuf and I do not know where he will want me to sit. Does he regret what passed between us last night? Will he ignore me? Will he refuse to let me sit in council, even? He had not wanted me to join the council in those early days and now that he leads this army it is his command that must be obeyed.

I brace myself, meet his gaze as steadily as I can.

He meets my eyes and then flickers them to one side. He gestures minutely with one hand to the empty place by his side. I am to sit in my usual place.

Carefully I lower myself to sit beside him. When I sat by Abu Bakr's side I never thought about how my body might touch his. I would lean across him or against him, the better to indicate maps. When I spoke my hands flew in quick gestures and if they brushed against him I did not draw back.

Now I sit very still. No part of my robes or body touches any part of Yusuf's. We both sit upright, our backs straight. We do not look to one another as Abu Bakr and I might do, laughing or challenging one another. We look to others in this confined space, we debate without turning our heads to see one another's eyes. Once we both look to the right, where one of the men is speaking, and I feel Yusuf's breath against my neck when, irritated with the point being made, he breathes out heavily. I feel the quick heat on my skin followed by the slow heat of my desire rising as my cheeks grow flushed. I shift my position, say loudly that this tent is stifling. I call for water, fresh air. The servants hurry to bring cups and to tie back larger parts of the tent's fabric that a breeze might be let in.

When the never-ending council session ends I am first on my feet, leaving the confined space before any of the men have slowly stretched to their full height. I go back to my own tent where the servants scatter before my snappish demands and finally leave me alone with the tent fully closed, cold water and cloths by my side, my body naked beneath a thin linen sheet.

I cannot sleep. I toss and turn, my body too hot as the sun rises above. Even as the evening cool descends I am too hot.

I have been a wife three times and three times I have been no wife at all. I am thirty-one years of age and I have been alone too long. I had resigned myself to a celibate life as wife to Abu Bakr, had been grateful for kindness since nothing else was offered to me. Now my fate has changed again and I have been given one more chance to feel love and desire for a man and to be loved and desired in turn. It has been a long time since I have wanted a man so badly. This time I will take him for my own and I will not share him.

Yusuf must be mine and mine alone.

Seductress

It is still dark when I awake. The call to prayer will come soon but for now all is silent. I sit for a few moments, drinking water that has been chilled by the night. Then I begin.

It is not long before Hela enters my tent. Her ears have always been sharp, you cannot stir, even in a tent ten paces from hers, without she will hear you. She stands just inside the doorway and observes me without speaking.

I ignore her. I am rifling through my great carved chests, throwing clothes and bed linen onto the floor. Down go my colourful silk robes, my intricately embroidered slippers, my shining veils, which are used to tie up my hair. I take whole chests; those studded with bright gems, and set them to one side, decanting their contents into plainer copies. I talk over my shoulder to Hela.

"After prayers you will find me the best carpenter and the best woodcarver in the camp. I want the best tailor of robes. I want the finest leatherworker. If the best are still tarrying in Aghmat you will send for them. Tell the traders when they come that I want fabrics, leathers and woods in black. It must be the finest, mind, none of their cheap stuff that washes to grey in three dips of water. Pure black. The traders of jewels you may turn away, for I want none of their merchandise. You are to take all of this – " I gesture at the piles of goods on the floor " – and give it to whomever has need of it."

I turn. Hela is standing over me in silence.

"Well?"

She speaks slowly, as though to an idiot. "He has to marry you whatever you are like. There is no need to change."

I come close to her so that she can see how my eyes shine in the thin light and feel my fevered breath on her cheek. "He is obliged to marry me. He is not obliged to desire me. Look at what happened with Abu Bakr."

She does not blink. Nothing intimidates her. "You think by moulding yourself to his image he will desire you?"

"He kissed me last night."

Hela nods as though this is not a surprise. "Exactly. So he desires you as you are now."

I shake my head. "I provoked him by speaking of lying together. He is a man. He is lonely here without a wife, without a woman. He is as good as my husband already, it might have been lust for any woman, not for me."

Hela's eyes roll. "And what are you moulding yourself into? What shape are you taking on now?"

I have lain awake for hours and even in my dreams I have fashioned this image. I pace back and forth within the tent as I speak – so great is my desire to make this a reality I cannot even keep still. "I will be everything he can desire. In council I will be his strategist. In the camp I will rule as his queen. Before his holy men I will be the most pious woman in the Maghreb. In our tent I will be the most desirable woman he has ever held."

"And what of his first wife?"

I shrug. "What is she to me? Or to him? If she was so precious to him he should have sent for her as quickly as Abu Bakr sent for Aisha."

Hela is picking up silks off the floor. "Why are you throwing these away?"

I kneel beside her to make the work faster, grabbing at items and stuffing them into one of the cast-off chests closest to the door of the tent.

"He wears plain dark robes and despises the riches of this world? So will I. Everything I wear will be black. I will have no embroidery, no bright gems."

Hela keeps packing in the silks. She pauses over a slipper, turning it this way and that. "Does he know that black silk is more costly than pink silk? Does he know that for leather slippers to be truly black they will have to come from a master leatherworker? You may dress all in black but your clothes will cost four-fold what they cost now."

I laugh and rest my head against her shoulder. "He is a man, Hela. What does he know of such things? If he wishes to see a pious woman who disdains finery then that is what he will see. And besides," I lower my voice, "when he holds me he must touch silk, not rough wool. He is still a man, for all his pious fervour."

She shakes her head and gathers up armfuls of my cast-off clothes. I see them later around the camp, worn by those women who can pay for such rich garments, worn by a queen.

"You are trying too hard to be loved," she says with sorrow.

"I have no choice," I retort. "He has sent for his first

wife now, even if he left it late. I saw the escort leave the other day."

Hela turns back in the doorway. "The one who lost a baby to a camel kick?"

"Why, how many other wives does he have?"

She sighs at my bad temper. "Only one. She is probably old and barren, Zaynab," she says gently. "You will shine beside her."

"Like I did beside Aisha?"

She shrugs. "That was bad luck. A rare love."

I concentrate on what I am doing, taking out all my jewellery and piling it in a heap. I hold back nothing. "She will not arrive for many months. It is unlikely she will arrive before the wedding."

Hela smiles as she leaves me. "Then if you can draw him to you, your wedding night will be as you wish it to be, Zaynab," she says and ducks out of the tent.

I sit back on my heels and survey my changing tent. It is growing more sombre by the hour.

"If I can draw him to me," I murmur. "If."

Three months are long when you are burning up for a man's embrace but they are short when you must stoke a tiny spark within him until it is a raging fire. There is much I must do.

By now the camp is entirely mine to rule as I see fit. Now I order those things that will begin to make a city of it in due course. The walls move on apace, outside them I ensure that the first shoots of palm trees are nourished and kept safe from hungry animals. One day they will grow above our heads, providing shade and sweet fruits, for now, they must be protected. I designate an area to be set aside for a souk, for by now the traders would far rather come to us than to dwindling Aghmat. As the souk grows so grows our access to what we will need in the future – spices for better foods, incense for sweeter smells about us. I order fresh herbs to be grown and a slave woman takes on that job. I see her sometimes, a twisted figure of a woman limping back and forth watering her small green charges. As they grow she begins to sell them and soon trade at her stall is brisk. I am glad of it, for fresh foods have been lacking and dried dates with coarse grains and camel's milk are a poor diet. It is only now that we begin to eat more fresh meat as the flocks grow in the fertile plains, that we can use fresh herbs and taste the cleansing bitterness of green leaves rather than endless stored grains.

The people of the camp are grateful. They know they owe this change to me and I gain greater respect for it. They stop grumbling about this new life as they can see a new city beginning to take shape. It may still take many years but people will do much with a vision in their minds. A few still grumble that I have too much power but they are mostly men and their wives will hear none of it. They fear me a little, as all servants fear their masters, but they can see that I am right in my commands and so they are carried out to the letter.

There are strange looks at first for my new robes, but those who are ignorant think I am thus unadorned because to keep rich bright silks clean in this place is almost impossible, no matter how many servants and slaves you have at your disposal. Those who are pious see in me a new piety, a bending of my will to my husband-to-be's choice of garments and they nod approvingly. Only those who know fabrics and leathers smile when they see what I am wearing, for they know that no matter how unadorned I might be the clothes and slippers I wear now are those of a queen, as they have always been. Any fool with a few coins can buy cheap shining silks in a myriad of colours. Only a queen knows the value of quality and has the heavy gold coins to pay for it. In the council I see Yusuf's quick glance when I enter council in my new garb and his softened gaze. I know he never liked my opulent attire and when I continue to wear the same simple style day after day I see him look upon me with more favour. Gone are the disdainful stares when I would arrive with some fresh outrage of vivid silk held tight to my body with entwined belts of silver and gold. Now I am hidden under soft folds of black silk, which promises but does not deliver my true from. My hair falls loose and straight without shining silver veils or clasps to tame it, mostly it is only lightly covered with a black veil. Its softness brushes more than once against Yusuf's hand or arm in council and he does not draw back.

The robes have the added benefit that they accentuate my new-found public piety. Where once I prayed in my own tent now I pray ostentatiously in public. I pray when many are gathered, where the greatest gossips and the most pious pray. The gossips spread the word and the pious are pleased. I have no private moments of prayer now, all is done for show. My face is suffused with a holy fervour, my bows are so deep that were it not for Hela's precious unguents the skin of my forehead would grow calloused as it touches the rough ground over and over again. The holy men, who used to mutter in corners against me, finding it unwomanly for me to sit in council, are appeased. They talk of Yusuf's influence on me, of how their teachings are converting even those, who like me, enjoyed the riches of Aghmat in all their glory, showing little true belief. They believe that I have seen the error of my ways, that their pure interpretations of the faith have been heard. They tell Yusuf about these new changes and I see him glance at me when I arrive for prayers, a careful, considering glance. I do not return his gaze. I prostate myself and after a moment he does the same. Only once in these three months do the holy men falter in their new praise of me.

The man sits where he has been told to sit, despite his mortified protests. Slowly word carries through the camp. All make their way past my tent on one pretext or another. Even shepherds, who have no business being in camp at all, come from the fields and hills. No-one can resist the sight of which everyone is speaking. They stand a little way off, watching as day after day as the curls of dense black wood fall to the ground. It is slow work, for the wood is harder than most.

Mostly our beds lie upon the ground and they are made of soft weavings with stuffing of one sort and another. The poorest sleep upon the earth with only a rug to keep the chill from entering their bones. The rich, of course, have grander beds, but even so they are made mostly of soft things – thick woollen blankets, fine silk cushions. The wood or metal that holds all of this softness is rarely of much interest. It may have a few carvings or be bent to better please the eye, but no-one has ever seen a bed like this one.

From the hard black wood begin to emerge flowers, and fruits. The children squat close to the wood and reach out a finger to touch them. Life-size and perfectly formed, were they not black and hard their little mouths might try to bite the perfect pomegranates and figs, their small noses sniff out the perfume of the roses and jasmine which twine about the legs of my bed, growing more beautiful by the day. When the carver begins his next stage of carving, however, these children are shooed away by their parents, and virtuous women blush as they walk by, their husbands glowering but then casting one quick backward glance as they walk on, unable to resist.

In the dark wood there are figures entwined and as the carving goes on, so their lusts grow stronger. There in the darkness are men and women whose bodies merge with one another in ecstasy. In the last days of its preparation the carver puts aside his sharp tools, takes up soft leathers and fats and begins to rub at his creations, bringing lustre to the writhing skin of the lovers. The women of the camp who have no children, whose business here is the pleasure of many soldiers are the only ones who dare comment now. They walk past with swaying hips and jangling jewellery, each claiming to have been the inspiration for the carver's work. They giggle amongst themselves and when a man walks by who looks more than once they call out and suggest he might like to taste such delights in soft flesh rather than in hard wood.

Hela watches me as I mix ingredients with pestle and mortar, a servant hovering by with hot water.

"What is that?"

"Nothing," I mutter, head down, arms aching with the grinding motion. The hot water is poured into the mortar and a deep intoxicating smell emerges.

"It is an aphrodisiac," says Hela without even inspecting the contents.

I do not reply.

"Who is it for?"

I continue grinding.

She sighs and gets up to leave. She pauses in the doorway. "You are not skilled with herbs, Zaynab. These drinks are for enhancing what is already there, not for forcing what is not."

I shake my head and keep grinding. "It is already there," I mutter to myself. "It *is*."

It is the heat I feel first, throwing off one cover after another until I lie naked on the bed. In the darkness with only the dying fire outside the bodies carved into the bed flicker and move, their movements lewd. I reach out to try to still them but find myself caressing them as though they might include me in their embrace. The silks of my bedcovers brush my feet where I kicked them away and I drag them back onto me, slipping them over my too hot and tender skin.

It is Hela who hears me moaning in the darkness and comes to me quickly, silently, muffling my mouth with a silk sheet while she searches around her for substances that will bring me back to myself. She pours cool water down my throat and dampens a cloth to pat me with but I turn towards her touch as to a lover, taking her hand and pressing it to my most intimate parts. She waits until I loosen her and then returns to her task, seeking to cool my fevered body and mind.

By morning I lie still and quiet. Only faint images of the night come to me. "What did I do? What did I say?"

Hela is mixing a new version of what I made. "You are not competent to mix such a drink. I should not have let you. I will do it myself now even though I think it should not be mixed at all."

"I wanted it for him. But I thought I should try it myself first."

"It was too strong. You were wild with passion."

I sit up eagerly. "I *want* him to be wild with passion."

Hela shakes her head. "If he had drunk this and been with a woman he would have hurt her. His passion would not have been contained. You can be passionate without being driven mad with lust."

I lean forward watching her closely. "But you will make it strong enough?"

She sighs. "I will increase it over time. Otherwise he will become desperate for a woman. He'll find a whore before your wedding if it is too strong."

I laugh."He is too pious to use a whore."

"He has slaves."

"A good Muslim should not wed his slave," I recite piously.

"Who said he had to wed a slave to bed her?"

Well before the bed is entirely finished I am visited by one of Yusuf's religious advisors, who is appalled by the forms taking shape under the carver's hands.

"It is said," he begins with great firmness and keeping his eyes on me rather than the object in question, "that the angels will not enter the home of one who displays pictures or images such as…" he gestures rather weakly towards the offending carving, visible outside my tent.

I shake my head. I have been expecting this moment, I am ready. "It is *said* that when all souls are brought back to life those who have made images will be asked to breath life into them and if they cannot they will be cast aside for their presumption in taking the place of He who is greater than us all. That one should not make images of living beings for no mere mortal has the power to give them true life."

He nods, agreeing with what I am saying, but he looks doubtful. If I know all this, why am I proceeding with such shamelessness?

I stretch out my hand towards one of the finished parts of the bed. "They are not living beings," I say.

He frowns at me. I gesture back towards the carving and he reluctantly follows my hand's path to gaze at the blasphemous images. When he looks more closely a blush appears on his face but a frown begins to steal over his brow as well, for he can see that I have outwitted him. None of the men and women depicted have heads. There are no faces. Their heads are thrown back in ecstasy such that they cannot be seen or the carving, so detailed and accurate in every other way, so well planned, seems to be so large that where a head should come there the wood ends and when another figure begins the head must be imagined for it seems that the diligent carver has quite forgotten to place it there.

"But, but – " he splutters.

I smile meekly at him, my face the very image of a good and pious woman. "I would not dream of showing a living being in sculpture such as this. None of my figures may live, for where would their breath be since they have no mouths?"

He stares at me incredulously.

"Blessed is Allah and the teachings of His Prophet Mohammed," I say and he can only mumble a reply and retreat, confused.

I know the holy men argue amongst one another for days. By the time they have decided that the carvings are anyway a disgrace and should not be on public view it is too late. The bed is ready and has been taken into the privacy of my tent where it is assembled. But by now all of the camp knows that in my tent I now have a bed that is obscene, lustful, shameless. There is not a man in the camp who would not wish to lie in it with me, nor a woman who does not think of it and blush at the thought of Yusuf's power, his hard arms and dark eyes.

I make sure Yusuf drinks the potion Hela grudgingly prepares. I slip a little into his drink during council and see him grow flushed with anger over a disagreement, he who is always so calm. I mix it in his food and see him slip away in the early evening to his tent, where he lies restless. I hear him toss and turn late at night, standing quiet by his tent in the darkness. I hear him call out and moan in his sleep.

Traders from around the world provide bedding that shines like jewels within the darkness of the bed's embrace. There are blankets in wool so fine it is almost transparent.

Sheets of delicate silk that slip over the skin like a lover's caress. Cushions of thickly woven silk embroidered with thread beaten from gold coins. In my tent now there is nothing of ostentation save this bed. There are large chests of perfumed black wood carved with only the most simple of designs. There are prayer mats displayed as though holy in their own right. All is black or the colour of sand. Only the reds, yellows and oranges of the bed burn like hot coals. The last of these covers arrives one day. It is a fine wool in a vivid orange with tiny discs of silver. I stand outside my tent and shake it out, turning the midday sky to a searing sunset. Through the colour I see a dark figure and when the cloth falls I see Yusuf before me.

"Yusuf," I say, bowing my head.

"Zaynab," he replies. He has little to say to me when we are outside of council. He bows his head to me and walks on but as he does so I see he glances slightly to one side, the better to glimpse the glowing bed through the open folds of my tent.

His long stride falters and I smile as I watch him go.

That night after mixing the potion, now stronger despite Hela's reluctance, into his food, I go back to the field outside the camp where I saw him that night and he is there again. I stand and watch him and he does not speak nor turn his head but when I turn to go he speaks. His voice is husky, I have not heard him speak like this before.

"That bed..."

I laugh softly. "There is nothing carved into it that

I would not do when you are in my arms," I whisper. "Nothing."

He takes a deep breath and as he turns towards me I slip back behind the camp's wall and leave him alone.

The next morning a servant stands outside my tent, holding out a small pouch. Inside is a simple string of black beads and silver discs, the engagement necklace of his people. I wear it under my robes where it cannot be seen, the cold silver warming my skin.

There are small battles from time to time. Soon there will be greater ones but for now it is a matter of crushing small rebellions, challenging those tribal lands closest to Murakush, that its borders may grow piece by piece. When men return to us wounded it is Hela who provides their care. She walks from tent to tent, her healing salves and knowledgeable hands changing destinies. There are men who do not lose their limbs because of her care and men who lose limbs rather than lives. She is feared, for she has no gentleness in her manner or speech, but she is also revered. There is no wounded man who would refuse her ministrations. Meanwhile the stores in her tent grow every greater, with chests filled to brimming with bottles and measuring spoon, strange pouches and more mortars and pestles than any woman could use in a lifetime. The council can re-calculate their possible losses because of the knowledge that she is waiting in the camp.

"Perhaps Abu Bakr was right," Yusuf says as we leave the council tent.

"In what way?"

He looks across the camp, still growing larger but becoming more ordered under my guiding hand. It is no longer a random maze of tents, there are pathways which have been created, making it easier to move about. There are boundaries between what one day will be quarters.

"He said that if you were to read the maps and I was to lead the battles there was nothing that could not be done," he says.

I lift one hand to my neck, touch the tiny necklace given for our engagement and through that quick glimpse between the folds of my robes he can see that I have spared this one jewel from my purge of sober dressing. I do not reply and he does not speak again. We gaze, side by side, at the camp bustling around us and then we walk away from one another.

I have done everything I can to bring Yusuf to me with desire in his heart. I have thought of every thing that may make the warmth in him grow to a burning fire. When he turns his head in council he knows that by his side he has a woman who is shaped to his every desire. I am robed all in black, less adorned than a slave. I am pious in my speech and ruthless in my strategies. I rule the camp better than any man. He knows that in but a few days he will be my husband. When the words are spoken he knows he will come to me in the magnificent black tent which stands at the centre of this camp and lie with me in a bed of shameless desire. No man could hold the cool night air within him who has felt the flames of my desire lick at his skin for the past three months, growing hotter as our marriage day approaches. His blood has been heated with Hela's drink, day by day, drop by drop, growing stronger in its intensity as the marriage draws closer.

The words of the Holy Book are read out, the crowd murmurs and sacrifices are made. I stand in my black clothes, unadorned. One would think me a slave rather than a queen coming to be wed, were it not for the fineness of my delicate leather slippers, my rich silk robes. No jewels dress my hair or neck, nor jangle on my arms. I am still, and quiet. I stand as tall as Yusuf and looking at us the crowd murmurs again. They think we are alike, the two of us so still and dark, so sure of our rule. They see in us the truth of my false vision and they are content.

I am in ecstasy, for by my side is the man I desire and within a few words he will be my husband. His first wife has not yet arrived, her voice will not speak out against this union – or if it does, it will be too late. This all makes me happy but what brings me the greatest joy is Yusuf's hand on mine. His skin is burning up, his grip on me is tight. I slide my eyes to one side without moving my head and I see his gaze is fixed, not on the speaker of holy words, but on my lips. *I am desired,* I think, and a wave of happiness rushes through me. I have achieved what I had set out to do and only a few short hours hold me back from my reward.

I want to turn from that place as soon as the words are complete and run to my tent with Yusuf by my side. I want to feel his body on mine but it has been otherwise decided. It is still morning and there is a council to be held. After that, as dusk falls, there will be a great feast and then, only then, will I be satisfied at last. I watch him bow to me and turn to leave. I will not attend council today, for there is too much to do. I stand to watch him walk away and when he reaches the council tent I see a hesitation. He turns his head and looks to me, one glance, one quick look before he is gone. I let out my breath and turn to prepare for the feast.

There is food everywhere. Every slave has toiled for this day, every woman has brought her finest food to celebrate my wedding day. The ovens have been hot for many days and nights, blood has run freely as one animal after another has given up its life to feed this multitude. Now rich smells waft through the air and children cannot listen to the storytellers who are gathering, for their noses are filled with food and their mouths drip with hunger for all those good things now prepared with such abundance.

There is hot bread in great baskets and sweet cakes that drip with rosewater and honey. Cooking pots are filled to their brims with stews laden with every kind of spice. Pale golden with saffron, thick red with heat, the sumptuous brown of meat juices, carried with care to the central space where the feast will be held. The tents were moved back today, for fires the height of a man burned since dawn. Now their molten coals are ready to receive the whole bodies of camels, goats, sheep, cattle. The fat and herbs hiss and spit together to create a haze of taste in the air.

Rough rugs were laid out though those sitting are only the elderly and infirm for now, along with the children and the storytellers who are embroidering on my legend yet again. Those strong enough to be pressed into service have too much to do yet to sit and listen, but they joke and laugh as they go about their work. The women of pleasure are slowly emerging from their tents, hair oiled and curled, jewels tinkling, hips making a short journey a far more interesting one for those men who care to watch them pass. I watch and smile. Many men will lie with a woman tonight, and one of them will be Yusuf.

A little boy comes running towards me through the crowd. I stand still, heart beating, when I see his speed, how he darts like a fish round the many people, rushing to my side. It cannot be. It *cannot* be.

"Lady Zaynab!" He is panting with excitement as much as with the speed of his feet.

I grab at his hand and pull him into my tent where he gazes in awe at the surroundings, so different from his own family's humble tent, a ragged affair of worn colours and many mouths to feed.

"Speak quietly," I hiss at him. "What do you have to tell me?"

"She is here."

"*Now*?" No, not today, please not today. Let me have one night, one night where I am Yusuf's only wife, his only love.

He nods, eyes bright. He knows that this information is what I had asked him for, that coins will slip now from my hand to his and that his family's fortunes will change because of his quick feet and sharp eyes.

I struggle to smile, for no-one must gossip of how I looked when this woman arrived.

"She is my sister," I say, forcing a kindly tone. "And I have longed for her embrace."

"Allah be praised!" says the boy, aiming to please. "She is here for your wedding feast!"

My teeth clench so tightly together I think he will hear them grinding. I feel for coins and press them into his hand. He gapes at them, he will never even have seen some of these coins.

"How long?" I ask as he bows to me and makes for the door.

"An hour, no more, lady!" he assures me with a smile.

Hela shakes her head.

"You knew this moment would come," she says stubbornly.

"Yes," I hiss at her "But I did not know it would come on my wedding night."

She shrugs.

"You have been working on him for three months now," she says. "If he is not yours now, he never will be."

"His first wife is about to arrive," I say. "And if he goes to her tonight, my wedding night, I will die."

Hela is not impressed with my dramatic words. "You will not die," she says. "Besides, what kind of a man goes to his first wife on the wedding night of the second?"

"A man who has not seen his first wife for more than two years!"

"You will have to share him, Zaynab."

"Perhaps," I say. "But not tonight, Hela."

She sighs and gets out her mortar and pestle.

"Make it strong," I say.

She looks up, challenging me. "How strong?"

I look into her dark steady eyes. "Strong," I say. "Strong."

She hesitates, then opens a chest and pulls out the red cup.

I am shaking. My tent is too large. I long for a small place that will hold me in its warm embrace, not this mighty structure, which commands me to stand tall when all I want is to crouch, to curl up and brace myself for the unknown threat to come. I know that even now she is walking towards my tent. I sent Yusuf to prayers before our wedding feast knowing that while he prayed she would come to me.

I pray harder than any man or woman as the call to prayer echoes through the camp. My piety, though, is all for me. Let her be ugly, I pray. Let her be old. Let her be barren forever. Let her be stooped, stupid and too stunned by her new surroundings to take her rightful place in my world. Let me take Yusuf for myself over her reaching hands.

In the midst of my prayers a man's voice calls my name and I know that she has arrived. I think of the light in Yusuf's eyes, how it shines now when he looks at me, how his hand was hot on mine when we stood together to be married. I think of his growing desire and how tonight at last he will be mine. I stand tall and I walk to the door of my tent. Unseen to those outside Hela holds back the folds and I emerge.

In front of me is one of the guards sent to escort her here. He is following orders as he should, he has brought her here quickly and without taking her to Yusuf first as she no doubt will have begged him to do. She has already been betrayed. My eyes slide past his anxious face and at last I see Yusuf's first wife. Kella.

I keep my face still although I want to grimace. She is not old, as I had hoped. She is nowhere near Yusuf's age, indeed I would say she is younger than I, although she is weary with fear and travelling. She must have been almost a child when he married her, no older than when I married my first husband. Is this what Yusuf wants from a bride? A child-girl, barely rising past my shoulder? She should be rounded and pleasing to the eye but she is haggard with lack of food and water. She must have ridden day and night to come here so quickly and it has taken its toll on her. But underneath the worry and the exhaustion, the weight dropped too quickly from her breasts and face, she is pretty. A sweet face, a slender body but well formed. Bright robes, though dust-covered, wrap round her body. A young, pretty wife, heartbroken at the sight of me.

I have waited a heartbeat too long in silence. I know without looking that the escort is worried. I should have spoken by now. There is only one thing I can say in front of this man. I hold out my hands and smile at the child-wife.

"Sister," I say, and my heart shudders for the times I have spoken this word, the times it has brought me nothing but sorrow and another failed marriage.

She holds out her small travel-dirtied hands to me and dutifully repeats that untruthful word back to me. Her voice trembles as though on the brink of tears. I can only pray this means she is weak, that she will be easily swept aside so that nothing can stand between me and my last chance to be loved.

So begins my fourth wedding night.

Rival

THE FIRES BURN BRIGHTLY, PLATE after plate of food is brought out. There are stories, music, much chatter and laughing. I sit in near-silence, so close to Yusuf I have to stop myself from reaching out to embrace him. He will come to me tonight.

He has no choice. The drug Hela mixed was stronger than she has ever made it. As we eat the wedding feast Kella sits in hopeless silence as each mouthful he takes makes his heart beat harder, his face turn ever more my way, his skin aching for my long-promised touch. She must have thought he would be glad to see her, and indeed he is solicitous, but she is a dish he has already tasted. I am new, and have been promised to him for so long that he can think of nothing else.

She sits on his other side, freshly robed. Under the dust that has been washed away her facial tattoos have emerged, claiming love and protection from her far-away people, who cannot see her present humiliation. Her hair is piled up in bright swathes of coloured cloth, her woollen striped reds and yellows are tied to accentuate every part of her slender body. Silver jewellery cascades from her. She should be glorious. Younger than I, bright and shining, while I am a childless woman growing older with every marriage.

But she looks like a colourful wild bird caught in a net, hopelessly seeking a way to escape while I sit freely, robed in my black rippling silks, back erect, surveying my domain, a sharp-eyed, cruel-taloned falcon to Yusuf's right hand. Perhaps before, in her desert tribe, she was ruler of her own domain, knew her own strengths. Here she is out of place, weakened, uncertain. There, Yusuf would have seen her bright spirit, her courage. To a man about to face an uncertain future these qualities may have drawn him. Here, where he feels safe in his conquests and dreams of more to come, he sees my power and it draws him more strongly. What can she offer when I have given him everything he might desire in a woman?

The feast drags on too long for my liking. I grow restless and at last, in a rare moment when Kella is not staring pitifully at him, I allow my hand to brush Yusuf's as I pass a dish. He turns as though burnt, with a quick low intake of breath, and meets my gaze. I lower my eyes but it is all the encouragement he needs. He stands and announces that we are retiring. This, of course, is met with cheers and whoops, with comments relating to my beauty, Yusuf's bravery in battle, the great bed awaiting us and other such ribaldry. Yusuf waves it all away, smiling, but his hand grips mine tightly as he leads me away. I look back for one second as we walk towards my tent and see Kella. Head down, her shoulders are hunched over as she sits in barely contained misery. I should feel sorry for her but I do not. It is the first time that I have been the woman more desired than my co-wife, the first time that I have longed to be in my husband's arms and known that he longs for me also. I cannot feel pity, for I am too happy.

He barely lets the folds of the tent close behind us, my foot is still outside the tent when he grabs me and throws me bodily onto the bed. I had thought to entice him further, to dance for him, to let him touch the figures on my bed, to then turn and touch my own warm body. I had thought I would slowly display my body, then let him discover my skills, taught to me so long ago, for another man in another time.

But he is wild with desire. He cannot pause for even a moment, grasping my silken robes and ripping them from me. I gasp, for I am afraid now. I know Hela made the drink strong tonight at my own request but now I doubt my choice. He is like a madman, tearing away all the fabric, leaving tatters of it on the floor and pulling at his own clothes. I would reach out, would try to stroke him gently to soothe his fire a little, to bring back some control, but I am pinned beneath him and he is moving too fast.

I think of my past husband, lord of Aghmat. I remember with fear his tortures and my body after a night in his rooms or mine. I try to remind myself that Yusuf is not intent on torturing me, indeed he holds me tightly and groans my name as might a gentler lover, but now he spreads my thighs and I brace myself for what is to come. I have not been touched by a man for many years now and I am afraid as though I were a new bride once more and not a woman lying with her fourth husband.

I have no choice but to try and tame him. He enters me too fast. I cry out in pain, but grip my legs around him and try to move in his rhythm. The tighter I hold him the faster he thrusts inside me and I cannot help but cry out with every stroke. But even as I cry out in pain and even as I feel his hands too tight on me, bruising my arms, my waist, my thighs, still as he groans I know I have a triumphant smile on my face although my teeth are clenched. This man would not look upon any other woman in this moment, he wants only me, he needs only my body and as he cries out I hold him tighter to me and feel his release.

He does not stop. He does not pause all night. Every time he is granted a release, a moment of sweetness in my arms so he begins again. He cannot stop, he is driven on and on by the potency of the drink. Sometimes he is gentle with me, whispers to me and kisses me, sometimes he forgets his soft caresses and once again I try to contain my cries. There are moments of sweetness for me too, when he is gentle enough and I can find my own rhythm and revel in his whispers, in his voice grown husky with love for me. But pain grows through the night, as parts of me that were made tender in his first passion are bruised and stretched again and again.

The days pass and despite the pain I cannot help but long for his presence.

"Too much," says Hela, as she smooths my bruises with her ointments. "You are mistaking pain for love. You have been twisted by Luqut and his ways."

"I never mistook what he did for love," I say.

"You think that love must be painful," she repeats. "You have known nothing else."

"My first marriage," I begin, although my voice dies away.

"A different kind of pain," says Hela. "Can you not

trust that he loves you, that he will come to you without being gripped by a false desire?"

"It is not false!" I say too quickly.

She looks at me. "He would come anyway," she says. "I can make the drink lighter. Night by night. Then you will see that he comes out of true desire. And he will be gentler."

For a moment I am tempted. For a moment I contemplate giving her the order, imagine what it would be to have Yusuf come to me in gentleness. But I cannot give up the burning desire I see in him. I cannot give up being so badly wanted, no matter the physical pain. The feeling of being so greatly desired is something I cannot give up. I look away and Hela waits, but I stay silent and so the drink is made again and again.

One night I wait for him and he does not come. The drink waits, untouched. Restless, I pace about my own tent while time goes by, until I hear his voice close by. For a moment I feel a wave of relief, before I realise that he is not coming closer. I hear him laugh and I run to the door of the tent. In the darkness I see lights flickering in Kella's colourful tent and see his outline on its walls.

Hela refuses.

"You will take this to him," I snarl.

She shakes her head in silence.

"He must come to me," I say.

"It is too late," she tells me. "He is with her tonight. Let him be. You know he will return to you."

I shake my head and lift the cup.

"Be careful of what you do," says Hela.

"It will bring him back to me," I say.

"You cannot know what it will do," she says.

When I hold out the cup it takes everything I have to speak softly. My voice shakes a little and I can only hope that they think I am speaking from duty, one wife to another, a meek and obedient woman. I see her hesitant face and I return to my own tent and pray that she will not stop him from drinking it. I wait for him to come to me and instead I hear her cry out and I know that he has drunk the cup down to its very dregs and that his passion, his poisoned lust, has been unleashed upon her. I turn out every light in my tent and I kneel all night in the darkness, hearing their sounds, unable even to raise my hands to my ears. I do not want to hear and yet I must.

He comes back to me. I see that Kella no longer seeks him out. She keeps to herself. I know there will be bruises fading on her body. She is afraid of such passion, knows it for the sorcery that it is, knows herself unable to withstand it. And so I hold Yusuf to me again and endure the pain in order to feel myself desired. *What can she offer when I have given him everything he might desire in a woman?*

I am happy. I have defeated my rival. She stays away from me and from Yusuf. She seems well enough but she is no danger to me now, no threat.

Yusuf kisses me each morning, a lingering kiss that has him hesitating before he leaves my tent but I let him go, certain that he will return to me even as darkness falls. As he strides away I note with satisfaction that he does not even turn his head towards Kella's tent. Hela emerges from her own dwelling and comes towards me, her back warped from the night. She may be able to cure others but her own bones begin to grow old and it seems she will not or cannot treat her own suffering.

She stands on my threshold and I am about to gesture her inside when I hear retching. I turn my head and catch Kella as she staggers against her slave woman, her face white as she gags again, as she catches my gaze. *What can she offer when I have given him everything he might desire in a woman?*

A child.

Of course. There had to be something.

"You did it for my mother!"

Hela will not even look at me. I have to kneel before her, sink low and twist my face to make her see me. She turns away. Her shoulders are slumped, her hands tightly held in her lap. She looks old, defeated.

"You did it for my mother. Do it for me."

She tries to turn her face away. "I did nothing."

I pull her shoulder to make her look at me. "You took the life from Imen's womb!"

She shakes her head.

I will not let her forget. "Well who did, then? It was no accident. She was a healthy young woman. So who took the baby from her and left her to die in a river of blood?"

She answers but it is a mutter.

"Speak louder."

Hela looks away as though she cannot meet my eye. "I gave her a drink to put a child in her belly. I did it without your mother's knowledge. I thought if your father had a child from her he would no longer seek your mother's company, that she would be left alone to live her own life while Imen bore the sons he wished for."

"Why would my mother wish to be put aside?"

Hela shakes her head. "It does not matter now."

"Did you change your mind? Put a baby in her belly and then have a change of heart?"

Her voice is so low I have to lean towards her. She speaks cheek to cheek with me, the words coming straight to my ear, her eyes wandering elsewhere, back to the past we have shared. "Your mother tried to make a mixture that would take the baby from her and I stopped her, I told her she would kill Imen with the strength she had made. I tried to persuade her to leave Imen to bear children but she could not bear it. What she felt, it was so strong it tainted the cup. The next time Imen drank from it..." her voice grows thick with emotion, even after all this time. "I could not save her. You loved Imen. You would do to this girl what was done to her?"

I think of that night, how Myriam and I prayed in the darkness long before the dawn call to prayer. How the bright sun rose on Kairouan's walls as Imen's pale light left her. I think of my tears and the silence that descended on our house after she was gone, broken only years later when my first husband laughed low in the darkness of our courtyard. I think of Imen's fluttering pale silks, her giggles. I try to think of Imen with love but above the memory of her swelling belly I see the face of my new rival. My face darkens and I turn back to Hela's imploring gaze.

"Do it your way," I say. "Or I will do it mine."

Hela leaves my service for Kella's and I wait, impatient.

"Tell me what you need," I say when I see her. "Tell me what you need from your chests. I will have it brought to you. Whatever you need."

She turns away.

"Do you need the cup?" I ask, my voice low so that Kella will not hear me.

She shakes her head, makes a gesture as though to push the thought away. "I will do it my way," she tells me. "Do not interfere."

I watch and wait. All I can see is that Hela serves Kella well. She cooks for her, she cares for her as a devoted servant would. I feel fear grow in me, that Hela has turned against me and will protect the child growing within her until it is too late. But at last she comes to me one evening and her face tells me the news I have been waiting for.

"I will not forget what you have done for me," I tell her.

"Neither will I," she says and her voice cracks.

But I cannot dwell on what has been done in my name. I have a greater fear. Kella fell with child after one night with Yusuf. She is fertile.

"Give me a child," I say to Hela.

"That gift lies with Allah," she says, not looking at me.

"That gift lies with the cup," I say. "Give me a child."

"You have enough to do," she says. "There are rumours that Abu Bakr has subdued the Southern rebellions. What if he returns?"

"I need a child in my belly before she falls with child again," I say.

"Why must you always measure yourself against another woman?" asks Hela.

"You think no-one else does?" I ask. "You think if she bears Yusuf a son and I do not that everything else I do for him will count against a mewling babe? I could conquer the whole of the Maghreb for him and it would be forgotten against a son and heir."

"Spoken like a woman who longs to be a mother," says Hela.

I sigh. "Do it, Hela."

She does not speak but later she brings me the cup. My hands shake as I take it.

"What if I am barren?" I ask, my voice trembling.

"Is that what you are afraid of?" she asks.

"I have been married three times," I say.

She shrugs. "Were you expecting to bear a child to one of your previous husbands?" she asks.

"I am old," I say. "I am more than thirty and I have never yet born a child. She is barely twenty and she has fallen pregnant twice by Yusuf already."

"Drink," says Hela.

I drink and pray.

Hela sees my white face and nods.

"I am with child?" I gasp after I have vomited up everything I have eaten.

She nods again, her face unsmiling.

I beam. "I can tell Yusuf," I say.

"Wait," she counsels.

"Why?" I ask, touching my belly as though to ward off any ill luck.

"Too early to tell him," she says.

I shake my head and tell a servant to ask Yusuf to eat with me tonight. I send another servant to Kella's tent, inviting her also.

"Too soon," warns Hela, but I ignore her.

I have been unable to eat all day. Great waves of nausea roll over me, the smell of any food is disgusting to me. But I nod when the servants place great plates of food ready and swallow down the sharp bile that rises in my throat. When Yusuf comes and then Kella I welcome them with a smile. I pick at my food, trying to eat as little as possible, while they dine. When they are done and we have washed our hands I turn to Yusuf, a smile spreading on my face.

"Dearest husband," I say and my voice shakes a little. "I have been blessed."

I feel Kella shift next to me. I meet her gaze and smile, my words directed more to her than Yusuf. "I am with child," I say. "Allah has answered my prayers. Blessed is His kindness to this unworthy woman."

At once Yusuf's arms are about me. I am swept over with relief. I have beaten Kella. She has nothing to bring to Yusuf, I have given him everything.

But Kella is speaking and I pull away from Yusuf, unable to believe what I am hearing.

"I am also with child, blessed is Allah," she says brightly and I want to strike her. Instead I must exclaim, I must embrace her once she has emerged from Yusuf's arms. I put my arms stiffly about her, but as I am about to pull away I hear her whisper in my ear.

"My son will be born before yours."

If it were not for Yusuf by my side I would strike her. How is it that everything I do is thrown back to me, poisoned?

"Do it again!"

Hela shakes her head. She will not look at me but her voice is clear. "I will not."

"You did it the first time!"

"That was different."

"How, different?"

Hela fixes her dark eyes on me. "It was early that time. It is too late now."

I cannot stop myself pacing until she grabs me and forces me to sit down. Even so my legs pace, my feet tapping against the floor. "What can I do, then?"

Hela tries to soothe me. "Nothing. You must do nothing. You must rest and be well. You must think of your own child, not hers."

Seeing my angry face she tries to make me see it in a different light. "They will be born close together," she says. "They will be brothers." She sees a brightness in my eyes and mistakes it for happiness. "You see," she says, relieved, "it is a pleasing thought, no?"

I look at her and her smile fades.

"It is a race to be born," I say, my jaw stiffening.

"No," says Hela, trying to turn my thoughts.

"It is."

She reaches out for me. "A child comes when it is ready. A child born too soon is a child weakened."

I grasp her arm so hard I can feel my nails digging into her skin. She flinches.

"My son will be born first," I say. "You will make it so."

But I do not trust her, for Hela can be stubborn and I can see that she does not wish to bring the child early, that she will try to find ways to dissuade me. And so I ask here and there and find that the slave herb seller is a healer. She is from Al-Andalus but has lived here long enough to speak our language well enough.

I have her sent for when Hela is elsewhere.

She stands before me, her face still, as though she is adept at mastering her thoughts, at not allowing them to show to the outer world.

"You have knowledge of herbs? Of medicine?"

She nods.

I look her over. She limped when she entered the room, she stands a little crooked. I wonder whether she was born this way or whether something was done to her. Her face bears scars.

"Can you bring a child before its time?"

"Why would you wish to do that?

"I have my reasons," I say.

She looks at me, her eyes settling on my robes where there should be fullness and there is not. "I would do nothing to harm a child," she says. She raises her eyes back to my gaze. "And nor would its mother," she adds.

"Leave me," I say.

I am so sick I think I will die.

"I cannot even hold down water," I tell Hela. "This baby will die within me."

She shakes her head. "The nausea will pass," she assures me.

"When?"

"Soon."

I watch Kella and see that she is well. She looks at me apprehensively if we pass, as well she might if she knew my thoughts towards her, but otherwise she is well. I see her eat without flinching, I see her touch her belly and know that beneath her robes it is beginning to change shape, that soon she will show. My own belly is flat, I am afraid that perhaps there is no child, that I am only sick, that I may die of something unknown.

"You are with child," Hela reassures me.

"How can you be sure?"

"I feel life within you," she says.

I make her touch me every morning, I press her hand to my belly and look fearfully into her face. Each morning she nods and I feel my shoulders drop with relief.

But the sickness begins to take its toll on me. "I feel as though I can barely stand."

"So rest," says Hela. "Rest. Leave Yusuf to rule. Rest and you will feel better."

"I cannot," I say. "Abu Bakr is returning."

She shrugs. "Let him return."

I shake my head. "Yusuf wishes to be Commander. The men are loyal to him. Abu Bakr is old, he does not have Yusuf's vision."

"Yusuf wishes to be Commander, or you wish it for him?"

"It is the same thing."

"If he challenges Abu Bakr for the leadership and fails, he will be executed for treason."

I nod.

"Still worth it?"

"I will not allow Yusuf's rule to come to an end. I will make him Commander."

"How?"

Yusuf is uncomfortable, he believes my plan may fail and he is all too aware of the consequences if it does. Besides, I am asking him to challenge his own cousin for leadership, his own kin. But I know that underneath his reluctance he desires what I desire.

"You are making your own prophecy come true," he half-jokes.

I think of the moment when I realised what I had done with my false vision, of my first husband's eyes the day he took me to Aghmat, the pain I had unwittingly put there. The pain that came after that. Something good must come from that pain. I tighten my lips. He needs the lie to give him resolve. It seems this lie is irresistible to men.

"It is my destiny," I say. "You are my husband and you will rule all of the Maghreb. But first you must deal with Abu Bakr."

The planning takes many days. Our only chance is to make enough of a show of strength to make it clear to Abu Bakr where the power now lies. Yet we cannot overtly threaten him. We must loudly offer honour and praise while silently warning what may happen if he does not accept what we want.

I inspect every part of the plan as it comes together. A personal guard for Yusuf, made up entirely of black-skinned warriors from the Dark Kingdom. I have them dressed in identical armour, their giant shields matching. The armourers work day and night to my command. Meanwhile the craftsmen build vast chests of carved wood and each is filled with treasures: weapons, silver, gold, robes of honour, jewellery, the finest skins and woven cloths. These are kept locked and ready. Meanwhile the carpenters are set to work, building the sections of a platform that can be quickly assembled.

"You are doing too much," says Hela.

"I am doing what has to be done," I tell her.

"You are not even eating," she says.

I look down at my robes. They are covered in dust. I know that they smell of sweat. My hands are bony, as is the rest of me. I still do not see any sign of my belly growing and yet I can swallow nothing but tiny sips of water and unleavened bread, one mouthful at a time. I stride by Yusuf's side so that all can see that we are as one and yet I think I may fall at any moment. Often my vision fills with a swirling darkness and I have to fight not to faint away.

"When will this sickness end?" I ask Hela.

She shakes her head. "There are women for whom it does not end until the baby is born," she admits reluctantly.

I gape at her. "I will die! Or the baby will."

"Most women survive," she says. "But it would be better if you rested, Zaynab."

"I will rest when this is over," I say.

"And when will that be?" she asks.

"I do not know," I say.

We wait.

When the children spot riders on the plain and soon after the sentries confirm that Abu Bakr's men are on their way, I give the signal and at once my plan is put into place. I watch as the platform is erected, the guard of honour takes its place, the great fires are lit and servants carry vast trays of food to be cooked.

"Be strong but kind," I whisper to Yusuf, and then I hurry to my own tent where Hela waits with fresh robes.

"Make me beautiful," I say.

"You said not to use makeup," she says. "You said Yusuf did not like it."

"I need it now," I say.

She uses rich creams and powders on my face, she tints my lips and cheeks.

"Drink this," she says and holds out the cup.

I turn it in my hands. "What is it?"

"It will give you energy," she says.

I drink it and leave her, almost running to the platform to take my place before Abu Bakr's advance guard arrives.

The platform has been covered with rich rugs, it is surrounded by Yusuf's guard of honour. Yusuf himself is already seated. He looks uncomfortable.

"Show that you are their Commander in all but name," I hiss.

"Abu Bakr," he begins.

"Is not with them. This is an advance party. He already

knows that there may be a claim for leadership and he is not making his claim. He knows his time has come. These are your men. They will be loyal to you, if you can show them a ruler they can follow."

Crowds are flocking into the central square. I see Kella among them, her face turned up towards the platform in surprise. *How little you know of what must be done for a man like Yusuf,* I think. *You think bearing an heir is enough but that is worth nothing if his command is undermined.*

She is helped up onto the platform and takes up a place a little behind Yusuf and I. Now we see Abu Bakr's men arrive, a smallish party: a few high-ranking generals and then their officers, a handful of common men behind them.

They make their way through the crowd, then stand before the platform, their faces showing their shock. These are Yusuf's men, they have fought under his command for many years. When they left Murakush it was nothing but a city of tents, a garrison. Now they see city walls rising, the first buildings springing up. They see Yusuf sat side by side with a consort queen, surrounded by a fearsome personal guard. He looks like an amir. I lift my chin as high as it will go and look down on the men. There is a silence. Then Yusuf stands.

"In the name of Allah, I welcome you back to Murakush, my brave and noble warriors."

I smile down on them as though they were each and every one my own beloved and see them swallow. Yusuf has spoken to them as if they are his men, not Abu Bakr's, while I, his beautiful queen, have welcomed them with warmth.

"Come, eat with us, my brothers, for you must be tired and hungry," continues Yusuf. He claps his hands and slaves step forwards with jugs of scented water. The men, dazed, allow their hands to be washed. The more senior join Yusuf and I on the platform while their common soldiers gather close by. Slaves bring huge platters of rich meats and fresh breads, spiced stews, piled-up fruits and other good things to eat and the men, unused to such food after many months away in harsh fighting conditions, eat heartily. Yusuf speaks with them as though they have returned from a mission he himself has commanded, praising their bravery and prowess without ever naming Abu Bakr. I watch as their shoulders relax, as they settle more comfortably, eat and drink well, smile at Yusuf and bow their heads to me. The common soldiers are given gold coins while their superiors are led to our own tent and offered gifts of honour. I stand by Yusuf. There is more than one man who glances at the lustfulness of my bed and blushes, whose eyes slip over my body in desire. They will remember the prophecy and believe they are witnessing it coming to pass at last.

"Now send back only a handful of the men," I tell Yusuf afterwards. "Only mid-ranked men and commoners may return to Abu Bakr to report back, and only a few of them. He must see that their numbers and loyalty are much diminished."

And so the smaller party of men returns to Abu Bakr and we wait again.

The messenger who arrives brings us good news. Abu Bakr agrees to our request to meet away from Murakush, at a place midway between here and the humbled Aghmat.

"He is no fool," I tell Yusuf. "He knows what is coming. We have only to play our part."

We ride out at dawn, Yusuf and I at the head of an army of several thousand. Just behind us, clearly visible, are the senior men Abu Bakr sent out. Also behind us somewhere is Kella, part of a group of people of importance: the tribal leaders who have sworn allegiance to Yusuf, generals. His guard surround us. Behind them, thousands upon thousands of men in full battle armour, a show of absolute power, of unbeatable strength.

"And if he has brought all of his army?" asks Yusuf. "You expect us to begin a battle? Cousin against cousin?"

"He will not have his army," I say.

"How do you know?"

I think back to Abu Bakr's kindly gruffness, his good nature, his growing weariness when more battles were spoken of. "He will be alone," I say.

I am right. On the plain is a tiny shelter, a simple thing made of a few poles and cloths. As we draw closer I can see less than twenty men around it, armoured but with their weapons sheathed. Beneath the shelter, protected from the heat, sits Abu Bakr himself. A little greyer, a little wearier, but otherwise the same. For a moment I think of his gentleness to me, how he treated me like a daughter, how he praised my intelligence and knowledge, gave me a voice in council. I think of calling off my plan, but we have gone too far now and anyway I can see that Abu Bakr is already resigned to what is about to happen.

We halt before him and there is a long silence. As his military subordinate and younger relative, Yusuf should dismount, should embrace Abu Bakr. Instead I make a tiny gesture and the guards step forward with the great chests of treasures. They unlock them, the turning metal keys loud in the silence. The lids are thrown back to display the treasures. It is the completion of our show of wealth and power, of transferred loyalty.

Abu Bakr looks out across the plain, filled with thousands of men in tight fighting formations. He looks at the chests of treasure and then, instead of looking at Yusuf, he looks at me. His eyes crinkle in a wry smile, an acknowledgement of what has happened and at whose command. Then he holds out a hand to Yusuf and speaks clearly, for all to hear.

"Will you join me, cousin?"

Yusuf waits just a moment longer, as I instructed him to. Then he dismounts and makes his way to Abu Bakr, sits down at his side. The men tighten their grips on their weapons but already Abu Bakr is speaking again. The words are smooth enough that I can tell he has already rehearsed them, knowing what was to come.

"My cousin Yusuf. My true brother before Allah. There can be no man more worthy than you to command this army of holy warriors and to undertake a holy war in the name of Allah."

I feel the tension lower, hear the tiny sound of every man loosening his grip on the hilt of his sword, magnified many thousands of times over. I meet Abu Bakr's gaze and he nods. I nod back, an acknowledgement of his good grace. He speaks again.

"I am a simple man, one who loves the desert, home of our families and seat of our power. I wish to return there with a small force of my own men. There we will continue our work, fighting back the rebel tribes and securing the trade routes for our own needs. Brother, I ask you to assume command in my name. I will return to the desert with all speed, for this is no longer my place."

Documents are to hand to be agreed on, already worded to my order. The transfer of power was over long before now. By the time Abu Bakr remounts his horse and gathers his men about him many of the soldiers have already been sent back, some with instructions from me. We turn our horses back towards Murakush, but not before Abu Bakr speaks with me.

"Aisha sends you her greetings."

I smile at the thought of her. "Send her mine," I say.

"Are you happy?" he asks.

I think of Kella's swelling belly. "I try to be," I say.

"You have a brilliant mind, Zaynab," he says. "You should have been a man, the world would have recognised your greatness."

"It still may," I say.

"I do not doubt it," he says. "I thought it before and I know it now."

"I have a warrior at my side," I say.

He smiles. "It is the superior warrior who wins without bloodshed," he says. "Goodbye, Zaynab."

"Goodbye," I say. Our hands touch for a moment before we turn away from each other. I look back over my shoulder before I join Yusuf at the head of the army again and see Abu Bakr's party, small on the vast plain, heading away from us.

I have won.

Murderess

THE UNENDING SICKNESS OF MY pregnancy cripples me but my spirits lift at Yusuf's new status. Abu Bakr's name may remain on the gold coins but Yusuf is now leader of the Almoravids in all but name. And at last my belly swells and I feel life growing within me.

Now we can plan for greater conquests. The army is made vast by new recruits, each of them trained to Yusuf's standards. I watch them myself as they are drilled on the plain, over and over again. Money for armour comes from taxes levied on Jews and the merchants who follow the now secured and safer trading routes.

I think of what Abu Bakr said, that to win without bloodshed is the greater victory. The army is now so vast that I advise Yusuf to send out only a small part of it to Salé and the region quickly submits to his authority without fighting. They know that should they choose to fight, Yusuf will simply send the whole of the army and they will be utterly crushed. By offering their allegiance they will come under his protection, which is worth a great deal. Having seen the success of our strategy against Salé, it becomes our way forward. To each region, each leader, we offer a choice: submit to us, pledge allegiance and receive honour and protection, or face the might of an army the like of which has never been seen before. Meknes falls, its amir moving out of the city and setting up a humble settlement in the region, leaving the city open at Yusuf's command. It is an important win for us, for it is close to Fes, which may be harder to take. It will act as a provisioning ground for us, supporting any siege required.

While Yusuf builds the army, I build Murakush. I command the builders to work harder, faster, longer. The city's walls and ramparts are complete. Now they turn their attention to the homes and buildings that must rise within the walls. Bakeries, hammams, a mosque. The mosque is large although not large enough for Yusuf's liking, he will want a bigger one in due course. Homes spring up. First a large and imposing palace for Yusuf and I. He makes a face when he sees the plans for it.

"You are not in the desert now," I tell him. "You are the leader of the Almoravids and you will receive fallen amirs, new leaders who must pledge allegiance to you. They will not do so in a tent when they have come from a castle."

"I do not want splendour," he says.

"You need splendour," I retort.

And so the building is large, so that it can accommodate leaders and their entourages, the servants needed to offer feasts, the great chamber for council meetings. But it is simpler than many leaders would have created. I allow the craftsmen in but they must work to a difficult brief. Carved plasterwork yes, but only using calligraphy praising Allah. The paints and designs on the doors must be simple, none of the flourishes and elaborate designs they might usually offer for an amir. Carved chests for our belongings, but again they must be simple in design, although I have them made from perfumed woods, the better to care for our clothes and other belongings. The garden courtyard is lavishly planted but the pool is tiled with a simplicity that makes even the craftsmen look doubtful. But I am right, for the courtyard becomes one of Yusuf's favourite places, its simplicity and use of nature pleasing to him. Sometimes he even takes a blanket and sleeps there, as though remembering the old days when he slept by his men's side and ate only bread and meat.

He complains again when he sees the meals I order when we have visiting dignitaries staying.

"They are your honoured guests," I say. "You cannot feed them only bread, meat and dates. They are not your men on the training ground."

Reluctantly he allows me to order what is appropriate, although if we are alone then the servants know to bring only the simplest dishes.

Kella I place in her own house nearby. I do not want her too visible to Yusuf and by her face when I show her the new home I can see that she is relieved not to be too close to me. I eye up her swelling belly, larger than mine, with fear. I dare not ask when she is due, I am already afraid of what I will have to ask of Hela, of bringing my unborn child into the world too early, perhaps risking its life. So I have her placed elsewhere but tell Hela and two other servants to keep a watchful eye on her, to let me know if anything strange happens in her household, if she seems to be near her time.

Murakush grows under my hand. One tent and then another is taken down, our city of cloth becoming a city of mud bricks, rising higher each day. The people of wealth commission tilework and pools, painted wood and beaten metals to adorn their homes. Craftsmen labour night and day, there is more work than they can keep up with. The last tents fade away as even the common soldiers and their families have their own homes built. Arches curve into shape, great gates are hung and painted or wrought in metal. Different quarters spring up: the armour-makers, the metalworkers who create jugs and platters, handles, hinges and locks, their great hammers beating, beating. The weavers' workshops turn out fine cloth and rugs, vast carpets to soften the newly-built homes. The leatherworkers, the vendors of street food, take up permanent positions rather than trading where they find themselves. Fresh fruits and vegetables are brought to the markets from the huge gardens growing up around Murakush, for a great city has need of many farmers to feed it. I have vast water tanks built, to save winter rains and melted ice from the mountains so that we will have water all year round and the gardens will be irrigated.

The people begin to grow proud of Murakush. They belong to a great city, they are no longer making do in a garrison camp. Now they crave finer clothes, better food. They wear perfumes and choose elaborate scabbards for their swords. Merchants seek out the city, it becomes a major point on the trade routes.

"You should be proud of what you have done," Hela says.

"There is still so much to do," I say.

She shakes her head. "You need to rest," she says. "You are coming into your final month."

I look down at my swollen belly, which sits oddly against my bony hands. Kella has grown plump, soft. Her cheeks are rounded, her hands have little dimples showing. She eats well and has not been sick since her very early days. I still struggle to keep food down.

"This baby has been grown on nothing but bread and water," I say fearfully.

"All will be well," says Hela. "But rest."

"I must attend council," I say.

In council we are entirely focused on Fes. It is a strange city, made up of two cities side by side but with a wall between them, with two amirs, one for each part. It will be like taking two cities at once. The first move has been made: we have sent and asked the amirs to submit with grace, to pledge allegiance and give their cities to us without a battle. Both have refused.

"There will be a siege," says Yusuf. Heads nod around the room.

I nod along with them. It is I who will provision the army, who must ensure Meknes will be ready to support the siege and act as a garrison for our men. The order to take Fes is no small matter to me. For a moment I envy Kella, no matter how much she has been put aside by Yusuf. She has nothing to do with her days but eat and rest, to feel her growing child within her and triumph in the knowledge that it is due before mine. Meanwhile I am racked with sickness and feel my body grow weak beneath its burden, yet I must continue, must plan strategies by Yusuf's side and carry out feats of military planning that would put a man to shame. If Fes falls it will not just be because Yusuf's men are strong, well trained and vast in their numbers. It will be because I moved thousands of men and animals there, because I ensured their weapons were fit for use. It will be I who feeds them, ensures there is water for the men and their mounts, that there are fresh troops ready to relieve them from our garrison in Meknes, that the armourers are ready to make repairs at night while the men fight by day. If Fes falls it will be I who will order the documents that will ensure peace, who will decide where and how the fallen amirs may live. I shake my head. She may have a son. But I will have many more. And if I can do her son harm, I will do it and I will not hold back. Every time I see that life grows in her womb I will find a way to take it from her. Before or after it is born, while I still live each one of her children will die. I will not be usurped by some nobody, some girl who thinks she is entitled to give Yusuf an heir when I have been everything to him, have been his right hand and a better strategic mind than his best generals. I will not have the baby of a foolish girl push my own children out of the way of inheriting Yusuf's kingdom, for it is a kingdom I have created alongside him, it is as much mine as it is his.

"Her shutters have not been opened today," reports a servant.

At once I am on my feet. Her time has come earlier than I thought. I have not had the time I needed.

"Leave her," says Hela from the back of the room.

I ignore her. Heavy with my own child I hurry to her home and catch the sound of a child's cry as I open the gate, although I cannot be certain where it comes from, whether Kella's own home or somewhere else. Inside the lanterns have not yet been lit, even though it is already dark. I make my way partly by feel inside the house, where a dim light draws me upstairs to Kella's rooms. My heart thuds, my weak legs ache at each step.

She lies alone, half-propped up on cushions, her face a little dazed. Her belly still protrudes, but not as it did before. At the sight of me in the doorway she startles and looks over my shoulder as though expecting someone else to join us. There is no baby.

"You have a son?" I ask. I cannot see a baby anywhere, I wonder whether one of her servants has taken it away, whether they knew I would come.

She does not answer, only stares up at me like a frightened animal.

"It is my own children who will follow Yusuf," I tell her, and I hear my voice tremble even though I meant to sound fierce, meant to intimidate her.

"Why do you hate me so much, Zaynab?" she asks, tears falling down her face. "I am nothing compared to you, yet you hate me and pursue me. You seek to do me harm at every possible opportunity. I have done nothing to you."

I look round the room again. I barely hear what she has said. She knows nothing of my life, this silly girl who wanted the freedom of the trade routes and ran away from her family to follow Yusuf and his army as though she were some lovesick fool, without a thought for what her future might hold, for what kind of mission Yusuf was embarking on. At her age I had already lost my first love and been thrown into the clutches of a monster.

"I am always second," I hear myself murmur.

"You are a queen," she whimpers. I want to laugh at her for thinking that being a queen must mean that I am happy, that my life must be good. Only a child thinks like this. And still I cannot see the baby. I think to search the house but then shake my head to myself. If there is a baby, I will find it soon enough.

"Before or after it is born, while I still live each one of your children will die," I threaten her and see her eyes widen. Now I know there is a child and it is alive. She cannot command her feelings well enough, they are visible all over her face.

"Get out," she says, her voice shaking in fear, while her eyes flit behind me again.

She lies. She claims that the baby died and Yusuf weeps with her.

"She is lying," I tell Hela. "That baby was alive when I went to her home."

"Did you see it?"

"No," I say.

"It might have died afterwards," she says.

I look at her.

"Forget the child," says Hela. "It is gone."

"Gone where?" I ask her and she does not reply.

"Find it," I tell her.

My own son must be destined for life as a warrior, for I gave instructions for the siege of Fes even as I birthed him, sending messages through gritted teeth to Yusuf with one servant and then another.

"The pain will be over soon," Hela tries to soothe me.

"It is never over," I say, panting. "It is one thing and then another, my whole life long."

I think I will split in two.

"Scream," says Hela, watching me.

My teeth are so tight together I think they will break, my jaw aches from my silence.

"Cry out, Zaynab," she says. "You cannot hold the pain inside."

But I do. I hold it until I am lost in darkness and when I awake there is a baby beside me.

"You have a son," says Hela.

He is tiny. I look down at him in silence. A fierce joy runs through me, a love so violent I am afraid to touch him in case I crush him.

"Hold him," says Hela.

I put out one hand and touch his face. At once he opens dark eyes and cries.

"Call a wet-nurse," I say.

Hela frowns. "You can feed him yourself, Zaynab," she says. "I will help you learn how."

I shake my head. "I cannot," I say. "I must attend council."

My son is named Abu Tahir al-Mu'izz and Murakush erupts in festivities for him, celebrating an heir for Yusuf, a sign of Allah's favour, surely. Why, I have been married three times before and have never born a child, I am old for childbearing and yet as soon as I wedded Yusuf I have been proven fertile after all. Abu Tahir is surrounded by nursemaids and an eager-to-please wetnurse, more servants and slaves are allocated to his service, whatever service a tiny baby has need of.

Hela shakes her head. "He only has need of a mother," she says.

"He must have everything," I tell her.

Council sits long hours and now the men begin to march North, joining the ever-growing garrison at Meknes, ready to take Fes.

I am regaining some strength, now that the nausea of the past nine months has left me. I eat hungrily, seeking to cover up the too-obvious bones of my hands, my neck and shoulders. When I look in a mirror I stand tall again, a women of power. I cannot help but feel a little sorry for Kella. She is nothing but a foolish girl who tried to take from me what was mine and now has lost everything.

Except that I catch sight of her one day and when I do I summon Hela.

"That is not a woman who has lost a child," I say. "Look at her. She is well fed, she smiles, she goes about her life as though all were well and yet she claims to have lost her son, her third child."

Hela says nothing.

"You will follow her, wherever she goes," I say. "That child is not dead. Find it." She makes to speak but I wave her away. "Find the child," I say.

The two amirs of Fes are given one more warning but they do not show wisdom, only stubbornness. The siege is about to begin.

"Have you found the child?" I ask Hela.

She shakes her head.

"It is somewhere in this city," I say. "I know it."

"Kella has not been anywhere near a baby," says Hela, holding Abu and half-singing to him. Her face lights up when she sees him.

I walk in the dark streets of the souk and ask for the merchants who will not flinch when I tell them what I need. I send Kella a ring set with a tiny box that contains a perfume, the use of which will kill her. If I cannot be certain of the babe, I will be certain of the mother. I will not have a baby hidden from me and then revealed as an heir who can topple my own children. I have the servant who delivers it to her claim it is a gift from Yusuf and she, the innocent, wears it with pride.

The siege begins.

Each day I await news. I sit in council or in my own rooms and I do not hear what goes on around me. I think only of the ever-beating war drums, how their endless rhythm makes the enemy uneasy at first, before they grow unable to think clearly, their ears and minds filled with the constant sound before they have even been engaged in battle. The soldiers and their families will look out from the walls of Fes and see an army the like of which has never been known before. They will swallow and wonder what it will be like to fight such an army, whose tight formations are so unlike anything they have encountered in previous local skirmishes.

The siege goes on day after day and while the armies of the amirs begins to diminish, our own stays strong in numbers. Now the people of Fes will beg their amirs to reconsider, for their fathers, brothers and husbands leave the safety of the walls to fight and do not return.

The drums beat on, I hear them in my mind even though they are in Fes. They are my waking pulse, my sleeping breath. I sit on the walls of the city and look out across the plain, think of our army, imagine the dark mass of our soldiers, slowly advancing on the men of Fes, crushing them.

"Lady Kella is in your rooms," a servant tells me.

I make my way to her, my feet swift. I am amazed she is still alive.

She looks drunk. Her eyes are unfocused, she moves her head this way and that as though she can hear something.

I sit above her on my bed, look down on her.

"What have you given me, Zaynab?" she asks, blinking at me as though she cannot see me clearly. "I thought the perfume was from Yusuf, but now I know it was from you. It does strange things to me, I see visions of terrible things and I hear things I do not wish to hear. My feet stumble and I feel that I might fly like a great bird if I were only to leap from my window. I talk and talk, telling all that is in my heart, no matter who is listening. I feel light, and then the colours grow so bright they hurt my eyes until I grow afraid." She talks too fast, then too slowly, too loud and then too soft as if she cannot hear her own voice, cannot control it.

"You are strong," I say. "I thought it would kill you."

She stares up at me. "Why do you hate me so much, Zaynab?" she asks, tears starting in her eyes.

I sigh. It is like speaking with a child. She cannot see

beyond her own concerns. She is still speaking, not even waiting for an answer from me.

"I have not tried to fight you. I want only to help my husband succeed in his mission, to bear him children, to build a great country. Yet you treat me as your greatest enemy. What more can I give you? You have taken my husband. You have taken my children – one from my womb, one from my arms – "

I gasp and slide down from the bed so that our faces are suddenly barely a hand's breadth apart. My heart is pounding. I cannot believe she has let this slip.

"*Taken?*"

She tries to pull away from me, her eyes wide with the fear of what she has just revealed. "He is dead."

I shake my head. "You said I took him. He is *alive*?"

She tries to lie. She begs again for me to soften towards her. Her voice is nothing but an annoyance to me, her innocence enraging. And at last she says something of interest. She rises, unsteady on her feet.

"I am leaving, Zaynab. You have tried to poison me. No doubt you will try again. What do you want – my life in exchange for my son's?"

My heart is pounding. "I might consider such a bargain," I say.

I watch her walk away, clinging to walls as she goes. Behind me Hela enters.

"Watch her," I say.

Still we wait for a messenger from Fes.

"She is shopping," says Hela.

"What?"

"Kella," says Hela. "She is buying things in the souks."

"I do not care what she buys," I tell her. "What am I, a housewife? Do not bring me useless information."

"A saddle? Piles of household gifts? A sword?"

I frown. "For her own home?"

"Most has been sent away, back to her people's camp."

"Most?"

"She kept a racing saddle."

"She cannot be allowed to leave," I tell Hela. "I need to know where she is. She and her child."

"If she leaves she will no longer trouble you."

"Why?" I spit. "You think she will stay away forever, not return with a fully-grown son she can show to Yusuf and claim his place as heir?"

Hela shakes her head. "I do not think she will return, if she goes. I think she would leave to protect her son."

"I will not risk that," I tell her.

We look at each other.

"Command me," says Hela.

"You know what to do," I say.

"I want to hear you say it," says Hela. "I will not take a life on hints and whispers."

"Kill her," I say, the words out of my mouth so fast I am not even sure I have said them. They hang in the air between us.

She gazes at me as though she believes I will add something, as though I will countermand what I have said.

I hold her gaze. I hear footsteps running and a messenger stands before me, sweaty and dusty.

"Fes has fallen," he pants.

We are jubilant. There is feasting and celebrating throughout the city. Fes is now our stronghold in the North. Our army is unstoppable, we have conquered not one but two cities side by side. Now the great walls that separate them will be torn down and we will command one great city to rise from the ruins.

Yusuf and I sit late into the night, maps of the Maghreb spread out before us, our bodies slick with sweat from our coupling. With Fes falling, more and more leaders will submit to us without fighting, for they have been shown what it means to defy us. Yusuf's fingertips trace the contours of the regions that lie before us.

"The Mouluya valley," he murmurs.

"Tlemcen," I return.

He raises his eyebrows. "So far East?"

I shrug. "Why not? And further: Algiers."

He laughs. "You are unstoppable, Zaynab."

"I am," I say, curling my body back into his hands. "I am."

The dawn call to prayer comes and Yusuf leaves me in the half-light. I do not follow. I am lazy with relief at our plans coming to fruition. I lie in the tumble of blankets and listen to the world around me, the servants clattering about, the merchants in the alleyways. I have created a great city from nothing, from sand and tents. And I will create many more.

"She is gone."

I blink and struggle into a sitting position. Hela leans

in my doorway as though unable to stand unsupported. Her face is white. In one hand she clutches something wrapped in a rag.

"Gone?" I repeat.

"Gone," she echoes.

"Dead?"

She shakes her head.

"I told you to kill her," I say.

"She broke the cup," she says, her voice shaking.

I frown. "What are you talking about?"

She lets go of the rag in her hand and two pieces of wood clatter out of it onto the floor, two halves of her carved cup. We both stare at it. I feel a sudden fear: what if the drink that drew Yusuf to me, that has kept him filled with desire for me, can no longer be made? What if it is not Hela's skills with plants but the cup itself that has done the work?

I swallow. "Did you poison her?"

"She spat it out."

"Did she swallow enough?"

"I do not know."

"And where is she now?"

"Gone," says Hela. "Her camel is gone. As has a man from her tribe, one of Yusuf's soldiers."

"She had a lover?" This, I had not expected.

Hela shrugs. Slowly she lets her body slide down the doorway until she is sat on the floor, her hands close to the cup's broken halves. She strokes one half, as though it is an injured pet, a dying creature. It makes my skin crawl.

"Does Yusuf know she is gone?" I ask.

She shakes her head.

"Do not tell him yet," I say.

I dress quickly and leave the room, brushing past Hela, who does not move.

I send out scouts in all directions but it is too late. Kella has gone, there is no trace of her. Her two slaves are also gone. Not much is known about the man when I enquire. He served in our army, he was from her tribe, perhaps they will return there although she cannot be so stupid. It is more likely that she believes we have made a pact: her disappearance for her child's safety. Perhaps she will return to the trading life she had before she met Yusuf.

I cannot keep the information from him for long. When he finds out that she has disappeared he, too, sends out scouts. I already know they will not find her but I stand by to comfort him. I remind him that her child died and that perhaps she has ended her life. I hold him when he weeps for her. But the days go by and then a month passes and he grows resigned, he no longer speaks of finding her. There is gossip of course but we weather it, it is nothing compared to our successes and I make sure my son's nursemaids show him off in public, that he is seen with Yusuf, a reminder that this is his heir, that I am his wife and queen.

I should feel relief. Kella is gone. I am Yusuf's queen, the mother of his heir. Our army cannot be stopped. If there is a baby, if Kella has actually left her child behind, then I cannot find it. Perhaps Kella wanted only for the baby to be safe, for if she is not here then how can the child ever be proved to be Yusuf's? A passing similarity of their features would not be sufficient. If there is no mother to claim its father, it will be one child among many hundreds, thousands in our kingdom. It cannot stake a claim. I should feel relief.

But Hela is sick. I think of the moment when she told me that the cup was broken and I think she has been sick from that moment onwards. Her skin has taken on a strange pallor, as though there is no blood beneath it. She no longer walks, she shuffles and she does not speak, only mumbles replies if she is asked a question or talks to herself when there is no-one nearby. The broken cup sits in her room, set into a niche in the wall as though it were something of beauty to be admired or something holy to be worshipped. When I visit her in her rooms, which she leaves less and less, I find her in half-darkness, the shutters closed. She sits on her bed, huddled in blankets as though she is permanently cold and she stares at the cup.

"Throw it away," I say, standing in the doorway. I do not want to enter the room, it feels heavy, as though it were full of something unseen.

She shakes her head.

"I will do it for you," I say, although I do not want to touch it. There is something about the cup that still seems alive, even though it is broken. I cannot but think about what it did to Luqut, how it took away his lust for me and then took his life when he went into battle. I think of the lust it stirred in Yusuf, a lust that has not yet faded. I owe the cup many things but I am still afraid of it. I think of Imen and Kella's lost children.

But Hela sits up at once, shaking her head. "Do not touch it."

"You are a healer in your own right," I tell her. "You do

not need the cup." I am not sure this is true. I know she is a gifted healer and that she has her own powers, her skill for sensing the feelings of others, but still I am not certain how much of her power comes from her own abilities and how much from the cup. Her sickness frightens me, it is as though her life force has been broken along with the cup.

"Tell me what you need and I will have it made for you," I tell her. "Or a servant can bring your herbs here and you can make it yourself."

She shakes her head.

"You cannot die just because a cup breaks, Hela," I say, trying to sound light hearted. But my voice does not sound light. It trembles.

She does not answer.

"I command you," I say, trying a different approach. I make my voice hard. "You must rise up and serve me again, Hela. I have need of you."

"You are set upon your path," she says. "You can follow it alone now."

I feel a heavy weight settle in my belly. "I cannot manage alone," I say and my voice wavers more now, I can feel tears coming to my eyes.

"I have failed," she says.

"In what?" I ask.

"I swore to bring happiness to your family," she says and her head slumps down, she does not meet my gaze. "I failed."

"You served my mother," I say awkwardly.

"She was not happy," says Hela. "I tried but I failed. Then I looked to serve you, for I felt my obligation was not yet complete."

"Obligation?"

"And you are not happy," says Hela, ignoring me.

"I am Yusuf's wife and queen," I begin, then stop. "I have given him an heir," I add. "The army... our conquests..."

"You have spent your whole life desperate for love," says Hela from the darkness. "Desperate to be loved, to be the only object of a man's desire, to be his only thought, to be of supreme importance to him."

"Enough of this," I say. I do not like her voice, it sounds like a message from another world.

"It will kill you," she says. She sounds weary, each word an effort. Her breath rasps in and out and every time I think there may not be another breath. "This terrible need to be loved, Zaynab, it will kill you. It robs you of every moment of happiness you might otherwise claim."

"Enough," I say. "I will not listen to this, Hela."

I leave her but cannot settle to anything. I wander through the rooms of the building, I sit with my baby son, dandle him in my arms, ask questions of the servants to be certain he is being cared for. If I hear of anything in his treatment that is not right I have them whipped. He is too precious to me, the thought of anything happening to him fills me with dread. I take my place in council, but I cannot focus on what is being discussed. I send servants to Hela, offering food, drink, lanterns, healing herbs, blankets, whatever she has need of. She refuses them all. At last I return to her rooms. I can hear her breathing before I even reach her, the desperate sucking in of air and then its slow release. The room is dark, only faint streams of dusty light trickle through the closed shutters. There is a musky smell, as though something is decaying, rotting nearby. I stand by her bed.

"Finish this," says Hela. Her voice startles me.

"Finish what?" I ask although something in me already knows the answer.

"Release me from my vow," says Hela.

"I do not know what vow you made, but I release you from it," I say. "You have stood by my side, Hela. You have made me who I am today."

She sighs, as though my words are painful to her. "I know," she says. "I am sorry."

"I meant you have made me a queen, a wife. A mother," I say.

She shakes her head, a slow movement to one side and then the other.

I stand in the half-light and wait for her to speak again but she only continues to struggle for breath. Slowly I make my way to her side, sit on the edge of her bed, take her hand in mine. Her hands have always been sturdy. Now they have lost their strength and they feel like bones bound together with ragged skin, limp in my clasp.

"Release me," she says again, a croaking whisper.

"I do," I say. "I have."

Again the slow side-to-side shake of her head. "I cannot go," she says. "I have tried."

I swallow. "What can I do?"

Her spare hand feels about her until she finds a blanket. She tugs at the corner of it, pulls it until it touches my hand.

"No," I say.

"I cannot go," she says again. "Let me go."

She goes quickly. I do not have to hold the blanket for long, but when I pull it away again it is already wet from my tears. I wonder if she tasted them before she died, if my grief trickled through the warp and weft and touched her lips as the breath left her body.

I sit in council while the deaths are tallied. Fes has been crushed, thousands lost their lives, but we also lost men. Their names are listed so that they can be prayed for, so that the correct rituals can be carried out. I know that there are families in Fes who think of us as murderers, who curse Yusuf's name and would curse mine too if they knew my hand in their loss.

Back in my rooms I hold Hela's broken cup. It does not feel strange or powerful now, it feels like what it is: two broken pieces of wood, lifeless in my hands. Hela is the only person who saw the gaping emptiness within my outer perfection, the fear inside my utter control. She saw me for who I truly am.

Now she is gone. At my hand.

Spy

WITHOUT HELA AT MY SIDE I feel vulnerable. Now I must stand alone, must hold my power without her help.

I have feared for a while that my knowledge of the Maghreb and all its rulers, its secrets, deceits and counter-deceits, the certainty that the Almoravid council craves from me, would end. I have stretched out all I knew and of course I have learnt from them as they have learnt from me. But I feared the day would come when I would have nothing else to offer. Today I glimpse a different path to tread, and at once I realise its power, for it offers endless possibilities.

The man standing before me bows deeply and asks in a low voice if he may visit me in private. I wave him into my own bedchamber, call for servants to bring sweetmeats and cool drinks. His eyes widen when he sees the bed, of course, but I am used to that by now. He sits on the cushions laid out on the floor and we make ourselves comfortable. He has been in our council today, offering words from his lord, chief of a tribe to the North. A minor tribe, but one who wishes to stand at our side, one who fears a possible onslaught if he does not pledge allegiance to us.

"Your master is a wise man to become our ally," I say,

trying to understand why he would want to delay his visit by idly talking with me rather than resting before his return to the North.

He nods. "Although…"

I sense he will not speak unless I make it easy for him. "Although?"

"He can be… changeable."

I know this word when used in such circumstances. "Can I trust your lord's stated intentions and promises towards us?"

I ask it with great bluntness. The man blinks. Perhaps he thought more discretion would be used. He pauses and I lean forward. My perfume envelops him and he leans a little closer. He will tell his friends that he sat alone with the legendary Zaynab, queen of Aghmat, now queen of Murakush and Fes. They will not believe him but they will want to know more.

"I – I think perhaps you would be wise to put your trust in others before my lord," he says, stumbling over his words.

I put one hand on his and he trembles a little at my touch. "Can I put my trust in you?" I ask gently.

Now he cannot speak fast enough. "My lady – yes – yes, I would do anything to deserve…"

I am thinking as fast as I can. I lean forward a little more and place another hand over his. His hands are bound in mine now. "I would pay you well," I whisper. "And I would like to see you again – to hear from your own lips whatever news you have to bring me."

Just like that it is done. It is a matter of days before another man is ensnared by my hands and whispers, by my perfume which fills their senses. They cannot resist the idea of serving me, of being known by name to a woman whom the storytellers have already shaped into a legend.

Slowly I gather informants across the Maghreb. My two eyes become four, eight, sixteen, thirty-two, sixty-four... many hundreds. When I blink they blink, when I look to the right or left their eyes move with me. When I sleep they keep watch. Now I have information from across many lands.

Yusuf frowns when I begin to reveal changes to loyalties or successions, when I share the secrets of leaders, but when I am proved right time and again the men begin to lean towards me when I speak and Yusuf waits for my knowledge before choices are made, new allies approved. My power in the council is undimmed, indeed it grows stronger. I hear the storytellers call me 'the Magician' and claim that I speak with djinns to know all that I do. I laugh in private at such claims, but in public I let them think what they like. Let them fear me.

My son Abu Tahir grows. I see him take his first steps. I give him a little wooden sword of his own, I have a shield made for him, give him a drum and teach him the slow drumbeat of the battlefield. When Yusuf sees him pretending to be a soldier he laughs, but he is proud and I see that he grows closer to the boy because of his warlike nature. My only fear is that some harm will befall him. One child is not enough, for any child might grow sick and die and always I remember that Kella's child may be somewhere in Murakush. I must have more children, although the thought of it makes me want to weep. The endless sickness I endured weakened me so badly that to willingly undertake it again seems madness. Besides, I am growing older. I risk my life by birthing more children. I hope that perhaps, perhaps, the sickness will not come again, that the first time was the worst.

I am wrong. It seems I am fertile enough after all, for despite my age I fall with child again but the sickness is so great that I do not know how I will get through the pregnancy alive.

I send for one healer after another and all of them are useless. I am made to drink foul brews and wear meaningless amulets. They do nothing. I eat unleavened bread, one tiny fearful mouthful at a time, I sip water constantly, for I can only swallow a tiny amount at a time or risk losing everything I have eaten or drunk that day.

"Rest," says Yusuf, worried as my hands turn bony again and my skin grows pale from keeping indoors.

But I have spies who will speak only with me, I must sit in council. I must tend to my son. I must weave the endless warp and weft of Yusuf's kingdom.

I send for the herb-seller, the healer from Al-Andalus. She stands in my presence and waits for me to speak.

"I suffer with great sickness from this pregnancy," I tell her. "I have need of your healing powers."

"I do not have powers," she corrects me. "I only have knowledge of herbs and I pray to my God for His guidance."

I say nothing. I note her stubborn clinging to her own god, her Christian god. Much good he has done her, a scarred and crippled slave girl far from her homeland.

"What have you tried?" she asks.

I list various things: eating acrid things such as capers,

not eating such things, avoiding chickpeas and other such legumes and rue, the use of fresh air, gentle walks, wool placed over my stomach. Various wines, diluted with one thing or another. The never-ending amulets.

She shakes her head when I have finished. "I will make you a syrup," she says. "Take it when you feel the sickness and at least twice a day even if you do not. Eat small meals and often."

"I can barely eat anything but unleavened bread," I say. "Everything else I vomit."

She shakes her head again. "I will send the syrup," she says.

"You must tell me what is in it," I say, suddenly wary. I do not like her stillness, her steady eyes that look me over as though she judges me.

"Pomegranate syrup with yarrow, stinging nettle, comfrey root, cinnamon, turmeric and bentonite clay," she says. Her tongue is quick as she names each ingredient. There is no hesitation, no subterfuge that I can see. There is nothing I have not heard of.

I nod. "Send it to me," I say.

The drink, when it arrives, has a sweet-sour taste to it, with a spicy warmth from the herbs. Luckily I cannot taste the clay. I sip it gingerly but it does not cause me to vomit and after a while I call for some food: the plainest couscous and white meat and find I am able to eat. It is the first real meal I have eaten since this child was conceived.

I send for her again and she stands before me.

"Did the drink work?" she asks.

"Yes," I say. I nod to a servant, who passes her a large pouch, heavy with money. "You will continue to send the drink throughout my pregnancy," I say. "You will be well paid for your service." I should say more perhaps, should be more fulsome, for I am overwhelmed with gratitude that she has taken away the gnawing hunger and the endless violent vomiting, that she has opened up the path for me to birth more children without suffering so badly each time. But her stillness, her dark eyes, her watching me does not make me feel close to her as I did with Hela.

She takes the money without gratitude, without bowing. "I can tell your servants how to prepare it," she says.

"No," I say. "I want you to prepare it."

She nods and steps away, making to leave.

"Wait," I say.

She pauses.

"You could work for me," I say. "My own handmaiden Hela has passed away and I have need of a healer in my service. Will you be my handmaiden?"

"No," she says simply.

I frown at the speed of her reply, she has not considered the proposal at all. "Why not?"

Her brown eyes fix steadily on mine. "I do not wish to serve you," she says. "I cannot serve a woman who has such darkness inside her." Without asking my permission, she turns and leaves the room.

I call for one of my spies. "Find out who she is," I demand. What I am really asking is, *who is she to speak to a queen as though she disdains her, disdains me?*

It is not long before they return with information. They tell me she is from the very Northern kingdoms of Spain, above Al-Andalus, even. That she is a devoted Christian, was a nun in a convent but got caught by a raiding party and sold as a slave to a rich man in Aghmat who, it seems, maimed her. Certainly she walks with a limp. She followed the army to Murakush, as did most of Aghmat's population, and set up her herb stall for a while, before some man set her up in a house of her own. No-one is sure of his name, he is one of the thousands of soldiers in our army.

I dress in the bright colours any woman here might wear, my long hair hidden under a wrap, my face overshadowed by a shawl. No-one would recognise me in such attire, even those who know me well would struggle to find my likeness at a distance.

The street where she lives is cramped, a hidden alleyway. The door is small: narrow and poorly painted. My knock sounds too loud and I look over my shoulder but there is no-one about. A servant's face appears in the half-open door. An ugly girl, one shoulder set too high, her skin coarse.

"Is this the home of the healer?" I ask.

The girl nods. "She's not here, though," she tells me.

I look beyond the girl. All I can see from here is a half-open door and a few plants in pots. Already I can feel my interest fading fast. Whoever keeps her here is no man of importance: some soldier whom she healed, perhaps, and was grateful enough to feel something for her, scarred as she is. He does not have much money or she would have better servants and be kept in better style. So she will not serve me? I do not care. She has given me a cure for what ails me and I have paid her well for it. It is enough. I would not want such a woman by my side all the time. She can make me the syrup when I ask for it. I do not even need to have her in my presence.

"It is not important," I say and turn away. Behind me I hear the door creak shut and think, so little does her man care for her that he does not even see to oiling it.

I see her from time to time, when she brings the syrup or in the streets. Occasionally I see her with a young child balanced on her hip. Perhaps she is too busy to serve me if she has a child of her own who must be cared for.

I do not have such a luxury. When my time comes and the pains grip me, I have no-one to cling to now that Hela is gone. There is no other woman I would summon and so I hold onto my own carved bed and birth a daughter, Fannu, all alone. I sigh when I see her, for although I would be glad enough of a daughter, I am always mindful that I must provide male heirs and so her birth forewarns me that I must endure another pregnancy. I know that some slave girl has given birth to a girl child named Tamima whom Yusuf has acknowledged as his own. I narrowed my lips when I heard of her but Yusuf still comes to me and I am still seated at his right hand. I am greater than the unnamed girl will ever be and she would not expect to become a wife. She would fear such a position, not crave it. So I look at Fannu and whisper to her that she will be a great queen one day, I will see her married to an amir, she will learn to rule as I have.

"Should I continue to follow the Spanish woman?" asks the spy.

I think about her and then shake my head. "She is not important," I tell him. "I have better things to think of."

He bows. "And the other slave girl?"

I shake my head. Yusuf may have rolled with some girl or other but she is no danger to me, he does not suggest her as a wife. "I am not interested in slave women who whelp bastard girls," I tell him. "Look beyond. I would know how Ibrahim the son of Abu Bakr fares."

It seems from what my spies report back to me that he seeks to challenge us again for leadership, in his father's name. I sigh at such stupidity, but I send gifts of honour and many fine words. My belly swells again and I provide a second son. I name him Abu Bakr, honouring our distant so-called Commander. Sure enough the boy-Ibrahim gives way at these meaningless honours and gifts, acknowledges Yusuf as amir, as his father will already have counselled. Such is the brashness of youth. It makes me feel even older than my years. But the power of my many eyes allows all such challenges to be swept away, for I know they will come our way before they are even spoken and can plan accordingly. I hear foolish tongues claim that I speak with djinns, that the spirits of the air tell me what is to come. I laugh at the very idea. People speak more loosely than any spirit, are easier to command than any djinn.

Mother

I AM GROWN TO BE THE mother of a great kingdom, of a future dynasty. Altogether I give Yusuf six sons and three daughters, more heirs to choose from than any man could need. Many of those years taste of the sour-spiced syrup from the Spanish healer to me, when I look back at them. The remedy saves me from the unending sickness I would otherwise suffer each time, for it seems I must always struggle to bring a child into this world. Two slave girls with whom Yusuf has brief dalliances provide one daughter and two sons between them, all of whom he acknowledges, treating them with care but keeping them well away from me. From time to time I wonder if there is still a ninth son, Ali, who was born first, but I hear nothing more of him, nor of Kella and as the many years pass I no longer fear for his re-emergence, nor hers. She is no doubt far away on some trading route with the man from her tribe. The child could be dead by now, many children die young. And if not, well, then his name is lost and there is no-one to speak it and make his claim.

We have come to the last of our battles, or so it seems. Yusuf sends his troops out to capture the Northern port of Tangier, from where Al-Andalus itself can be glimpsed across the sea. Its ruler Suqut fights for two days but then the sky grows dark and he dies as the sun hides its face in fear at Yusuf's coming. His spoilt son Diya' al-Dawla flees to Ceuta, a tiny outpost of land nearby, jutting into the sea and is promptly cut off from the Maghreb by our army. Meanwhile we take Algiers, just as we once dreamt of.

Poring over maps together Yusuf and I divide up the whole of the Maghreb into four great provinces, two in North and two in the South. Each is placed under the command and care of a governor and every leader and tribal commander is brought to us to pledge loyalty.

We have created peace and prosperity, in a kingdom larger than was thought possible, a kingdom beyond what anyone could have dreamt of, with wealthy cities set as jewels within a crown across it. The tents of Murakush are long gone. Now it is a wealthy city. Fes is restored and grown ever greater. We command the trade routes, especially those of salt, slaves and gold. We have great riches at our disposal. I laugh when I think of the miserly treasure I once showed to Abu Bakr, enhancing it with mirrors in the darkness to hide its paltry amount. Now we could fill that storage room a hundred times over and still have gold to spare.

Yusuf, of course, still wishes to live as though we were in the desert. There are nights when he leaves my side and I find him the next morning lying in our courtyard gardens, wrapped only in a blanket, as though to turn away from all that he has at his command and return to the simple life he once led. At banquets for our allies he still waves away the rich spiced stews and honeyed sweets, eating only plain roast meats and bread, perhaps accepting some fruit. Our children sit with us, many of them grown tall now, our sons ready to take their places leading men into battle, our daughters beautiful, their hands already sought by suitors.

"There is not much for you to do," Yusuf jokes with our sons. "You have only a peaceful kingdom to govern. You will grow fat and soft like the Taifa kings of Al-Andalus."

Still, I ensure that all of our sons train with the soldiers and sit in council, so that they will learn to rule. Our eldest sons are given small regions to govern, so that they may see what it takes to lead our people. Our daughters will marry allies, to further strengthen our bonds. They are taught to read maps, to run a city. They take their places in council, for no-one will raise an eyebrow at a woman sitting in government, knowing what I have done for this kingdom. I will see to it myself that none of our children will be like the Taifa kings of Al-Andalus. Princelings only, each holding tiny regions of Al-Andalus and thinking themselves great rulers. If they had banded together they might have taken over all of Spain but they have grown fat and lazy living their lives of luxury. They squabble amongst themselves and therefore have ended up with the humiliation of paying tribute to the Christian king of the North, Alphonso.

"They do not follow Allah's way," says Yusuf, frowning when we hear news of them. "They cannot call themselves true Muslims when they tax their people so harshly."

"They are none of our business," I say. "They are fools. They have accomplished nothing but a comfortable life for themselves."

But a letter arrives from Al-Mu'tamid, the amir of Seville,.

"He did what?" I ask, appalled.

"Killed Alphonso's messenger," says the scribe who is reading the letter to our council.

Yusuf and I look at each other.

I shake my head. "Start from the beginning."

It seems that Al-Mu'tamid was late in paying the annual tribute demanded by the Christian king, Alphonso the Sixth.

"Alphonso most unjustly and violently demanded not only tribute but also the delivery of many strong castles in my region, in punishment for the delay in payment, blaming me with many untrue accusations," reads the scribe.

"And then Al-Mu'tamid killed Alphonso's messenger?" I ask again.

The scribe nods.

"And now he wants my help?" asks Yusuf, eyebrows raised.

"He asks that you, as one Muslim king to another, do advance in support of him and fight off these unreasonable demands by the Christian king. His scholars and other scholars of Al-Andalus agree that this is righteous."

Yusuf is silent for a while as the members of council murmur amongst themselves. "We need to take Ceuta," he reminds us at last. "It is the only part of the Maghreb not yet under our control. The late amir of Tlemcen's son still lives there, they say he lives a dissolute life. He is surrounded by our men but we cannot advance further for Ceuta juts into the sea and we have no sea-going ships."

I think of my spies, of the words they have brought from Al-Andalus, which until now seemed useless. But I listened to them anyway. One never knows when information will prove of use and now its time has come.

"Al-Mu'tamid is building a great ship," I say. "Tell him that we need it for Ceuta. Only then can we come to his aid."

Yusuf's eyes brighten. "Yes," he says. "Write to him and tell him that if Allah lets me take Ceuta, I will join him and gather my strength to attack the enemy with all my soul. But first we have need of his ship."

The ship towers above us, the men on board look like insects. It is like a fort rocking on the water, it cannot be resisted. The young amir of Ceuta, soft from his luxurious lifestyle, protected only by the sea, suddenly finds himself captured and put to death.

But now the kings of Al-Andalus send word that Alphonso has grown more aggressive. He comes to the region around Seville, on Muslim territory and ravages the land and people. He captures Toledo and the Muslim kings, frightened by this new move, ask Al-Mu'tamid to write again to us.

"Alphonso has come to us demanding pulpits, minarets, mihrabs and mosques, so that crosses may be erected in them and monks may run them."

The council members look appalled. I can see my sons tighten their grips on their swords, as though they are about to fight here and now.

"Allah has given us Ceuta," says Yusuf. "We will cross the sea and stand by our brothers. Pray with me. Oh Allah! If you know that my passage will be beneficial for the Muslims, then make it easy for me. If it is the opposite, then make it difficult for me so that I do not cross over."

"The Maghreb is quiet," I tell Yusuf. "You are free to do battle wherever you wish." I try not to smile at the eagerness of Yusuf and my sons to go into battle. They are trained soldiers, eager for combat. This kingdom we have created is too peaceful for the liking of warriors. I will remain behind, the Maghreb held safe in my able hands while our army supports the Muslim kings.

"Remember not to be too trusting," I remind them all before they depart. "The kings of Al-Andalus are weak men, their lifestyles have made them soft. They do not remember what it is to truly fight, nor are they always honest with one another. They have paid tribute for years to a Christian king whom they could have dispatched if they had banded together, instead they have bowed to him. He has been their lord and master all this time. They may have called on you but you are new to them and they may quickly return to their old lives and the tribute if the change is too hard for them. Be on your guard."

The crossing is blessed. The weather is perfect during the sailing and when Yusuf disembarks in Algeciras Al-Mu'tamid has sent splendid gifts, the inhabitants open their doors in welcome and the peasants of the region have been ordered to provide provisions. But Yusuf remembers my words and he has the men repair the crumbling walls and watchtowers of the city. After this they dig a deep trench around the city and fill it with weapons and provisions. He takes his best solders and creates a garrison to support any future military needs before he sets out for Seville.

"The amir Al-Mu'tamid embraced him and gave him many gifts," says the scribe.

"Gifts mean nothing," I say. "Did the other amirs join their forces with us, as they promised?"

The scribe looks back down at the letter. "The amirs of Seville, Granada and Badajoz joined forces with Yusuf."

I look down at the map laid out in front of me. "And the amir of Almeria?"

"He pleaded old age."

I snort. "He wants to wait and see what will happen before he commits himself," I say. "We will not forget his cowardice, nor his lack of loyalty."

"Yusuf wrote to Alphonso to offer mercy," reports the scribe.

I nod. This has always been our way, since we had an army large enough to command fear in the hearts of our enemies. We offer them the opportunity to avoid battles, to become our allies. "What did he offer?"

"He invited Alphonso to take one of three options. Convert to Islam, pay tribute, or fight."

"And?"

"Alphonso was filled with rage. He responded, saying: 'How can you send me such a letter when my father and I have imposed tribute on the people of your religion for the past eighty years. Advance towards me: it will not please me to meet you near a city which may protect you, for it will delay me from seizing you, killing you and assuaging my hatred of you.'"

I shrug. "A king who cannot control his temper," I say. "More fool him. He will find out what we are made of.

He has only done battle with the kings there and they are not like us. He will realise it soon enough." I think that he has no idea what he is about to face. Our army is without equal, led by Yusuf who has more experience of battles than any man I know and supported by our sons, eager for glory. Our army is backed by a vast kingdom of huge wealth and power. While Yusuf heads up the army, I stand behind him with supplies, with more soldiers to call on.

Alphonso cannot win.

The two armies come together and as I predicted Alphonso is not ready for us. His camp is burned to the ground by a small party of our men while he is engaged with the rest of the army. Alphonso is grievously wounded in his knee and finds his troops enveloped by our own, a move the men have practiced time and again. He is forced to retreat.

Yusuf returns to us covered in glory but doubtful of how long this victory will last. "I have told the amirs that they must band together. It is their infighting and soft lives that has brought about their own ruin and weakness. They must unite, they must face Alphonso as one."

"And will they?"

He sighs. "I doubt it. Of course they swore to do so, but that was after a successful battle, when any man will swear to anything in his pride and exhilaration. It will be a different matter when they return to their palaces. They will go back to their old ways soon enough. And Alphonso has been lamed for life, he will not forget this humiliation."

"I too have news," I say. "Sad news. Your cousin, our

Commander Abu Bakr, has died. He fell to a poisoned arrow in battle. A warrior to the end. "

Yusuf is sorrowful. "He was a good man," he says. "And he did great things for this kingdom."

"And kept his word to us," I say. "He did not go back on our agreement."

We praise his name and his deeds: the quelling of the tribes in the South, the re-opening of the salt route towards Aulil, the strengthening of the commercial trade routes. And above all, most recently, the conquest of Kumbi in Ghana, from where vast amounts of gold make their way to our mint, where dirhams are moulded and accepted as coinage not only across our own lands but far beyond, known for their quality.

Now it is Yusuf's name that is pressed into each coin at our mint. He is given a new title: Amir of the Muslims. His new title brings Al-Mu'tamid himself to our shores. He crosses the Strait and stands before us in council, full of words of praise and fine gifts. I do not trust him.

"We ask that you join us again, Yusuf," he says. "We will gather together as one under your command."

"As one?" I ask.

Al-Mu'tamid looks somewhat taken aback by my seat of honour in council but he knows better than to show it too much. "As one, oh Queen Zaynab," he says smiling. "I will even set aside my differences with Bin Rashiq of Murcia, who will join with us."

But of course the reality is not as smooth as the amir's words. Once the armies join together Bin Rashiq of Murcia tries to woo Yusuf with gifts so as to push out Al-Mu'tamid as our closest ally. In turn Al-Mu'tamid accuses him of favouring the Christians, which proves true. Bin Rashiq ends up loaded down with chains while his kingdom of Murcia is given to Seville, much to Al-Mu'tamid's pleasure. But the inhabitants of Murcia stubbornly refuse to provision the troops and at last Yusuf, disillusioned and weary of the infighting, returns to the Maghreb. At once Alphonso forces 'Abdullah of Granada to not only resume paying him tribute but also to sign a treaty declaring Granada against Yusuf and Seville.

Council is taken over with scholars, who argue that the amirs of Al-Andalus have been shown to be libertines and impious.

"They have corrupted their own people by their bad example and forgotten their religious duties," says one.

"And commanded illegal taxes, against the law of the Qu'ran," says another.

"I made it clear they were no longer to levy such taxes," says Yusuf.

"They have continued, regardless of what they agreed to when you saw them," I say. "They are nothing but liars."

"More than one is in alliance with Alphonso," reminds a scholar. "They prefer to bind themselves to a Christian king than their own Muslim brothers. It cannot be bourne."

Yusuf is wary. He dislikes the infighting, the disloyalties, the effort of trying to command poorly-trained troops, so different from his own. "How can I be certain this is the will of Allah?" he asks. "Perhaps it goes against His will. In which case I will not take action."

The eldest scholar stands. "We have sought assurance

from the great scholars of Islam as far away as Egypt and Asia and all of them confirm our ruling on this matter. We take it on ourselves to answer for this action before Allah. If we are in error, we agree to pay the penalty for our conduct in the next world. We declare that you, Yusuf, Amir of the Muslims, are not responsible. But we firmly believe that if you leave the Andalusian kings in peace, they will deliver our country to the unbelievers and if that is the case, then you will have to render an account to Allah of your lack of action."

"Leave us," says Yusuf.

Alone, we sit tracing the contours of the map showing Al-Andalus, the kingdoms of the amirs, the kingdoms held by Alphonso.

"I am seventy years' old," says Yusuf. "I am too old for this."

I laugh. "You are still a greater warrior and leader than the amirs of Al-Andalus," I say. "They are like children. Squabbling and telling tales to their mothers."

"They are impossible to help," he says. "They go behind my back, they switch loyalty. I cannot trust their word, nor even their men in battle, for they are weak and poorly trained."

"Then do not help them," I say. "Command them. Rule over them."

"Do you not think the kingdom we have created is great enough?" he asks.

"Create an empire," I say.

"Go there without being summoned?"

"Yes," I say. "The fight is between you and Alphonso now. The petty kings must submit to you now, for they have been proven unfit to rule. Your greatest scholars have declared them so. Remember: do not trust them. Their lips speak honeyed words but they come only from the sweetmeats they fill their mouths with, not from their hearts."

Yusuf crosses the Strait again with his scholars' blessings but without being summoned. Once in Algeciras he leads his men towards Cordoba to begin a siege. As they pass Granada its king, 'Abdullah, meets with them and humbles himself before Yusuf, begging his pardon for displeasing him. But Yusuf is wise to their ways now. He replies that he has forgotten any grievance and invites him to enter his tent, where he will be honoured as an ally.

I sit in council and look down at 'Abdullah kneeling before me. I can barely keep from laughing.

"And so you entered the tent?"

"Yes," he mutters.

"And?"

"I was taken and bound in chains."

"You deserved it for your lying ways," I say. "Granada has been taken by Yusuf. Your people praised his name when he abolished all your unlawful taxes. They were not allowed by the Qu'ran. Are you not a good Muslim?"

He mutters something.

"You and your family have been sent to me in chains," I say. "And I am sending you to Aghmat. It is a poor city now, a humble city loyal only to Yusuf and I. You will live there for the rest of your days."

He looks at me with angry eyes as he is made to rise.

"You bow," I inform him. "You bow to me as your queen and you give thanks to Allah that I am merciful."

He has no choice but to do as I say.

Only a month passes before Yusuf sends me the king of Malaga, whom I dispatch in a similar manner, to live out his days as a prisoner: a luxurious life, perhaps, but still a prisoner, watched and held at our will. I feel the vast power I wield as I dispose of these fallen kings and it gives me pleasure. Yusuf and I created a kingdom together. Now, we will create an empire.

Tarifa falls, then Cordoba's siege breaks when its inhabitants open the gates to us. Seville's fleet is burnt and Seville falls, swiftly followed by Almeria and Badajoz.

The once proud ruler of Seville, Al-Mu'tamid, kneels before me in council, sent here in chains like all the others.

"Welcome back to the Maghreb," I say. "You must regret the day you asked for Yusuf's help. You will not be leaving us again. You may join your old allies in Aghmat. Do not plot against us, for your life will not be spared a second time. Believe me when I say that you will be watched."

"Gracious Queen Zaynab," he begins, obsequiously.

"Go," I tell him. "I have no stomach for honeyed words, only loyalty and strong deeds, neither of which, it seems, you are capable of."

Yusuf leaves the army in the hands of his generals. Only Valencia is not yet fully ours and must be held. But the army struggles without Yusuf at its helm.

"Alphonso has a champion," says Yusuf. "A true warrior, by all accounts."

"What is his name?" I ask.

"Rodrigo Diaz de Vivas," he says. "They call him El Cid."

The infighting between the kings goes on, infuriating Yusuf. Behind our backs the ruler of Valencia, Al-Qadir, sends for El Cid to support him, pledging allegiance to Alphonso. But a Muslim judge lets our army into the city, causing Al-Qadir to flee, dressed as a woman along with his wives. They take shelter in a poor house but are found quickly enough and he is sentenced to death. The judge is made ruler but then double-crosses us, agreeing to pay tribute to El Cid, who agrees that he can be ruler if he will stand against us. Yusuf sends more troops but his general is poorly prepared and El Cid not only calls on Alphonso for help but makes a sortie at night when the men are unprepared.

"Why were they unprepared?" rages Yusuf, pacing the room.

I frown. "Continue," I say to the scribe reading us the report.

"El Cid pretended to retreat towards Valencia but hidden soldiers came out and attacked our camp," he reads. "El Cid took a great victory and claimed much booty."

There are many pages of explanations and justifications, apologies and humbling from the generals, none of which soothes Yusuf, especially when we receive word again and again about battles fought, all of which El Cid wins. "It is not acceptable," he declares. "Al-Andalus is ours except for Valencia and Valencia *will* be ours."

"You had better go yourself," I suggest and he nods.

"I will defeat this El Cid," he says. "He will fall before my sword."

I nod. I do not doubt it will be so.

"El Cid's son Diego was killed first," reads the scribe. "In the battle for Consuegra."

I think of Abu Tahir, of the grief I would feel if I saw my son fall in battle. "And El Cid himself?" I ask, already knowing the answer.

"Died shortly after," says the scribe.

Of a broken heart, I think. I had heard great things of this warrior but it seems he was not invincible after all, for Yusuf broke him.

Now that their hero is gone the spirit goes out of the Christians. Valencia falls to us. All of Al-Andalus is now Yusuf's. The Christian king Alphonso has been whipped like a dog, creeping back to his Northern lands, to face the cold and fury of his people, outraged that an old Moor has beaten them, that their attempt to claim back the lands of the past has failed. One set of Muslims or another, it is the same humiliation to them. At least with the old Taifa kings they received tribute and could fool themselves that they ruled over them. Now they cannot pretend. They huddle in the North and we claim the South as our own, our kingdom grown to an empire for our sons and daughters to rule over after us.

My eldest son Abu Tahir kneels before me and I touch his head in blessing. He is a fully-grown man now, scarred in battle, his body made hard by war. He has a gravity to him, he knows that one day he will follow Yusuf and become Amir of the Muslims.

"You must study Al-Andalus," I tell him. "We must know it as we know our own people, as well as we know the Maghreb."

"It is a rich land, full of good and beautiful things," he tells me. "Now it is ours."

"One day it will be yours," I tell him.

Crone

In my rooms I like to study the maps I keep spread out, my mind wandering, as it often does now, back to the past. I am more than sixty years' old. I have aches and pains but I do not care about them, for I am at peace for the first time in my life. I can rest now. Our new-born empire is peaceful and prosperous. Whatever false vision I spoke and the men in my life believed in, none of us could have foreseen this moment of utter triumph. We hold an empire now, two lands spanning the sea. I wonder at it sometimes, that such a thing should come to pass and yet I know that every step towards such greatness has come about because of how Yusuf and I have worked together. He has led an army that made hardened warriors blench while I created first a rich and unified kingdom and then an empire from his conquered lands: managing a flourishing trade, the building of great cities, enacting good governance. We have done great things together, he and I. Our children will be worthy successors to us, for each of them has been raised to be the best: leaders, warriors, great queens. I once thought I would never find peace but here I am, an old woman, contented with the life she has made. I trace the lines of the maps once more, taking pleasure in their certainty for the future.

Yusuf stands in the doorway. He looks shaken.

"What is wrong?" I ask, unnerved. I have never seen him look like this. "Is there unrest? A rebellion?" I am think quickly about who I must summon, which spies will be of greatest help to me, depending on what has happened. I think of where our troops are stationed, how fast they can be moved, what supplies they will need.

"I have found Ali," he says.

"Who?"

"Kella's son," Yusuf says.

I feel as though I have received a blow to the stomach. "His body?" I ask, reaching for hope.

"He is alive," says Yusuf.

"That cannot be true," I say. My heart is thudding. I have to sit on the edge of my bed.

"She gave him to a slave woman to bring up," Yusuf says.

I think of the two slave girls who have given Yusuf children but I have seen their offspring for myself and they were born years after Kella left here. "Is that what the woman claims?"

"She has proved it," he says.

"How?"

He holds up something in his hand. I have to peer at it. A necklace, the long silver beads of his people. He gave one to each of our children, saying it would make them tall and healthy. "Where did she get that?"

"Kella gave it to her, to make Ali's claim when the time was right."

I try to laugh, although it does not sound natural. "She could have got those from any jeweller."

He shakes his head. "Kella's name and mine are marked on the necklace," he says and shows me.

"A jeweller can be paid for such work," I say, but I know that he is not listening to me.

"He is my son," says Yusuf. "And he has lived close at hand for all these years." His voice trembles and he looks down at me. His eyes are filled with tears. "Did you know of this?"

I do not hesitate, not even for a breath. "No," I say. "I believed Kella's son was dead. She told us he was dead. Why would she lie to us? Why would she lie to you?"

Yusuf's face is full of distress. "She must have thought him threatened," he says.

"By whom?" I ask.

"I do not know," he says. "But now he is found, he is safe. I will have him declared my son."

I swallow. It is a bitter thing to accept. But so be it. The children of the slave girls have been acknowledged too but my own children have always been given pre-eminence over them. "I am sure he will be grateful for your generosity," I say. "Not all men would trust such a claim."

"I know it for the truth," says Yusuf.

He stands before us, this lost son of Kella and Yusuf. Ali. I look him over. He has a slender build, unlike my own sons, whose years upon years of training, first alongside and then in Yusuf's army, have made them large of shoulder, their muscles rippling. His eyes, as he looks about himself, are wide and trusting. The shape of them reminds me of his mother. This is a man who has not been lied to by supposed allies, who has not carried a sword on his hip all his life and a dagger hidden in his robes. He speaks with the scholars at the far end of the room earnestly, as though what they have to say is more important than what the generals and governors speak of.

Yusuf stands. "I ask the council to welcome my son, Ali. Child to my first wife Kella, now no longer with us."

The council chamber ripples with interest. They have heard such announcements before but those were babies, bastards born to slave girls. They were of little importance. This is a full-grown man born to Yusuf's first wife. Where has he been all this time? Next to me, my son Abu Tahir shifts, a little discomforted by this disclosure. I touch his shoulder gently and he settles again, resigned.

"The woman who raised him will vouch for his birth," continues Yusuf. He waves towards the doorway, where a woman stands, her face half-hidden from me. "Isabella, join us."

I blench at the sight of her, my hands clench without my knowledge. The Spanish healer stands before us, her eyes calm and steady, her head held high. One of our eldest and greatest scholars questions her.

"I swear that this man is Ali, son to Yusuf bin Tashfin and his wife Kella."

"Do you know where Kella is now?"

"I do not."

"Is she alive?"

"I do not know."

"How did you come to have this child in your care?"

"His mother summoned me as a midwife when she birthed him. He was born into my hands."

"Did she give him to you at once?"

"No. She came to me in great secrecy. She claimed that the boy's life was in danger, that he must be raised by another. She begged me to take him. I did so."

"From whom was he in danger?"

I wait for her to name me but she does not, she does not even glance my way although my breathing comes fast and shallow. I feel the room swirl about me and think I am about to faint but I dig my nails into the palms of my hands so hard that the pain brings me back to myself.

"Give me a name," insists the scholar.

"I cannot."

"Can you prove this story?"

She holds up the string of silver beads and says they were given to prove his lineage, she asks Yusuf if they are the same beads he gave to Kella and he agrees that they are. I try to calm my breathing as Yusuf and Ali stand side by side before the council and the council welcomes Ali as Yusuf's long-lost son and acknowledges Isabella's righteous behaviour in having kept him safe from harm all these years.

"Has the boy been raised a Christian?" worries the scholar.

Isabella shakes her head. "He has been raised in his father's religion. I thought it right," she adds.

There is a murmur of approval. Yusuf declares that Isabella and Ali must accompany him to our palace, where a banquet of welcome will be served. I stand, legs shaking beneath my robes and keep my face still as I approach Isabella. Ali has already turned to me and is bowing.

"Lady Zaynab," he says awkwardly. "I believe you knew my mother."

I look at him, see something of her in him, a distant echo of her innocence. "I did not know her well before she left," I say and watch his face turn crimson at the reminder that his mother ran away in the night, leaving him behind as though she cared nothing for him, as well as her legally wed husband Yusuf, to whom she owed her loyalty.

"Come," says Yusuf and he gestures to Ali to precede him out of the door. Then he turns to Isabella, one hand extended. "Join us," is all he says but as he speaks I feel a heavy weight settle in my belly. His hand takes hers with gentleness, pulling her closer to him so that their bodies touch as they move forwards together and the way he looks at her, the softness in his eyes...

"I beg you will excuse me," I say to Yusuf and then I leave, quickly, before he can frown and ask me where I am going.

"Mother?"

"Attend your father," I say to Abu Tahir and hurry away from him.

This time I do not disguise myself. I run through the streets, ignoring the surprised faces of those around me, the murmurs I leave behind, *lady Zaynab running as though the very djinns of the air were after her*. I make my way back to the tiny alleyway, the poorly painted gate. I have been here only once, so many years ago. This time I do not knock, I do not wait for the ugly serving girl to come at my summons. Instead I push hard against the fading paint. The door gives way to me, it opens with the same creaking protest and I step inside, slamming it behind me. Panting, I feel the great heat of the day turn cold as I turn on myself, slowly taking in what has been hidden from me all these years.

Behind the ill-painted, creaking door and the ill-favoured serving girl I once dismissed as unimportant lies a secret, a secret I would have seen many years ago had I looked beyond the narrow glimpse I caught over her shoulder, had I pushed at the door and opened it wide, stepped inside.

The courtyard in which I stand is large. The tiles stretching across the floor are brightly coloured and arranged in pleasing patterns. Above me stretch not two but three storeys, set out in carved woods and exquisite plasterwork. On each level I can see doors to hidden rooms, each painted by craftsmen. By my side a large and well-made fountain splashes cool water in the sun's bright rays. There are climbing plants and even a palm tree, which reaches up towards the clear blue sky. This hidden home is a small palace deliberately concealed behind an ugly exterior, a dwelling fit for any one of Yusuf's family members.

Fit even for a wife.

I sit alone, thinking of the many, many hundreds of pairs of eyes I claim as my spies. Men, of course, who serve their lords near and far but bring me word of their foibles, allowing me to be certain of their loyalties. Women, too, for women hear and see what men pass over. They know unspoken secrets as well as those passed off as mere gossip yet which contain a kernel of truth. I even claim children. They come and go, are forgotten when voices are lowered, see things left behind, understand far more than their elders would ever suspect or wish them to. I think of the hundreds of men and women whom I have had followed and watched.

I curse myself that I allowed Isabella's service to me during my pregnancies, the relief her remedy brought, to let her refusal to serve me go too easily. I know that had it been a spy who had reported to me I would have demanded more, that I would have required they enter Isabella's home and tell me every detail of what they saw. But because I took on the task myself, because I saw peeling paint and an ill-favoured serving girl I saw what I wanted to see and turned away, believing there was nothing else to be seen. Now I curse myself for that failure.

But most of all I think of Yusuf.

I have trusted few people in my life. I have had eyes watching so many people around me, yet I never thought to have them watch Yusuf. Certainly, when the slave girls were mentioned as mothers to his bastards I had them watched long enough to know that they were of no concern to me. But Yusuf himself I did not watch. And yet there is something between him and Isabella, I saw it at once, any fool would have spotted it. How long has it been going on? I try to tell myself it is only gratitude to the woman who raised his son to safety, but I am not stupid enough to believe my own soothing. She has been living in that house for many years, since Kella had been gone only a year or so. Did Yusuf know where his son was all this time? Has he been watching me to see if I will harm the child? Surely not. He was shaken to know Ali had been found and yet all this time he has known Isabella, has cared for her enough to give her such a house?

I wander Murakush for the rest of the day, not returning

to the palace until I can be certain the banquet is complete and everyone has gone. I cannot face seeing Isabella sat at Yusuf's side, the looks between them. I had thought such fears long behind me, lost in my first marriages and yet here they are again, rearing up before me. Such love I felt and now it is swept away in lies and secrets. My stomach churns and from time to time tears well up in my eyes, I am carried on a swirling storm of emotions. I wander the streets without a plan, without a path before me.

But after a while the storm within me begins to subside. I look at the towering mosque, the bakeries, the hammams. I see the people going about their business, busy, proud of belonging to such a great city, I see the respect with which they greet me. *I have made this city,* I think. *I have made this kingdom what it is. I have made it even into an empire. My children will govern after me. Ali is nothing to me. If I should not have trusted Yusuf, so be it. I should not have trusted any man. But even he cannot take away what I have done, what has been achieved at my hand. My children will come after me. I will be known as the mother of this dynasty.*

When I see Yusuf the next morning I manage to hold my tongue about Isabella. She is a slave woman, not as important as the empire and dynasty we have created together. Ali may be Yusuf's son but he is clearly not suited even to take on such positions of power as our sons already have. He is a quiet, peaceable man, a man who enjoy study and the company of scholars. Perhaps he can be a scholar and advise on matters of faith. Yusuf might be pleased to have a man of God for a son. But I must secure Abu Tahir's place.

"You should announce the name of your heir," I say. "An empire needs stability."

He nods. "You are right," he says. "It shall be done. I will announce it today, in council."

I feel the tension in me drain away. We are still a formidable partnership. My legacy is whole. I smile at him. "It is a great day," I say. "Praise be to Allah for all we have accomplished in His name."

When Yusuf leaves I summon Abu Tahir.

"I have asked Yusuf to name his heir," I tell him.

I see him glow with the knowledge. His day has come at last. "When?"

"Today."

Abu Tahir and I are the first to arrive in the council chambers. My other sons and daughters nod to us when they arrive. They know that today is a momentous occasion, that even as Abu Tahir's name is announced their own future status is assured, that they will swear fealty to him, stand by him throughout the years to come as our dynasty is known throughout the world. The empire we have created may well expand further through marriage or battle, giving each of them ever-greater opportunities for glory. The scholars and warriors, the governors and chieftains who make up our council and court bow with greater deference as they greet Abu Tahir and myself, acknowledging what is to come. The room rustles with excitement. I even manage to nod to Ali, sitting amongst my sons and daughters. I know that Isabella is also among us but I do not look for her. She is nothing to me. Today she will understand that no-one can take my place, for I have earned it a thousand times over. I have earned the name of heir for my son.

Yusuf stands. "Today I will declare my heir," he announces. "Now that I command an empire, it must have a named heir, that there can be no doubt over its future, nor any disruption when my time to leave this world comes."

I smile. I look to Abu Tahir, seated at my side, who nods to me, his hand on his sword hilt, the very image of a young amir. He is ready to stand, to bow his head to Yusuf's announcement, to speak words of fealty and power. I feel such pride in him. Whatever sadness my husbands have brought me in all these years, my son has been faithful to me, a blessing to me. He will be a great ruler one day, the head of a fearsome dynasty ready for glory.

All of us turn our faces towards Yusuf, waiting for Abu Tahir's name to be spoken.

"Ali will be my heir," says Yusuf.

I do not move. My eyes slide sideways. Abu Tahir's face has drained white. He does not look at me, will not meet my gaze. I watch as Ali stands before his father then kneels for his blessing, his mouth opening and closing as he acknowledges Yusuf's command and swears to rule over the empire as his successor. I cannot hear him, it is as though he is making a dumb show. I look around the council and catch the faces of those who are not quick-witted enough courtiers, who have not yet smiled and nodded, who have not yet hailed Ali. These look to me, waiting for me to speak, to protest. But I keep my face stonelike, there is nothing to be seen. Quickly their faces accept the news even as Abu Tahir leaves the council, his siblings' faces frozen in silent disbelief.

"There will be a ceremony of allegiance," says Yusuf. "Here and in Cordoba. Each governor will make a pledge of loyalty to Ali." He does not look at me.

One by one the council members leave the room, filing past me in silence. They dare not look at me, they dare not speak to me.

I find Abu Tahir in his rooms, seated before a mirror, his back to me. I see myself standing behind him, both our faces rigid with rage and grief. His features are mine. I see in him the man I would have been, powerful and strong, destined to be a ruler and yet cast aside on the whim of a man. I want to tell him that I understand, that the whole of my life I have felt as he does now.

"Did you know?" he asks me and his teeth are so tightly ground together I barely understand him when he speaks.

"No!" I say. "How can you think so?"

"You should have spoken for me."

I gape at him. "You cannot blame me! I did not know what Yusuf was about to say!"

He snorts as though he does not believe me. "You two are as one, everyone knows that."

"I did not even know Ali was alive," I say.

"What, you who know everything, even the future?" he says, his voice full of spite. "Do you not converse with djinns as everyone whispers, did you not have a great vision? Did your spirits not tell you this day would come?"

"Abu Tahir," I begin, but he stands and pushes past me

to the door. I make to grasp his arm but he shoves me away from him and I find myself on the floor. Slowly I rise and see myself reflected in the mirror, all alone. For a long time I stand and stare at myself.

It seems the world cannot trust a woman who knows so much, who can hold a vision of the future in her bosom and bring it to fruition. Men look away when I meet their eye. Once they desired me because I was beautiful. Now they fear me because I am powerful, more powerful than any woman they have encountered in their lives and it makes them uncomfortable. Oh certainly, they still kneel to me, they still speak to me with courtesy, but the truth is they would rather I was not there. It humbles them to know a woman stands behind their leader and makes him stronger than he would be alone. Men do not like to be humbled. And even a great warrior like Yusuf would rather choose an heir for the sake of sentiment, for the long-lost memory of some old love or even for a new love than for the good of the empire. He will pass over my son, the son of a woman who has been the power behind his throne. Abu Tahir has been raised to be the amir after his father. He is a great warrior, a man of power and strength, a man raised in my own image as much as his father's. He is the man who should lead the Almoravid dynasty forwards and yet Yusuf has chosen what amounts to a boy, a man who has not yet been tried on the battlefields, who knows nothing of the empire we now hold, who has been raised by a Christian, of all things. For all I know she may have raised him as a traitor, he may join forces with Alphonso and restore Al-Andalus to a Christian rule, taking the Maghreb with it, reversing all we have done over decades in moments, should Yusuf die.

I am not sure how much time passes, only that the shadows of the sun have moved and still I gaze at myself in the mirror, unable to answer the questions in my mind. What am I, if I am not the founder of this dynasty? Have I created an empire from the dust only for my name to be forgotten, for my achievements to be gifted to another woman's son? Have I been punished by Allah for declaring a false vision all those years ago, a vision which has come true beyond anyone's wildest expectations? No, I do not believe that.

At last I stand up. I am done. I have spent my life forcing myself into one shape and then another: into every shape permitted to a woman and still it has not been enough. I have been a daughter, bride, concubine, queen, widow, wife, seductress, rival, murderess, spy, mother. Now I am a crone, an old and fearsome woman. I make my servants and spies tremble when they must be in the same room as me, for they are fools and believe everything they hear, that I speak with spirits and have visions of what is still to come. They do not, cannot, believe that a woman can shape her own life to achieve what she most desires. And I cannot believe that all my work has come to nothing.

I have been more than any woman is allowed to be. I should be remembered as an amir, as Commander, as Yusuf's right hand. Instead I will be remembered for my youthful beauty. They will make up stories about me and call me a magician. They will not see my network of spies, my insights, my endless hard work and military strategies, for they will not credit that to a woman, no, it must come from djinns and spirits.

At last I leave my son's rooms and walk down long corridors to my own chambers.

I am done.

Murakush c.1102

The taste is my mouth is beyond bitterness. I feel saliva drip down the side of my mouth, see it fall to the floor, a foaming wet whiteness.

There is a mirror in my room. I crawl towards it now, my silk robes brushing the floor, turning to rags beneath my knees. I cannot stand, my legs are too weak and my breathing too shallow.

My eyes are growing dim. Something cold touches me and I start back, then realise my face has touched the mirror, yet still I cannot see myself. I sit back on my heels, close my eyes and struggle for breath.

I reach out and place my palms on the cold hard mirror, bring my face close to its shining surface. I open my eyes wide and stare into its depths, seeking my reflection.

Daughter, bride, concubine, queen, widow, wife, seductress, rival, murderess, spy, mother. Crone.

I cannot see my face.

I hope you have enjoyed *None Such as She*, third in a series of four set in Morocco and Spain as the Almoravid army created their empire. Each book can be read alone but all the main characters recur throughout the series as each book focuses on one character's story and their version of events.

The chronological order is:
The Cup (a free novella which you can download from my website)
A String of Silver Beads
None Such as She
Do Not Awaken Love

Author's Note on History

It is both difficult and inspiring to write about someone when history does not give us much information to go on. Although she was famous in her era, the total information I could find on Zaynab amounted to little more than a couple of paragraphs. Zaynab was the daughter of a man named Ibrahim from Kairouan in Tunisia, a city known for its rose perfume and very fine carpets. She claimed to have had a vision that said her husband would rule all of the Maghreb (North Africa), at the time made up of many diverse tribal states. This drew a lot of attention and many important men sought her in marriage. However she ended up marrying Yusuf bin Ali, who was a chief, but only of a small tribe and a vassal to the amir (king) of Aghmat, which seems an oddly humble choice, especially as sources say she was a concubine (implying a first wife was already in place). There is no mention of Yusuf dying, instead it appears he then gave her up to Luqut, the amir of Aghmat, a wealthy city.

She was married to Luqut until the Almoravid army conquered Aghmat (and killed Luqut), when she was taken as a bride by their leader, Abu Bakr. It is said that she blindfolded Abu Bakr and took him to a cave filled with treasure, which she promised to him, then re-blindfolded him and took him back out again.

When Southern tribes started causing unrest, Abu Bakr gave the command of the army to his second-in command, Yusuf bin Tashfin, and divorced Zaynab (claiming that a rough desert life would not be suitable for her), giving her in marriage to Yusuf. In this way Zaynab managed to be married four times, an extraordinary thing for a woman in those times and somehow her initial prophecy came true, even though it took four marriages to happen, implying a certain amount of deliberate ambition. In my version of events, Zaynab naively makes up the vision to draw her first husband Yusuf closer to her, which backfires when Yusuf is then forced to give her up in marriage to his amir Luqut, ruler of Aghmat.

Zaynab became Yusuf bin Tashfin's right hand, acknowledged as a superb military tactician in her own right. She was highly important in negotiating the transfer of power from Abu Bakr to Yusuf. She is described in the quote I have used at the start of this novel: *In her time there was none such as she – none more beautiful or intelligent or witty … she was married to Yusuf, who built Marrakech for her…* as well as texts saying that she spoke with djinns and spirits. She was nicknamed 'the Magician' for her negotiating skills. Having apparently had no children at all in her previous three marriages over many years, she then seemed to have quite a few children with Yusuf (the information is very piecemeal but Yusuf had several sons and possibly nine to eleven children altogether, a good amount of whom were Zayanb's).

There is no clarity on when or how Zaynab died.

The Almoravids conquered the whole of the Maghreb (North Africa) and most of Spain. But Yusuf's choice of heir, Ali, was a peaceful and religious man, not much inclined to fighting and his empire was eventually lost to the Almohad army.

I wanted to try and put some reasons behind some of the things I found odd about Zaynab's story. Why marry a not very important chief as a concubine when supposedly she could have anyone? Why move from Kairouan in Tunisia to the West of Morocco, a very long distance in those days? Why was she free to marry the king of Aghmat? How come she had visions about her own future as the wife of the man who would rule all of North Africa when this prophecy actually took an unheard-of four marriages to achieve? It also seemed very odd that she had no children at all despite three husbands and then had as many as ten with Yusuf bin Tashfin. Finally, considering Zaynab's undisputed beauty and intelligence, her status as Yusuf's right hand and that she had given him several children, as well as his own devout Muslim faith, it seemed very strange to me that Yusuf would choose as his heir Ali, the son of a Christian slave girl. It certainly made me wonder how Zaynab would have taken such a choice when she might reasonably have expected one of her own sons (the Almoravids did not use primogeniture) to inherit the empire. My series of books set around the Almoravids takes this strange choice and creates a possible narrative around it.

Yusuf's first wife, Kella, is fictional, although again it seems odd Yusuf would have had no wife at all until he was nearly fifty. Isabella is not fictional, she is the Christian slave girl mentioned in historical records, although information on her is even more limited, to little more than a sentence, and so I have created her life to suit my storytelling. It seemed to be important that she was a slave and that she was Christian, for this is almost all that has been recorded about her apart from her Arabic nickname, Perfection of Beauty. The child she raised seems to have been very ill suited in temperament for ruling a newly-created empire, being described as studious, pious, peace-loving and not a warrior.

What emerges in this novel, I hope, is the story of a very powerful woman in history, one who had an unusual life and who was credited with extraordinary influence at a time of great change, but whose own child was denied inheriting the empire which Zaynab was at least partly responsible for creating.

A note on names: the names of some of the men (especially Yusuf's sons) have been tricky to choose, especially where they are called Abu-something. This ought to mean 'father of' and would be a name they used as an adult, referencing their own son, but as there is no mention of their childhood names, it is all I can go on and I did not wish to make up names entirely. So I have simply stuck to their adult names. It is not clear who were the mothers of Yusuf's children, except for his eventual heir, so I have made the assumption that most were Zaynab's, but not all: since Yusuf clearly had at least one son by a slave I assumed there might have been a few more. A few of the sons and all of the daughters do not even have dates of birth, so the order in which the children were born could be wrong. I have used Murakush (land of God), the original name for Marrakech.

If you want to see the inspiration for Zaynab's bellydancing lessons in the Concubine chapter, find a video of Rachel Brice, a world-class belly dancer, whose artistry I hugely admire and to whom this book is respectfully dedicated. Her combination of sensuality and spectacular physical strength and control must take huge amounts of work to create something that looks both magical and effortless, and is a model for how I think of Zaynab.

Your Free Book

The city of Kairouan in Tunisia, 1020. Hela has powers too strong for a child – both to feel the pain of those around her and to heal them. But when she is given a mysterious cup by a slave woman, its powers overtake her life, forcing her into a vow she cannot hope to keep. So begins a quartet of historical novels set in Morocco as the Almoravid Dynasty sweeps across Northern Africa and Spain, creating a Muslim Empire that endured for generations.

Download your free copy at
www.melissaaddey.com

Biography

I mainly write historical fiction, and am currently writing two series set in very different eras: China in the 1700s and Morocco/Spain in the 1000s. My first novel, *The Fragrant Concubine*, was picked for Editor's Choice by the Historical Novel Society and longlisted for the Mslexia Novel Competition.

In 2016 I was made the Leverhulme Trust Writer in Residence at the British Library, which included writing two books, *Merchandise for Authors* and *The Storytelling Entrepreneur.* You can read more about my non-fiction books on my website.

I am currently studying for a PhD in Creative Writing at the University of Surrey.

I love using my writing to interact with people and run regular workshops at the British Library as well as coaching other writers on a one-to-one basis.

I live in London with my husband and two children.

For more information, visit my website
www.melissaaddey.com

Current and forthcoming books include:

Historical Fiction

China

The Garden of Perfect Brightness

The Consorts

The Fragrant Concubine

The Cold Palace

Morocco

The Cup

A String of Silver Beads

None Such as She

Do Not Awaken Love

Picture Books for Children

Kameko and the Monkey-King

Non-Fiction

The Storytelling Entrepreneur

Merchandise for Authors

The Happy Commuter

100 Things to Do while Breastfeeding

Thanks

I remain grateful throughout this series to three scholars: first Aisha Bewley, for having translated *Les Almoravides* (The Almoravids) by Vincent Lagardère from the original French and making it publically available on her website which covers many things Islamic (http://bewley.virtualave.net): it was an extremely useful source of information on the Almoravids' complex movements and battles and I have taken a few quotes directly from it, such as Yusuf's letters to and from the kings in Al-Andalus. Also to the School of Oriental and African Studies for access to their wonderful library and the initial help and encouragement of both Dr Michael Brett for discussing my timeline right at the start and Professor Harry Norris for taking the time to read the first draft in this series and for sending me a lovely letter of encouragement which I still treasure. All errors and fictional choices are of course mine.

I am immensely grateful to the University of Surrey for funding my PhD in Creative Writing: a very precious gift of three years of creative freedom to explore my craft and many other creative outlets as well. Thank you also to Dr Paul Vlitos, my primary supervisor, who has taught me a lot about the craft along the way.

Thank you to Melitta Weiss-Amer of the University of

Western Ontario for her very interesting article, *Medieval Women's Guides to Food during Pregnancy: Origins, Texts, and Traditions* (1993 Vol 10 of the Canadian Bulletin of Medical History) and the DIY Natural website which lists styptic herbs (to stop bleeding). I used these two references to invent Isabella's syrup to cure Zaynab's ongoing pregnancy nausea: I don't recommend nor take any responsibility for anyone trying to copy my made-up recipe!

Thank you to Streetlight Graphics, who always take care of everything with no fuss at all.

Thank you to my beta readers for this book: Elisa, Etain, Helen. Your insights always make the books better. And to my family and friends for their ongoing encouragement.